b b b

b b b

b b b

b b b

glass

back

wards

b b b

b b b

b b b

b b b

b b b

b b b

b b b

b b b

b b b

GLASS BACKWARDS

ZEPH E. DANIEL

POISON VINE BOOKS

OAKLAND

POISON VINE BOOKS

All Poison Vine books are available from your favorite bookstore,
amazon.com, or from our 24 hour order line: 1.800.431.1579

Library of Congress Control Number: 2003104214
Publisher's Catalog-in-Publication Data
Glass Backwards/Zeph E. Daniel
ISBN 1-930859-66-X
1. Murder——Fiction.
2. Human Sacrifice——Fiction.
3. Occult——Fiction.
4. Necrophilia——Fiction.
5. Sadism——Fiction.
6. Bestiality——Fiction.
7. Satire——Fiction.
8. Satan——Fiction.
9. Mind Control——Fiction.
10. Assassination——Fiction.
I. Title

This book was written, printed, and bound in the United States of America.

To Mother, with love

ENO

My name is Vincent Damien Del Monte. When I was on better terms with the prep school athletic department, I was affectionately called VD. I suppose anything connected to toilet humor or sex would be funny to the upper rungs of polite society, many of whom had no birthright by blood, yet made up for it in secret.

One must always understand, either you serve the womb you were transmitted from, or you find your true calling.

In my case I was hired by a king, my Lord, who is seemingly at odds with many a human grouping. Human groups would not call it an organized society or sophisticated or anything of the sort—they would say *misfit*, I say *innocence*, they say past, I say *inheritance*, for this is about the future.

I was a soldier in a realm not of this world, not exactly, a servant of my Lord and Master, always referred to in remembrance, since remembrance is how we were trained to know all things. The future happened, my faithless one.

One rule you must remember, and that is this: What is in remembrance is happening as we speak, my Recorder. What is in the future was through remembrance, which also resides in the future. In such a world, I had to avoid getting caught in certain repetitive behaviors and thus continue to keep objectivity, especially when killing was involved, as it directly propelled us into certain yet implacable aspects of reality, perhaps making it a bit more certain through time. I say this perchance as a cautionary problem, not for you to be concerned with now.

As I was telling you before, though you still may be truly amused at the connection made between politics and entertainment, and indeed, evidence of Grand Design, my people mean business. By that I mean we will not be mocked.

Was it any wonder a bloodbath was in the offing? Do you still doubt the causes and effects? Perhaps you were impressed with the Titanic, or the World Trade Center, or the Temple Mount. Or your cache of journalistic prizes. Or your own understanding.

I know why you're here: you would like to know how such an industry, indeed a country, like Hollywood, could fail, indeed, could be sold into the hands of those with nothing but war on their minds—war towards us, here, now.

From little things, I tell you, from little things. I shall prove this at least.

Was there any other way? Was there, for instance, any other mode of reality that offered sustenance? Would you mean negotiation? Or self-help? Or charity? Or self-pity and grand partying? Venting? Vetting? Fundamental fairness, would that be your personal bias or proclivity? Would that be something you would apply to today's power elite, after all your saber-toothed media jocks left the latrines and barges for something more submerged? I would hope you would say, of course there is no other way—pray tell!

So in the hopes that some publicity would reach forward in time to my Lord and Master, I will reveal, for a price to be divulged later, the extra-linear information, part prophecy, part history, and when you check your paths of power, you shall find that I was accurate. Though you may not survive the mind-quake about to befall you, Mr. Nunn.

The benefit for you is that it hasn't happened yet. A forward mover such as I will never truly be captured, no matter how many die and are forgotten, no matter how secure you think I am in this prison. Answer: it's not me who is in prison. You cannot understand that with all your sophisticated information systems, your zero-logic cash-outs and panty-boy confidantes, your extra-perceptive glib-speak conversations and lugubrious bartering, you've got *nada* compared to infinite advantage, wouldn't you say? And to think, you're not here to understand omniscience, but gossip, for that is how you think. Past tense.

Don't worry, I'll get to what I did to Flavius in a minute! You need context. In the end, you'll beg me to stop. I am the greatest sword ever sent, and you are the greatest reporter, and together, you will say *history*, and I will say this: I am going to become you. And then I will destroy you.

Oh, you'll listen, won't you? What I have to say will make you famous again, because I sell—everything about me sells, the public wants to know. Dying to know, your readers. And they'll pay, oh, my friends, they will buy it all.

To think that I was heinous, even callous, if my killing began to lose its fervor and clamor and rigor, considering how yours would kill without thought, was entirely the wrong train of thought. Truly, if they weren't so steeped in their failing flesh, they might have made something of themselves. But the blind cannot see—they can only react, and that is the whole sad history, from top to bottom—L.A., D.C., Big Apple...global war, famine and guilt, easy perversion, *wolf-like* and wasted. Your entire history is one of *backwardness*, seeing how the nozzle goes into the hole once it has come out.

Imagining it backwards, you would, even if it kills you. But you don't care about the profundity of my persuasive message and particular mission; you want to know about gossip. Sexual details, dark rooms, behind closed doors, in private chambers...initiations, abominations, yes, worship of the Beast...but you won't write it, because you *are* it, Mr. Nunn.

For the rest of you, life is the cheapest commodity going, especially the iconic, the insolent and the baleful. Certainly the overblown—when after all, flesh is so soft and weak. Or in Leonard Kruzmar's mind...smooth, youthful...pliable, *suckable*.

Okay, okay! As I was saying, I was invited into the foyer, and I had already told my men to stand down, that I would go in alone. What does it matter how I got there or where I came from? Even this: who she was and who I was.

As I told you before you so rudely interrupted me, I was let in by a sickly manservant by the name of Flavius. Once I had entered the foyer I instantly knew that inside this *faux chateau* was what my Lord called a Queen of Abomination—a-sowing but not a-reaping, and I knew that Flavius had quite a few seasons of envisioning himself as the heir and supplicant to Her Highness. Yes, the intelligence briefing indicated she had once been a beauty queen, and she harbored some cockamamie idea that all the men wanted her, which propelled her rise to this rarefied height. She was warned in the beginning, before she killed her husband, or her son, or any of the other hopeless men whose testes got into her jar, that there would be a day such as this—didn't she know? Why was the press so shocked?

She was no longer a beauty queen, at her age, but you'd think she was from her manner and expectation, especially around the attorneys and accountants. She was Queen Margot, maiden of the beautiful, priestess of the pageant, and the ultimate recipient of all blessings into manifold black hole alliances, slaves providing furtherance of wealth and prestige, a swirl of false fucks in an atmosphere of anus worship.

It was fair that she did not know my true identity, though I popped out of her womb and into the gauntlet of her best friends, those gentlemen who in an organized fashion broke us all in at four years old. It was like a dream, grown men exposing their shanks to little boys and girls while Miss America watched. It was thus to insure obedience to her realm, so old and true, the not-so-secret society, the bee-hive...another set of *rules* from a faker who apparently abandons his subjects at just the wrong time.

Surprise, Mommy dear! I've come home!

I had always tried to help her, and indeed, this was my mission—not to expose my true identity, but simply to reconcile the truth of things, that dead is dead. I was no profit to my men, and so they went to reap the reward a few kilometers over, at the golf clubhouse.

When her manservant opened the door, I used a maneuver I had used many times before—I lunged with the blade for his gut, then wrenched it up, right through quick and deep into the cavity of spongy lung and shutting down the heart of Flavius like a switch. Then I pulled out and quickly thrust into the side of his neck, severing the jugular easily, as we were trained so meticulously by those who had once been the enemy. Poor Flavius' body reeled in surprise back onto the black and white checkerboard marble, adorned by Fortuny fabric, under the glare of a Louis XIV crystalline chandelier, a quick death though the gold he sought was bleeding from his hands. The rouge spiral of blood pulsed out to the rhythm of a Muzak Brandenburg. The poodles were barking as I made my advance upstairs. (He did have a semi-auto nine holstered, but did not have time to use it. I did not ask to be trained by mercenaries, but it happened.)

"You remember me, don't you, Queen Margot?" I said, and she marveled in quaint recognition of one long since dispensed with, she apparently never having understood the story about chickens roosting. I might have told her this: "I have come that you might recall the parallel situation, when you told that man who was my father to kill his competition with a golf club, and he did it. The body was thrown into the sea far to the north, and the witnesses were threatened. That led to his chairmanship of the Western Insurance Corporation, where his father had rebuked him and promised that his son was not talented enough, was indeed too upright a man to have what it really took to achieve power. Then he was killed, and in that rattle I heard him say *Poison*! By that I knew your Flavius the Bolivian had used his family remedy. When he died I saw the look of peace befall him like the Dove of Peace descending on humanity."

Margot Del Monte stared at me with incredulity, muttering something like: "...But I, we, I mean, you know, those of us who missed you...we heard you were homeless, on the streets of Phoenix. I tried to find you—we didn't know whether you were dead or alive. Oh, come here, my son—come here, baby. It's all right now. Mommy will take care of you."

"Mommy, it is me—and I am not dead. Your servant is dead. What, you heard I was on the streets of Phoenix begging for bread? You put a hit on me but I blended in with all the homeless veterans of future wars."

"You're...you're crazy," she said. She was seventy-nine years old, but looked like sixteen. She said, "Look, honey, you're still in my will."

I wondered who was I, and who was she and what good would a will do me at this point when my supply was more than pro-vided for—all moot, money like water, easy to get and plenty of it. I had to humor her for a brief moment.

"Now look, Mother Sweetness, your servant is dead—because he did not kill me when he had the chance. And now you're an old withering female who believes herself to be a beauty queen. And I can verify that you *were* once a beauty queen, my dear lady."

She smiled, convincingly. She was still primping, still one hundred three pounds and would not fluctuate one feather. Al-ways in the shade and not the slightest difference in her diet, to the extent of not leaving the house for years on end so as to not interrupt the routine, thwarting her from gabbing endlessly with all the ladies of the competition, from far and wide. Oh, my, she was the best!

"I thought you were dead, Vincent," she said boldly, lighting a cigarette, sure that I would do her no harm.

"I did die, Mommy—but you won't understand because your eyes lie to you. Just as your servants do."

She was thinking the maid had called the Beverly Hills Police Department, and that I would be arrested for killing someone who had become expendable anyway. I had done her a favor, and her mood lightened. Her auburn hair had been coiffed that very afternoon.

"You look as lovely as a bride, Mom," I said. "It's good to see you, especially after all these many years. I'd love to catch you up—"

"No, Vincent—I don't need to hear about your life right now. Would you like Maria to make you some dinner?" she asked.

Then I showed her my bloody knife and laughed because I was in the future. "Maria...cute?"

"Young, Vincent, *and* cute, if you must know—she can help you." She picked up the phone to call the maid, but I severed the line.

She preened a bit more, perhaps to get me to think she was confident that I wouldn't cut her head clean off.

Then she said: "Look, whatever I have...it's all yours, you know that!" She trembled, clutching her diamond necklace like a rosary, yet somehow knowing her angels would see her through once again, as they had in the eternal past, feeling the scar in her chin from the baseball accident, ripe and withering on the vine she knew, and she might have rested completely if I had been killed as she had commissioned, as all black widows leave no trace, and no men.

"But you didn't find me, Mom—your people were slow, and stupid. We scalped one of them outside the Scottsdale Hilton, remember?"

"You are so vulgar—right, I'm taking you out of the will. You are just too disrespectful for words, Vincent!"

"Well, then, shall we get on with it, Your Highness?" I drew the blade and then she began to see that things were not in hand the way they had always been.

"Whatever I did to you, I am sorry. I am truly sorry, Vincent. Look, one of my friends is a...a therapist—yes!—a family therapist and he's, of course he'd be willing to help you...us, I'm talking about healing our relationship, Vincent. Doesn't that mean anything to you?" she asked, poised. "Look, the police are on their way...Vincent, you are...my son, my only son! I need to leave all this to someone—and it's you...you're the winner, not me! Besides blood is thicker than water."

"We shall see about that, sister—we shall see about that!" I said, excitedly.

"Please don't!"

"This is for little Richie, Mom—remember? My younger brother that you poisoned and blamed it on his ex? Then sued for wrongful death? Brilliant, Your Highness. Now let's just see about how thick that blood is!"

"I..."

"You want to live, Mom? Why?" I asked, completely proud of my uniform of fatigues, flack-jacket and army boots. My hair was long and braided, my beard was dark with no hint of gray—I was fit...I had that mission given in secret, I had more than anyone could ever want or need.

"What do you want, Vincent?"

I lit a stogie, good and sweet and just primed to be my pleasure. "My men need me, and so you're in the way—I must deliver your head to the King. The Rubicon is crossed, the threads are bare, and you're surrounded. They wait for you—your head, actually—in the Holy Land."

She recoiled, to my amazement, and threw a lamp at me—I ran after her around her bedroom, the boudoir, the oval office overlooking the green. Oh, we had great frolicking fun! "Hide and go seek, eh, Mommy!"

She fell down the spiral staircase too easily, breaking her hip. I cut her throat like her servant who laid a few yards away, and then kept cutting with the serrated blade, through the spinal matter and finally I ripped the ex-beauty queen's head off and stuffed it into my laundry sack, a prize for my Lord, the glorious light from the east, to whom I am but a humble servant.

I needed her arms and hands, and used a saw for those.

When the mission ended, I set fire to the house and wandered away with my prize, disappearing onto the third fairway of the vast countryside adjacent to Century City. I handed over Maria to my men, the spoils of a fine victory.

Soon the sirens were wailing and I could see my brothers playing a mock game of golf and making utter fools of themselves (they have never been in polite society, they are warriors) as we laid down the rules for the girl—one at a time. By the time we arrived at the fifth green, under the canopy of trees, we were truly at peace. Spent, and full of lemonade from the refreshment stand. These club-hounds had it easy—and the last thing I wanted was for my men to get soft. At one point the Flagellator started using Mom's head as a bowling ball but gentle Millicet took it away and placed it in the bag.

"So where's the girl?" I asked. And that's when I saw that

Silas, a right sick ol' boy, playing croquet with Maria's head. "Silas! What do I pay you for? Give me your knife, you can't be trusted, obviously. What, you think this is a big joke?" I asked.

He looked around for a second, scolded. "I was just havin' a little fun...I'm sorry."

"Look, we're in foreign territory, we just bagged one of the beauty queens of the past (Jude was dispatched with it forthwith to deliver to our Control, who will remain nameless at this point.)

"Look, beloved," Millicet said. "We have a mission—we are behind enemy lines, and horseplay is certainly not appreciated, even from you, Flagellator."

"I related to her, not from the future, but from the past. Forgive me, my friends, my fellow servants," I said, aware of my mistakes.

"She was the queen of the past—you got stuck there momentarily...it happens, don't worry about it," said Silas, with corncob pipe and dirty long hair.

"Silas, how I love you—of course what you did to Maria—that's the kind of foul play used for combat, not tactical. What's wrong with just sex?"

"Can't get it up," Millicet said, stroking his beard and laughing.

"I needed another head," Silas said nonchalantly, and the men howled gleefully.

"Perhaps you're right," I said, trying to understand. "I suppose it's a calling card, of sorts."

We took her head with us, as a kind of mascot.

"Yes, Silas," I said, "how courageous you were at the convenience store of the future, sparing not even a guest, and even the gas, allowing it to flow into your torch to light up the midnight sky."

Silas took his sword and held it up toward the moon while taking a knee and proclaiming: "The Queen of the Past is dead. Vincent lives!"

Soon we heard dogs barking and soon more sirens, and then we were all awakened by bright lights of chariots blazing the night wide open and running right for us!

The five of us split up around the golf course with honed ears of higher octaves, as no conversation in the entire city could be held without one of us in attendance. A target-rich environment, our orders were to infiltrate enemy lines, to find and crush the next beauty queen and her armies. Mr. Nunn, I call you friend, for now—surely you would be surprised to hear that finding the next target was no easy task.

And she is multifarious, indeed.

OWT

"**S**o you're back. You're reading something and if it isn't what I am telling you, I might be very upset. I know you, Carl Nunn, but not *you*...who is he?" I asked.

When no answer came, I realized they might move me somewhere else, but my recounting of the factual events of this story would continue.

"Do you have any idea how much damage you've caused, Vincent?" the one who was with Carl said.

I settled down right quick to the task at hand. Was it debriefing, or briefing? The task was for my Lord, something these fleshly creatures could not understand. A rise in their pants, anger as sweat on the brow, more money than was fair—that, now that, they understood. So I laughed at them and the Voice (the one with Carl) became afraid.

It was a marriage made, a bed turned out and a masquerade—it was fitting how it just stood there and sung to all who might lend an ear, forgetting entirely that this was, after all, the

Kingdom of Leonard Kruzmar, the sort of kingdom that befits a Hollywood producer and confidante to over half the board at the Mount Triac Studio Facility in Culver City. What does this matter? You came to view the surface, and this is just the outer layer of the real *schlemiel*, but I will not hold it back from you, Carl, or your friend, numb-nuts.

Yes, Hollywood. Suffice to say, Trundle Pictures was Kruzmar's home, assuming that from childhood Kruzmar was upfront about his glorious past—frolicking around in girls' clothes at various women's functions, whether luncheon or paddle tennis or charitable tables. It was all really just one thing: a mad competition with the idea that all were perfectly made from the same alchemical reaction from deep inside the womb of woman—who was Earth itself.

Though Hollywood was populated with mean, spoiled kids, the jungle gym was political in nature, and a scientific analysis was never far from Kruzmar's Bel Air Estate. He had been the all-American, the festooned Crew and Q type—at least while he was climbing and the mysterious money would show up so that he could produce pictures, lots of pictures. Pictures with the best talent, all knew by now that this was no ordinary, bootstrap cherry pie sort of diligence—no, this was to be feared; too far from envy to signify. Low profile, not too much about the conservative parents who belonged to things that members couldn't even approach, much less enter—much less contemplate. The White House, Hollywood East—the prize, and occupied steadily—Kruzmar family implants. For Kruzmar, the politicians were what you might call men of the world, unfurled and striving after the wind—and Kruzmar would think of Milton Smith from Arkansas who knew about being a company man, yet fired because Kruzmar wanted bondservants, not individuals. Somehow, they all knew Kruzmar was behind all the significant careers in Washington, but it was a secret, and Milton's class ring would only go so far.

Wind was blowing down Culver Boulevard, down Motor Avenue, up the skirt of Sherry Lastlink, who stood a small distance away at the other studio, which had been Century and now became Monsoon. The children-who-marketed decided that a studio *should* be named Monsoon, just like a restaurant Kruzmar used to like, and there were secret merger talks with regards to Monsoon and others, and Kruzmar wanted a piece but his wife wanted a lot more.

He knew about a lot of things, a real Q, but it was all Italian shit, so that the penny loafers were very light and the plaid shirt was silk, the watch was Patek. The mood was very upbeat. So this shining, bright-eyed boy came to claim a paycheck, and right out of the box he hires Harry Batzer, no less, twenty-four mil a pop, and Leticia Wiles, goddess, swooner, and the best faker. So Kruzmar was trusted, you know, right down the middle, not too far this way or that, a confidence man for society, who had that secret stake in all studio business. His people didn't want to appear to be siphoning off all that pain from filthy media profits, show-biz people were so, non-aligned…no real blood, just mongoloid vessels. So having the Kruzmar son fit the bill. Oh, how cute he looked in the plaid ties!

You could put forty mil in his account and he would remain calm. He was always calm. If there were to be a glorious future in the land of inversion, it would rest in the transformation of Kruzmar. Mr. Leonard Cutlass Kruzmar, a Jew when you needed a Jew, a Wasp at a Republican Convention, a Catholic in a crayon convention. All white, blond and blue…man? Well, I'll let you say. What is a man these days? If a pair of testicles makes the man, he had 'em. He was the hope, the great hope of all the Los Angeles hilltop ghettos—that maybe, just maybe, little obedient Leonard would provide a way for the past to catch up, as if delusion was really worthy of senility.

And then he changed.

They would consider this the gentle move, the sharing with a woman move—yes, married…yes, divorced from the one who got fat and had the kids and backed him when he was down, keeping the name for some future assault, but the best she could do was run the new Azure into the jockey outside Kruzmar's new gate.

It was more of a calculated transformation. The press, the sociologists, the whole intelligencia mob had become tranquilized by fear. What if they talked about this? What if they mentioned Kruzmar's secret plan for transforming boyhood in

America? Every boy standing *against* God? The final solution—Kruzmar style. The glorious equanimity of Darwin's nonexistent but nevertheless Satanic theory of evolution, boys and girls as half-and-half! Boys pregnant, and girls developing the inward outward. It was more than just gay or straight or stupid or smart. Such extremes were outmoded, ridiculous. No, the man of the future would be literally di-sexed, as in both sexes, that is, hermaphroditic but with beauty, precision and genetic manipulation allowing for quick and easy conquests, self-abuses, and when the real man's man was around, the not so ubiquitous hero, enough of a woman so as to certainly and positively qualify in the morally mellifluous corporate culture of tomorrow. Oh, yes it was terribly hush-hush, just like Kruzmar had always liked. "We can't just let anybody have a key to the washroom! Not everybody's gonna get a seat at the table, unless...you can do something impressive. "But I've seen it all, so it better be good," he would say, and often.

All were terribly pleased with Kruzmar, their hidden god, because Kruzmar amplified a certain reptilian quality born of his subtle, week-by-week submission, and wouldn't everyone like to know where Kruzmar went for his material blessings!

He was considered a genius—yes, the lisp was a bit obvious, but the college boy thing had gone on for twenty years. The coiffed and streaked blond—yes, always blond—the precise grace of this coordinated man whose first real conquest was stabbing his best friend in the heart because he was looking for the way up.

His name was Whitley, and he was innocent—he was good, he was a little too good, and that did not sit well with the higher-ups. Kruzmar saw the opportunity of a lifetime—so it was goodbye youth, hello manhood! Kruzmar and only Kruzmar could have turned his senior year into the ultimate initiation and social climbing event. And sure, anyone would say that poor Whitley brought it on himself, especially when he proved he was a blab-all, an embarrassment, a potential danger to the rarefied society in which he was born. Nobody ever told him the true meaning behind the phrase "loose lips sink ships."

And so the motherfucker just stabbed him at Nancy Herrington's Coming Out party. Quite a coming out for one

Leonard Kruzmar, as he upstaged them all. Of course they understood, just as one must self-corrupt "on stage" as it were, so must one prove one's mettle at such things as elimination by any means possible. No one taught Kruzmar, this was all innate.

And so now Leonard proved he had a taste for human sacrifice; oh, how the reward was vast! Kruzmar moved up, and fast. He had the cachet, he had *push*, a fast track through college and then right into the family's global business: guns, drugs and slaves, not necessarily in that order. He was trusted with the keys, had a security detail that was nothing short of the U.S. military's best and brightest. Final destination? Movies...movies, and a mogul that no one would ever question. Nobody wanted to get stabbed! He had a brother somewhere—black sheep.

"Who the fuck cares? Let the dead bury the dead," he would say, misquoting the Bible. *Stabbed the fucking loser at seventeen and with no remorse!* So Whitley's body was removed from the club ballroom, placed in a car and dumped off a cliff somewhere in New Mexico. Meanwhile, Leonard was smoking cigars with presidents and kings.

They feared him mightily. He moved from mail boy for ten minutes to co-producer on the hundred mil sequel involving dinosaurs, then produced one low-budget horror film about witches and the occult—of course he knew all about that from Mother Kruzmar.

Yes, mother, responsible for it all.

Her name was Abacazzia, blonde, petite and would say things like *super* and *fabulous* and wore perfect little white pearls—a string of tortured victims, goodies for remembrance—ate a sandwich cut in two, leaving the second half and a nice bowl of soup, daily, of course. Yes, Leonard knew her three friends who prophesied many things they said they made happen. They were called practitioners, ladies of the Craft—or the three witches.

Leonard simply cranked all that funny money into production after production, garnering critical accolades for the mental hospital flick, then the revenge piece (curiously, about a guy who's murdered at a social event, then covered up by the whole town!), and all the while Leonard was still Joe-Preppy, all the while he could command a haggard power-broker down on his knees under the marble desk for that kiss of the almighty Kruzmar ring.

The feminine mystique—backing 'em all the way, in all productions, in all power seats. His genius for knowing when to jump—this strategy kept him. The unraveling gender master? The smiling flesh-eater? In a word, yes, the telling and the foisting, a'lusting and a'thrusting—power would be his, his, his, in perpetuity, ratified by everyone with a pecker. A man of vengeance would know and could voice the rage, outrage, insanity, cruelty and dishonor all the way to his definition of heaven—but he could only tepidly report this tale of ambition, and reluctantly so.

ⓐ   ⓐ   ⓐ

I wasn't impressed with Kruzmar, who orchestrated the *event* where Whitley was feeling frightened and alone as all the kids were laughing at him, teasing and mocking, joking an *a'plotting*. Whitley was the perfect hit, if you had to hit somebody. I, the witness, showed him how to thumb his nose at everybody. "Watch me, Whitley—I'll show you how to piss 'em off…"

For some reason I had no shame about such things, so I walked over to one of the patriarch's of the club, Mr. Goering, who was seated with his diamond studded, paddle tennis wife, pulled out my johnson—all the gray-hairs stood agog—and urinated gleefully all over Mr. Goering's sandwich. "Guess all I can do is piss with it, sir," I said and looked to see Whitley Marcus, seated at the table with Kruzmar, laughing his ass off. It was good to see him laugh.

But they hauled me away that day—that very moment! Security guards descending from on high—the once placid beach club became a battle zone. I was promptly shipped to a private psychiatric hospital out of state where I met many brothers and sisters. The news of Whitley's death came as a shock, and I wept for three days. I had tried in vain to save him, for there was no way out except a noble life of crime, and in their psychotic way of looking at it was called "service."

GLASS BACKWARDS

All this time I maintained a line into Kruzmar's mind, and that wasn't so much because of him, but because of his mother, a witch that my Lord called the Queen of Damnation. Mother Abacazzia Fontainebleau Himmelman Kruzmar.

After I easily escaped from the "Institute," I awaited my next assignment on the streets of Denver, and then Phoenix—out of sight, out of mind. I had contacts and this was how I learned every little thing you'd ever want to know about the man who killed your best friend. The present from the past, advantageous. The training camp was necessary, as was the Flagstaff log cutting job, which built me up and made me fast.

("I can see, Mr. Nunn, the story you want to hear is sociological, perhaps even scatological or pathological. What happened to Hollywood, you keep asking me? I am telling you that you need to hear it from the very bottom to the very top, from the slaughtered innocents, the liars and the witches, from even God Himself, or you truly haven't got a story," I told Carl Nunn while he kept publishing article after article about me. But slowly things were turning my way, and Kruzmar was the one they—the public—were beginning to disdain.)

For one thing, Kruzmar had changed—started speaking in a womanly manner while garnering himself a brand new wife named Lucy, not pretty, but ambitious and smart, a steel blade at any social occasion. Yes, Kruzmar could now be publicly effeminate, after all that was what was required of all the new men working at the studio; at least it was the written rule. You simply cannot have the uninitiated and undefiled wandering around into meetings or other private affairs and openly staring in shock or disbelief over anything. The new highway was wide; flesh was a smooth and fast road for Kruzmar. Little did he realize the need for prophecy, until he met his wife Lucy, who spent every day listening to the wind, and came up with marvelous visions to further the fortunes of unscrupulous merit and folly. What sort of spiritual advice would Kruzmar need if Lucy would do the worrying and complaining and climbing over the emasculated and cardboard, up to higher, more exotic levels before the crowd of onlookers who would never advance beyond deck chair jockeys on the Titanic?

Lucy knew from a very young age, from the orphanage, the brutes, the traitors, how she could turn them for a profit! But this, this! This new life of Hollywood was a joke, merely taking candy from an idiot. Her new life was easy. To think, a lowly writer gets hired by Kruzmar on a fluke because Kruzmar liked her treatment about a lesbian golf club, and then, the impossible...could she, should she or would she wind up on Leonard Cutlass Kruzmar's arm, in the dynasty of the Kruzmar name? For liberating a pent-up man named Leonard—whom she loved to pal around with—into his stereo sexuality, his will to be passive, but aggressive. His will to do all things well, including choosing a wife. His will to emasculate men worldwide for his private pleasure. His will to see a globe in the image of his own desires. His will to power.

His will to power, for what?

His will to control, for what?

His will to sex, for what?

His will, for what?

His, for what?

4 watt?

Her answer was never complete, and one day she swore to herself she would ascertain his true purpose, something behind his manifold pursuits, and she would learn the Kruzmar manifesto by heart and soul if necessary—she just wouldn't go back to slime and death and Frankie, Dave and Big Mike. And pimp Keshawn, and social worker Milda, and thief Snakey, or for rock and crystal and spread legs along the South Side and along the thoroughfare. Yes, Kruzmar knew all of this. It's what he needed, someone to fear, someone not in the system, someone he could infuse with power, all for his own use. A surrogate Kruzmar, an imitation...a ritual object—Lucy. A substitute. A multiplication of Kruzmarian supremacy.

Let her think what she wants, he mused. Let her think *anything* she wants...she's like everybody else, except for Vincent,

Kruzmar would think. Just knowing what happened to Lucy's mother, Martha, a waitress at Fido's Deli till she dropped dead of a mistaken bullet could help down the road; perhaps finding another Martha to hold sway if necessary, a tie-breaker, a manipulator, a mind-destroyer—like he had with his ex.

Acting was good for Lucy, writing was even better. She vowed she'd get off the streets, vowed she wouldn't wind up a junkie prostitute face down in the lap of a fat pimp. Mother was always watching those old movies with the best and brightest, the Princess Graces, the Ingrid Bergmans. "Lucy, just act like these girls...you'll go a lot farther if you do," she would tell her daughter. Lucy would pretend she was fabulously wealthy, utterly educated, and properly prim. What she did not know she would find out, she was a quick study, and until she met Leonard Cutlass Kruzmar, all she came up with were deuces.

He claimed that he loved her, bought her things, and doted on her in her room. They shared lovers together in the same bed and he always loved hearing Lucy-dish, Lucy-gossip, Lucy-imaginings, Lucy-paranoia, Lucy-consciousness...that's what he wanted. A filter...to wipe away the memories of cynicism and wretchedness, of nasty uncles and unwanted sodomy, of unneeded fondling and being told it was all love. Of quiet strategy and building on those who built the world...the Kruzmar Dynasty.

And she mistook him for an innocent! She would say, "Never mind, Leonard, you're too pretty for this kind of thing."

Oh, how he would delight in her bouncy, little way when her dark eyes would twirl around at how funny the rising and falling was—how weak they were (she and Leonard shared this reality) and how much fun she had dressing up and going out to meetings with all sorts of studio executives and how she began to influence Leonard to speak at the board meetings about changes. They would fall and she begged him to be there so she could watch the expression on their faces as they marched out of their ocean view offices down the hall and into their Mercedes. When Josh Banax blew his brains out she felt she had finally arrived. These were wussies, no question—she would rule over their incredible and implacable weaknesses; the men would have to go.

"I love you, Lucy—you're not only the best thing that's ever happened—I have a power I never had when I was a boy and I thought I had eternity in my tummy."

"Oh, you are so intelligent. I'd have a kid if we could get a surrogate."

"Boy or girl?"

"You and your science projects about boys getting pregnant."

The maids had heard it all through the intercom, and one was foolish enough to tape-record it, and there was nothing special written in her obituary, and certainly no investigation of her car the night of her accident on Mulholland when she was running an errand for Kruzmar. It was not even mentioned in his household. The word was always, "Next!"

To think that Lucy Shadrach, a poor girl from Chicago who blew her way into some shoestring scholarship to Vassar, would breathe the lineage of total ascendancy, a family with power and kingly heritage *all the way to the serpent*, someone told her once, laughing.

To think of Leonard Kruzmar's childhood, that picture she kept in her purse of her "man," just a little boy playing with an Indian knife and stabbing a cowboy doll with it.

GLASS BACKWARDS

EERHT

Styles' corporate persona hid perfectly his experience in the pornography world. His campaign to call it a communications company, with interactive internet, phone service, television, video, DVD movies and games allowed it to be funded by the world's largest banks and brokerage houses. In fact, agreeing to be named the studio chief of Mount Triac, agreeing as long as he could implement a total merging of his media empire into the vast distribution arm of Mount Triac. The board voted unanimously and all celebrated by attending the premiere party for The Young at the Hackfield Museum of Cultural Diversity, and at the Unction Parlor (UP or "Uppie") watching the slicers and piercers behind glass. Later, as the tide was stimulated, there would be early morning anything-goes girl fights at the Founder's Gym. The rules were simple, the participants had to be clad in g-strings and bare-breasted, which was obviously a handicap for some—and they had to slather themselves with oil, which made it impossible for a wrestling takedown, but great for all out slapping. To the victor went the tarts, the spoils and the underwriters—Styles was so proud—which meant that whatever the winner wanted to do to, or with, or in, or around and through the loser, it had to be done center stage. The audience laid around on gym mats and pillows, waited on by "trained and professional" waiters and waitresses. The lighting was methodically dim outside the ring. Styles was always partial to live entertainment, where the outcome was never secure, and where the possibility of failure enhanced every forward thrust.

Sure, Kruzmar had attended, but usually fell asleep. For him, pain, torture and sex were simply a means to an end—he loved to film his friends in compromising fare because that was useful in certain business encounters. He always kept his eye on the prize, and never forgot the purpose of such satanic conviviality—to the winner goes all! Why had they all forgotten?

Or were they never taught?

Lucy would say: "Look, Leonard, you have to go. You have to keep your hand in the game."

What a hand Leonard had put to excellent use, now that he did not exactly have to, now that his hands were bronzed, especially showing how an apron-strings wuss could garner such power, when a man of the field, brute and stringent, disciplined and noble, would get nothing. "Pity the poor man," Leonard would say, "get the motherfucker a broom."

Now, Styles was the man. The board was divided after the one hundred eighty-million- dollar war epic debacle. But he had the French Bond Company, his porn kingdom, turning out more and more profits for the studio—so they had to give him that. They had to acknowledge that he indeed brought something to the table.

And the growth charts were off the map. Thirty-five percent year-over-year growth in margins, twenty-eight percent year-over-year on the bottom line. That meant hundreds of millions of dollars with more and more products coming to market almost daily.

Kruzmar and Styles were camped at the Moroccan table in the back, sharing the agreed-upon delusion, where the victorious woman "co-testant" forces her victim into nearly everything: from shaving and the creative use of humanly incompatible devices to a lineup of endowed male mannequins (the real men would of course perform with each other, never with the women). So this was the zenith, the penultimate of good times, and a good time was in the offing, and a good time was had as the light of the morning glue stuck the minds into a tapestry of One.

"Look at them—good stock," Leonard said, amply.

"You mean the cattle?" said Styles.

"The sheep," Leonard said, thinking "better."

"The shit," Styles said. "Our lives are nothing but marvelous shit, but you, my young friend, don't know that yet. You will."

"Oh..." Kruzmar moaned, bored to tears with the has-been. Kruzmar was a bit weary, and wondered why Lucy didn't like the sort of pecking order violence that accompanies men and their fight to translate their will to sexual conquest and then into studio dollars and studio position. "But we know something they don't know."

"Yeah, *it's all entertainment*," said Styles, proud like a big sky rancher. High like a king. "And with it, we'll bury 'em all. Not bread and circus, *just circus*."

One thing about Kruzmar, at least from the standpoint of show—whenever he attended these events it was back to Joe-Preppy. Cardigan, plaid and brown leather, to be sure. Low-key. Styles would never understand the fabulous and suffused vision of grandeur Kruzmar harbored, and he would have to wait until someone of note could inform the board that Styles' vision for the future was as small as his purported genitals. A single studio, scaled back, more television, less celluloid—what the motherfucker wanted was a front! A lousy front to filter the skin *buckeroonies* through. A disgrace, he surely was, Kruzmar would always be sure. Oh, he knew it deeply, knew it completely. And he would know more as soon as he would let himself know what others were hoping for.

Big shareholders, board members, and every gin maker and shoe designer from Hong Kong to Baton Rouge was eyeing with uncircumcised abandon—the heathen!—a studio, a world, and a world view that Kruzmar felt he, and he alone, was responsible for.

But he, Leonard of Pedigree, whom everyone considered a pushover, was not violently disposed toward Styles. That which made him born of woman's apron strings forever and ever was that which would depress him one day—would make him question his little reality, the whole comedy of him he would resent in the form of his mother—but not yet. To think, therefore, that it was his own power, or under his own guise, that all these things happened, or more importantly, were going to happen, would be a serious mistake in perception. Remember, the operative word is Entertainment, which is illusion, falsehood, or false witness, which is sin, like lying or murder, like avarice, greed and no good.

"Trick or treat, Daddy!" Leonard's children would say, and he would say, "Can you spell M-A-U-I?" and they would cheer and Cari, his ex-wife, would wail for hours, days, perhaps indefinitely. He would see she meant business, so he dressed conservatively, as were his colors and his honor to do, well-bred, WASP training comes in handy on islands like Maui. With so much feast of foul, so many tethers and snares, crafted in glasses and away beyond volcanoes, the man of the world would throw his children down the volcano slide, work with his young male writers, and sashay to and fro between resorts on the Wailea coast with effortless abandon. Of course he would speak to the young flesh at the conferences and other places where his bowling-boy fronts would work swimmingly. No one knew Kruzmar as a murderer, and indeed, it was not something he ought to spend a lot of time contemplating. A double mind is good for the soul. A friend that used to be a conscience, a soothing presence, who would look through his eyes and be happy for the accomplishment of life in war, was worth it. A double mind was a good mind. A double mind is the only mind. A single mind is a fool, Kruzmar, pretty boy, all things to all people, would constantly remind himself.

For future reference, help would be hired. He had worked in the kitchen, he'd gotten the respect, and did not have to respect back, and it was all because of his new bride—Lucy. Yes, Lucy, who had hired an all-girl team to play office on the lot. The real game was whether Kruzmar would ever get caught for knowing everything so well. The real game was how long it could, or would last; the real game was not from a memory source, unfortunately, and Kruzmar would never understand himself as a cripple.

A creature of limitation, Kruzmar would never accept.

This would be his undoing.

RUOF

Now, Lucy would sit at the feet of Kruzmar's mama, Mother Kruzmar, or some ancient other name like Abacazzia Fontainebleau Himmelman Kruzmar, duchess of division and distress—creator of the double mind. Nevertheless, she was a whiz at dividing the root, the ancients would say. Her friend Margot Del Monte would be missed, and indeed, the heinous, Manson-like (you see, *Manson* is really an alliteration of the term *Monsoon*, not the other way around, and is a direct link to the new studio) murder of both servant and matron, and no head. "Really, Lucy, there is no head on the poor overlooked darling. You see, you really must make the effort to be social, or you become a recluse and then you see what happens. Poor girl, she was one of us once: Women's League, Cancer Society, Darwin Club. It's beyond something as silly as the mafia or even the annals of our torturous and incestuous boredom called polite society."

"I want to learn everything I can, so he knows I'm not an idiot," Lucy said, primping and preening like a little duck fresh under waterfall.

Abacazzia liked that. Her son chose well—Lucy could be in-

culcated, and no one else could be. No one else would accept the
indwelling. No one else but a street urchin could appreciate what
life was...hardball, cold steel, a knees-down blowjob for a kick in
the teeth if you weren't *inside*.

"He knows you're not an idiot—my lovely dear, I have more
than certified you at the outset—but there will come a time for
insemination, you understand."

"Yes."

"That's my girl," Mother Kruzmar, her bald spot prominent,
her one blue eye and one brown eye competing for allure and
sympathy. "It's horrible to get old, that's why we do this. The
only thing that makes it worthwhile is to see you lighting up our
family, and lifting up my son. A daughter of darkness cloaked in
light. You'll understand, it's about their flesh, not yours."

Mother Kruzmar took Lucy in, and she attended the coven
whilst the man of the hour was still island bound. It was a place
far from the Matrix Bar, the Peninsula Bar, the Bimbim Bar, the
MarBar, the Skat Bar and the day spa; there was no time to waste,
because the spell had been cast on, and the big cranes and high
office towers and lights and cameras and the very motion of their
dreams was grand and larger than life—everywhere the men
thought they were the owners and were out to play, and everywhere they were free from guilt and hard for pleasure, a man's
world, after all...and Lucy now saw how the women played with
all the parts like a chess game, like make-believe in the sandbox.
"They are in the field, but the field is formed right here—sym-
bolically," Abacazzia would tell her. "See them? The little minia-
tures running around thinking the other guy is smaller?"

Three of them, the three prophetesses, were all women of
color, all gray hair, husbands all dead, the three widows of the
truth, and Lucy knew to listen. She knew they were not going to
spin idle tales, that what was said would happen soon, abiding
and abiding, she would.

"Lucy, darling, I can't keep my eyes open, you stay here with
Serena, Asenath and Milaca. They will keep you good company,
and if you know of anything you think I should hear of, wake
me. One more thing: they were with my grandmother, and my
mother, and here they are with you...listen to them, for they are

immortal."

Mother Kruzmar's wheelchair ambled past her dead husband's war trophies and pictures of past presidents and Jewish Christmas parties.

"So it's a matriarchy?" Lucy asked in earnest.

They laughed and spoke of the root being the male *glans penis*—and that all roots in the ground were *imago-mundi*, or an image of the penis, which was an image of the world. To divide and conquer would be the quest, and men were the means to the ends for the controllers of the earth, Destiny's Goddess, represented by the three.

Lucy tightened the ribbon in her hair, and sat cross-legged in her blue jeans while they spoke rhythmically.

It was plump Serena, from the coast of Mozambique, circa 1800's, who knew of all things past and present. And spoke her prophecy: "There is no payment for death, and the death of one who is not worth his space alive, in style and out of style, the balloon goes up, and the blade comes down. But there is another one."

By now the breeze was wafting through the Polynesian room at the mansion, and they smoked opium from the pipe and spread about on pillows. The floor was sunken, its stones of copper slate and jade bejeweled were adorned by Afghan and Moroccan prayer rugs.

Lucy sat snug in her mind screen, so she could be inculcated.

Even the pool boy, Jerry, pretty, taut, innocent and boyish, a delish for anyone, buttoned up his shirt as clouds gathered overhead.

As the wind picked up and a summer rain commenced, though the humidity could not be stopped, the prophetess named Serena spoke, and the other two played with stones in a sandbox, moving them to her rhythmic tones—Lucy could see it all after another toke from the hookah.

"The style would go both ways, the Queen of the Past represents the Queen of All. Tragedy lies ahead, but whose will it be? She is revealed when the style of the day is no longer. And the blood washes all as clean as Leonard in the Lion's seat, King for the world to see."

Lucy stepped up, for these were servants and she had to treat them as such—for such was a test.

ⓐ　ⓐ　ⓐ

When I arrived in the house it was Peter Mallard, the well-to-do playwright and Queenie ® winning screenwriter who met me. I had apparently arrived just in the nick because his wife Sophie was pointing a gun at him, drunk beyond the pale, a few hanger-on guests still lounging at poolside, though the time was past the high place and lower than the cock-a-doodle-do. It was the time of the swaying palms in Santa Ana delight. Mallard had his back turned from her, and she laughed while shooting the gun into the air, hoping to hear the sirens she'd heard earlier—when Queen Margot was beheaded. She would swoop her way across the teak floor, waving the gun threateningly, but something prevented her from killing her brilliant husband. I was astonished how comfortable I felt in the Frank Lloyd Wright knockoff circa 1962, all the flat rooflines and palms, the atmosphere was swingin', man, and I was catching the rhythm! I felt at home, most assuredly.

I was accompanied, of course, by Millicet. But they ignored him, and I marveled at how he happened on the bowls of cocaine and the bottles of Crystal. Nothing had changed since the eighties, and it was immediately apparent by Mallard's guests that they had no idea who he was, Millicet that is, and so it was my duty, as a gentleman in the service of my Lord, to rescue Mallard, Peter S., from this white trash interloper with the big titties.

I sat with him at the piano and helped him with a Chopin waltz—he was so fast, I couldn't catch him. "Very good," he said in a standard British accent. "I say, dear boy, do you know the King's Fox Trot?"

He proceeded to play right eloquently and I was mystified why Millicet would not at least introduce us, since he remembered much better than I did.

"Do I know you? I like your boots," he said to me.

Indeed, I was wearing the standard-issue military boots from Quaker's Surplus down on Venice Boulevard.

"And your shirt, indeed—it's torn, and bloodstained; what are you up to, lad?" he said, drunker than his wife (I now realized that Mallard's big-tit mama was no skank from Reseda, and I would have apologized if things didn't start moving so fast).

"Let's play ping-pong," he insisted, and I followed him across the open-terraced living room, with the pool that snuck under the glass and into the play room, where it became a hot tub that you could swim away from out into the yard, all the way to the fountain that framed the swaying trees.

I took a couple of snorts along with Mallard, mainly because he insisted I be awake long enough to hear his new story idea. And so, indeed, I did what he said while Millicet, still in that blasted camouflage jacket, allowed himself to be seduced by Sophie, I suppose that was her name, who allowed him to take the gun and massage her on the pool table for the benefit of the five men who could not seem to keep their hands to themselves.

This was no concern to me, as I was involved in what might be called a police activity.

"Come, lad—you're about my size. Indeed, 5'11, 165 pounds? Believe me, having the 32-inch waist is an advantage. Here we are," he said while coughing and falling onto the cedar floor. I helped him up and took what looked like a satin smoking jacket, donned it with intrigue, while he fitted me into a pair of black Armani's and his favorite t-shirt, silky smooth. "Wore this one in Maui during the conference last year."

"Thanks," I said. "I'm glad I came. You don't mind Millicet, do you?" I asked, as any soldier would.

He stared at my Spyderco knife with the serrated edge. I had not wiped the blood off it, and figured he would know we were in quite a battle zone. But he did not judge, he did not try to assess anything. He took me to his study where there were many nude photos of his wife Sophie on the wall, as she was a stunning professional of some repute.

He would muse, "I simply call her by her last name, Haya. Sometimes I whistle for her to flash 'em in front of my friends so they can jerk off to something real. You like to jerk off?"

"My body doesn't belong to me."

"Oh," Mallard mused. "Are you a religious man?"

"We're trying to help you," I said, but he didn't seem relieved. "You of a double mind, sir?"

"Why...yes. Isn't everybody?" he asked, and perhaps he knew nothing of what I spoke. That would preserve his life, but only for a while, as my Lord is adamant about those with double minds—it's off with their heads, I'm afraid.

Peter S. Mallard showed me his six computers on various tables and how they were wired for games. Then he showed me his tape recorder used to write such classics as the *Innkeeper's Daughter* and *Rogue Assassin*.

He peered at me through a kind of square, Elvis Costello type glasses and he laughed. A man of a forgotten era, no doubt.

"Time for ping-pong," he said. "Maybe we can watch my wife get gangbanged on the pool table. Would you like that, Vincent?"

I hadn't thought about such an offer, and I thought I might rather like it, though not for the purposes of some sort of sexual emission. I thought I had told him, in as polite a manner as possible, that I was a eunuch (which gave me the strength of any ten men) for my Lord—that did not preclude sex with women, it just made things a bit more complicated. And so to somehow try and do away with the fear in his eyes, that was now the question before me. I wasn't quite sure how to handle it. It was as if he was giving me the run of the place out of fear and not truly because he valued our company, that is, me and Millicet, who had the ancient boldness in his baby-blues.

"I...would...you like money? H-how 'bout if I bang my wife and pay you to videotape me?" he was saying, as if pleading for mercy, as if he was making a plea for mercy.

"Truly, sir—for someone of your stature, Mr. Mallard? You needn't fear anyone, not after what you've accomplished."

"Call me...call me *Peter*. Peter, is that name alright with you, Vincent?"

When he picked up the phone it was Silas (don't ask me how he got in) who grabbed it and struck Peter Mallard squarely in the nose, shattering it, the nose that is.

"Silas! What the devil are you doing?" I demanded. "I'm sorry, Peter, this...this fool thought you were the enemy."

And then, curiously, Peter S. Mallard started pleading with me again. "Would you like money? Please, or if you like we could collaborate on a new story—how's this: a couple of guys break into a rich guy's home, rape and kill his wife, rape him, but don't kill him, and then they have group therapy and the...therapist— yes, he's...he's a...a psychiatrist, you know? Maybe his name is Haddon, sure, Dr. Haddon and his promiscuous wife, twenty years his junior, Sylvia, or ..."

"How about Margot?" I said, not able to think about a single name except that one.

"A yes, a little, how do you say, La France...francais, oui! Qu'es ce qe c'est maintenant?"

I said: "Oh...comme si, comme ça."

"Oui, bien tout! But of course!" he said as Silas ran after him down the stairs.

"Where did the gun come from—the .38 cal. Smith and Wesson?" I inquired of Peter Mallard.

"A gift, from...it was a souvenir from the movie...the Kruzmar thing, you know...oh, I don't know why the name escapes me now...it's—" Mallard started snapping his fingers while blood stained his goatee and white shirt. I figured he was all right.

"You mean the mental hospital piece? About the boy who was holy, but his parents accused him of being crazy? And his parents locked him up because they didn't understand?"

"Yes, you know it?"

"No," I said, and felt like eating the satin jacket as we watched Sophie, who was nude, spread-eagled on the pool table of all things. Millicet had kept Silas from stuffing her with various and sundry things. "Well, you know, Peter, this is the kind of help we get these days. Being a mercenary certainly isn't easy."

But he was so wrapped up in the television news he did not seem to hear what I said. Indeed, it was obvious that his wife had done this kind of thing so many times before. Why he gave me the gun with such a troubled look on his face was anybody's guess. We got rid of those overly sexed male friends of his, who seemed like movie people—and one committed suicide, which did not surprise me given the gravity of the drugs, and of course it was clear that they all needed help, Peter most of all. There were bodies in closets and clothes strewn all over, overturned lamps and chairs and CDs all over the floor. It was looking like bedlam, and I held Peter responsible. Someone had to. "Mr. Mallard, you deserve a better class of friends—look at this mess. I hope you have good help," I said. "You're not a cliché—you've done fine work! But this…this is a cliché, isn't it, unless you…" I trailed off—I was getting my orders by and by.

"I admit, I am sorry—I am sorry for having this party, and I am sorry that my guests stayed so long. Are you going to punish me for that?" Peter asked.

I knelt down to reason with him. I had to tie him to the chair facing his wife, because that's where he wanted to be. "Honey, sweet pea?" he would cry out.

We all listened. She grunted and groaned. "We had to gag her, sir," I said. "She was much too unruly."

"Did you have to rape her?" he asked me. Well, usually I am a kind man. I am tolerant. I had just spent time in his office and in his closet and in his master bedroom telling him how I was much like a eunuch, with no real sex drive, except to please my Lord.

"Did you escape from some loony bin, is that it? Did you kill Margot Del Monte, like the news says? What do you WANT FROM ME, YOU FUCKING CRAZY ASSHOLE!?"

"I hope you understand, sir," I said calmly, "I hope you understand that this sort of outburst is not the kind of fellowship and friendly discussion that befits a civilized man such as yourself. It's nothing personal," I said, while wrapping the duct tape around his mouth eight or nine times.

But he kept on with his eyes—outrage, fear, total distrust.

"I am disappointed, but not all hope is lost," I said. "I thought you might have had some manners. I do appreciate the offer of staying at the house. I just need to rest my men, as they'll need a little R & R—"

"Are you going to kill me?" he said through ESP, and he was insistent. And that's when I knew he wouldn't last too long, perhaps not even through the night. One thing was for sure: it was all up to him, as I tried to impress upon him. Perhaps one day he'll thank me for intervening in time, space and circumstance, as I had the keys to all these, and of course the advantage of doing all this from the future, as all was in my own remembrance.

Because I did not want to harm relations with my good friend, Peter, I quickly ripped off the duct tape from around his face, causing him to scream in pain, as the outer layer of skin came off along with a good bit of hair. "Please...she's my daughter—don't harm her."

"It's the Flagellator. He finds them, he does. I knew you were crying out something primal, as it must relate to your pretty daughter...well, she must be pretty," I said, looking him over...a handsome man, a perfect man.

He started crying. I wanted us all to somehow work this out, but with his crying like that, I felt, well what harm could he do? So I untied him just as Silas and Millicet moved his hateful wife Sophie to a private room, where she could rest from what the men did to her.

Silas threw a pool ball that accidentally hit Peter in the ribcage, and he started spitting up blood. His nose was already broken, and I felt that Millicet could easily set things right. But when he tried to straighten Peter's nose, it would only hug his cheek—indeed it dangled. Millicet looked at me and said, "Captain, he looks like a goner, it's best if we put him out of his misery."

"Permission denied. What this man needs is a doctor. Go dismantle the phone system until we can get this thing straightened out," I said, and bearded, burly Millicet went with great dispatch next door, where there was, of all things, a general practitioner and his wife, captive in our now quite successful infiltration of Kruzmar territory.

After reinforcements, I counted twenty-five men, and I told Peter about the plan to bring the heads of the matriarchs to my Lord's altar. I showed him the head of Mother Margot, and I showed it to the next door neighbor, Dr. Steinman, too.

He was thrilled to see someone doing something about the emasculated man in today's society.

I tried to impart to these gentlemen that I was from the future, that I was his sword, a scroll handed down in judgment and that it was not personal, though I felt the lives they were living were compromised, and worthless, destitute with money, deserted but surrounded...empty of all that is holy. However, short, bespectacled Dr. Steinman, a classy man of taste, perhaps fifty, proved to be more interested in betraying our position to the enemy than fixing Mr. Mallard's nose. For that he was executed in front of Mallard. Word came down to depart, but I was unable to leave Mallard alone. Besides, we were here—and Peter Mallard was fading.

"Not my daughter, please!" Mallard was saying when we took him down to the wine cellar to literally cool off. Millicet spoke to us about the mission. Silas, James and the Flagellator needed rest. This was easy to see.

Now, Sophie was dead, clearly—but not because of us, as the poor writer was saying.

"You want to collaborate, we can split the profits," Peter gasped, desperately. "Just leave my daughter alone! Look you've had your fun, but you didn't just fuck Sophie, you dismembered her!"

"I wouldn't exaggerate if I were you, sir," said Millicet.

I would have been there, with the others, down in the wine cellar, where there were thousands of bottles just waiting to be spoiled. Yes, I knew that Millicet and the boys would think that this was part of the war, the precious war that they had waged, to get the Queen of Nothing once and for all and deliver all the queen's heads to our Lord, some many years hence. It was simple, we would, for a time, set up here at Peter Mallard's house.

As I inspected the place, and I place the time at perhaps 3:30 a.m. I found the true purpose for my life.

As I proceeded with caution down the hall, and as I heard whimpering, as I heard music of a rock and roll nature, and as I entered the room and looked to find my long lost love, I was filled with a delight that became my epiphany, oh, glorious!

Nearly frightened by the sight of her, dazzled by the smell of her, I entered her room, and she was wearing earphones and did not hear me. I ensconced myself in the Tiffany-blue bathroom so I could get a better look.

Indeed, the love of my life, a lady—or rather, a girl—I would die for, sitting on a bed and wearing a long skirt and a covering over her high perky breasts. Her long blonde hair and frivolous way delighted me so. As I found myself living suddenly in the past, because I am no older than she, though I looked it now—certainly now I should have been considered a man of forty...but I was not. For my hair was dark, braided in warrior fashion, my beard was fine, and I had not lost my way. As I had fought for the right to court the highest lady in the land, and here, after all this time, I had discovered her locked away at Mallard's estate! My girl, kidnapped through time.

My one. My only. My soul mate. My figurehead. The one I let into my heart. I had saved myself for her. I had waited all my life, and through the lives of time, to be with her. Her beauty...captivating—it was the ancient memory that plagued me, a desperate love that brought kingdoms low and exalted the ways of the earth...oh, the earth, how I missed her.

Now, as for her name.

"What is your name?" I whispered, standing over her and smiling.

She said the following words, which almost corrupted me into being more of a father than an eternal lover, "I thank you for what you've done. I was grounded for doing this white powder."

"Really?" I said. "The very same white powder piled in little bowls for the party?"

"Party," she laughed, and pushed her long straight hair back over her shoulder. "Party? They have friends over and they all fuck."

"Is that really your language, my lady. Like mine?"

"I'm a poet," she said. "And it is just, and right, and true that you have slain my step-mother and all her stupid friends."

"My lady," I said, and now I felt silly wearing her father's silly clothes. "I know why I came now. Because I deeply love you."

Now, you must know, it DID NOT happen like that—I must have fantasized about it. What really happened is this: She opened the door, she let me in, and she, Anastasia Bailes Mallard, pulled me inside and gave me some of her white powder, and kissed me long and beautifully—and told me that we had always been lovers.

"How did you get those?" I asked her, referring to what looked like battle scars on her wrists, and cigarette burns on her arm.

"They schlepped me off to a mental hospital when I was thirteen. After my mom died. Or rather, overdosed."

"Overdosed?" I asked, unsure of this nomenclature.

"It means doing too many drugs, man."

"So the mental hospital movie that your father wrote—"

"Oh, yeah, he totally exploited me, man—fucking asshole."

"Oh," I said, feeling like a royal idiot. "I understand—when I was your age I did not know that my mother was at odds with All-That-Is, or at least, an enemy of my Lord, and the Realm, which is not of this earth."

"What are you flying on, Captain Crunch? You're a psychopathic killer aren't you?"

I was deeply hurt by her allegation, to be sure.

"Do you know what happened here tonight, Anastasia?" I said, hoping she was indeed one of us.

She said: "You killed Sophie, and you killed the men who were fucking her on the pool table, you hurt my father and others and forced them into the wine cellar—but you like me. Should I be worried?"

"Good girl!" I said. Now I understood, this damsel was not to remain a damsel, she is a woman of the field—a woman who could inspire us on to great victory. "No, of course you should not be worried…I will defend your honor, my lady."

"You don't know how long I wished I would have done what you did," she said. "But you let that idiot live—the idiot, I call him, because that's all he is, an idiot. You obeyed my mental commands…my deepest desires, but you let the idiot live!…how could you?"

"Your father?" I asked pertly.

"Peter, the idiot, there is no other word to describe him."

"You're mad because he—"

"Killed my mother? You might say that. Drove her to suicide? You might say that. His friends raped me? You might say that. His brother, Uncle Asshole, poked me? You might say that— hey, I know where all his guns are!" she exclaimed proudly, "You want 'em?"

"She is one of us, Silas!" I said and then wondered how Silas actually got into her room. "How did you get in here?" I said, and he looked at her, frowning. "Silas, your eyes betray you! Your still on duty. That's all, Silas," I said, waving him off.

"I came to ask you if we are to camp here," he said, eyes still fixed on Anastasia, who could not see him, well, not exactly.

"Hey, it's okay by me—as long as you tie up the idiot so I can throw darts at him," Anastasia blurted, not seeing Silas but responding as if he were there. I wondered if she could see us...which would be the ultimate test. I decided to call my men into her presence, and soon the rest of my contingent entered Anastasia's room overlooking the front driveway. Silas frowned, but she missed this. "And this is Millicet," I announced, a fact that I wanted to have happen. "This is not just some stupid little girl."

"Vincent, she's fifteen years old!"

"Actually, I'm fourteen," she said.

"Sweet fourteen," said Jude, who is usually silent on such issues.

She said, "You're really cute." Jude, of course, blushed and this caused a bit of a jealous streak, though I could see what she meant—Jude was beautiful to both men and women, to dogs and cats and anybody who could cast their eyes upon his perfect youth. "So you see Jude?" I said.

"I'd fuck him in a glass-bong minute."

"Get out of here, Jude!" I commanded.

"No!" Anastasia said, but I could see that she wasn't looking at him, she was looking at me.

"I want you too, Anastasia," Jude said.

"You will shut your mouth and do what our leader told you to do!" Millicet insisted, causing Jude to freeze in rebellion, as Anastasia's beauty was surely captivating to all.

"And these are your friends?" Anastasia said, with loving regard to all of us.

"Yes, my brothers. Jude, the—usually—quiet one."

"And beautiful," she added.

"Millicet, my general...Silas, our heretofore mother hen (yes, Silas, your mother hen days are over), and the Flagellator."

She laughed at the name 'the flagellator'—and Millicet proceeded to describe what happens to a man who feels he hasn't
lived up to something either his parents or his school or his peer
group believed to be a relevant goal—and in the Flagellator's case
he was one of those who just couldn't run the race, or even enter
it for that matter, all because of stumbling years before...so he
started flagellating himself...and he's been that way every since.

I said, "He was a bit more sensitive, like me. His problem
was that he was queer, you know. I mean, I'm not queer, but they
thought I was...you see, it gets pretty complicated amongst the
guys."

"Oh...yeah, guys can be pretty cruel if they find out you're
gay, or swish...or even bi—they'll try to rip your balls off. Or
rape you. But if you go totally gay, it's like cool again, because
they get repulsed...so you're left alone, and a lot of girls like to
hang around you...and if you can convince one of the guys chasing the girls to try you instead, you win."

"She's smart, Vincent," Silas said.

"But you have to like be so totally swish, you know, like a girl
or it won't work. But seriously, they'd fuck Jude, and so would I."

This was difficult for me, as the seeds of infidelity were already sown, and I was smitten and helpless.

But the Flagellator started whipping himself with one of
Mallard's belts.

"I want to see my daddy!" Anastasia said and leapt off the
bed and ran out of the room. The Flagellator was now jerking off
at the window and I told him there was no one there to look at
him. He was such a head case I wondered how and why I had put
up with him. Meanwhile, I had to follow Anastasia, who just
might be the love of my life.

"Thanks a lot, Flagellator," I said. "And as for you, Jude, lay a
hand on her, I'll cut it off."

"Yes, sir," Jude said. "But I don't think she can see me."

@   @   @

"So you mean to tell me we have two victims, a B&E on Grenmont Drive, in front of the whole world, dismemberment, and no suspects? Are you insane, Blue?" Captain Morgan asked.

"Captain, with all due respect," Detective Ashley Blue answered, "it's a psycho thing—we checked, she had a son, whose whereabouts we're not sure of. His name was Vincent Damien Del Monte—"

"And why isn't he here? Why aren't you and McPherson stomping Del Monte's head in for a confession! We've had Menendez and a dozen others who went unpublished. Rich kids hate their parents, it goes without saying—why, I don't give a fuck. But because they do, because perhaps they think it's unfair they should have all that money when some friend of theirs from the wrong side of the tracks has nothing, maybe it's their better nature gone askew, that gets these punks to do such sick-brained shit as matricide, patricide and rape of young kids. And sure, maybe after you catch the guy, he'll cop crazy and go up north to a nice country club for the insane. Maybe you won't make captain some day, and yeah, your pay, at the zenith is about fifty pre-tax with a take-home of maybe thirty. I would think, Mr. Blue, that you would love this kind of case."

Blue stirred. He stood up in the morning zoo, at the chalkboard no less, and announced a manhunt for one Vincent Del Monte, and the only picture they had, incredibly, since Vincent did not have a driver's license or any other proof of life, was a high-school picture taken when he was sixteen, since he did not graduate from high school.

"That's all we know," Blue would say, and then he'd adjust himself and his collar like the football hero he was once upon a yesteryear in Cleveland. He was tired of fixing things for the approved-of rich—now, when one of their own turns on them, it was truly a disease of social justice. If folks outside the Beverly Hills Police Department knew how many kids got away scot-free while their counterparts in tougher neighborhoods got three-strikes, that is, twenty-five-to-life, they might sit back and let a little cancer work its way around before excising it. They all felt his way, Blue, Short, McPherson, Annie Potter, Blue's partner—they just didn't have the guts to admit it.

EVIF

When Kruzmar returned from his adventurous trip to Maui, in which he visited his children in-between sojourns of the smooth kind, he was gratified to find Lucy, his ever-loving wife, presiding not over the office, but the kitchen. He was greeted with champagne, and her friend and his—a kind of his-and-her affair, of the young teen kind. "Brother and sister—aren't they cute?" she exclaimed. "I had the best time with your mother—she is so cool."

"Cool? She's a thousand years old," Kruzmar said. "What's his name?"

"Scot..."

"That's cute," he said, watching them work out in the weight room.

Yes, the young son had moved into a lavish Bel Air house, which had belonged to Howard Hughes, and sported a keen 7th green location to the Bel Air Country Club, just as Howard had belonged many decades earlier. He had managed to move within a five-minute radius of *mommulus*, or 'mother' Kruzmar, and Lucy had her own dance studio, which doubled as a meditation room when she would entertain the wayward Tibetans for talks on world peace and tea. When she would ask her friends for money to support the relocation of the *holy men*; when she would pass out books about the Dalai Lama, and when the Dalai Lama spoke, he said that Abacazzia Kruzmar must have known His Holiness in an earlier incarnation, because that kind of care and loving kindness could only come from a holy person.

Only from a holy **PERSON** *such as His Holiness..*

He would have said "woman," but he learned *person*, and indeed, Kruzmar was more than pleased to watch Lucy at work. The most difficult people to know would always come for the Dalai Lama—"He's like Santa Claus, the Easter Bunny and the Tooth Fairy all in one!"

The little monks were of no interest, and indeed, the idea of sex with them horrified Leonard, who was simply more interested in the twenty-something newbies who were wanting—desperately—to work their way up.

Besides, he enjoyed a roll in the hay with Lucy too, and her friend, but there always had to be that extra element, and if she was so darned wonderful at providing it for her bunny-kneed king, so much the better. Better that than to cry for a quarter century like Cari, who went to church, who took the kids to Sunday School at, of all things, an evangelical center in the Valley.

One day he would rectify that, if she ever stopped crying.

Kruzmar showed the young teenage lad around the grounds of the authentic Italian villa, across the stones from Tuscany. The secret entrance underneath the house from the garden, a secret passageway that Scot, *beautiful Scot*, with his surfer good looks, his boxed abs, his sinewy defined arms, he could use anytime.

Any ol' time.

Lucy was showing Arnica, with her athletic charm, all around her dance studio.

And they had a little dance class with Penny, who came over to help with Arnica's *motivation*.

That night, just as sure as hunter-and-huntress in residence, and this was Sunday night, to be sure, with just the right amount of narcotics and wine, the nude chase games were on and they

were fun. Scot thought it was so hilarious how Maria would order her husband around. "Haven't you ever heard of matriarchy?" he asked Scot, who was swimming nude in the evening air.

"He's like this totally stupid wimp. I'll never be like that."

"No, you're a strong warrior, and you're going to go far in this
town, I'll make sure of it," Leonard told him, in his bikini and
fish-net top, the newest gift from Lucy, who didn't bother telling
him she only shops the women's section for men, and the men's
section for women. "Your mother's a good woman," said Leonard.
"And your father—"

"He's dead," Scot said.

"Well, here's to moms. I don't know what I would have done
without—"

"My mom killed my dad, the way she ran him around."

"Well, lad, that's not you, is it—you're cool, man."

Leonard was quick to slip off his little suit and enter the bap-
tismal waters of the 100-thousand gallon pool that cost $3572
per month to heat at 88 degrees, while the two spas were an
additional $1000 each. The tiled spa, converted from an Italian
fountain from the turn of the century, was now being used by
Penny, Arnica, and Lucy. Maria made her famous margaritas and
all were playing like happy kids. Maria of course approved of all
this, and she was Lucy's resident witch, who instructed her husband to plant all the strange plants that had very deep roots.

"Tomorrow, Mr. Leonard, they come over for a talk. To tell
you what happens. Miss Asenath, Miss Serena, and Miss Milaca,"
Maria said, fresh in a starched white uniform.

After Scot and Arnica left, Leonard wondered why it was so
important; he already knew what Lucy wanted—*the studio itself.*

"They'll be back—that was fun. Oh, the dailies came in for
Cat Chaser," Lucy said. "I thought they sucked. Your virtuoso
director is amping on crystal again. Last time he thought he was
Cher and in love with Steve, and then he dons a freaking general's
uniform and threatens to shoot Denny Davis in the face. The
bond company's about to pull it and the cost is not a moderate
seventy-two mil, and we have another month of shooting left."

"It's no problem...he can have a car wreck, or contract a para-
site at Luigi's...he's a good friend of mine. Don't you know who

knows? *Me.* Don't you know who makes the sun set and rise? *Me.* If anybody fucks with me, I'm so far up their rectum they see God...Lucy...don't ever try to fix things yourself, we have a company, a network you might say...all problem solvers."

"Yeah, well...I don't want to know what you have to do to make things work," she said, primping in her compact, and wondering why he married her in the first place, then dismissing the thought because she wanted it all very badly. "Do I make you comfortable to be yourself? I mean, did I...do I help you? Why do you have me around?"

"You're part of my plan. You are my plan. I can be me because you're you. But like everything else, if you get in the way, you pay," Leonard said, threatening Lucy with more than his eyes. Making sure she knew that she had still not bridged the gap between hired employee and beard. Utilitarian. Sleazy.

She went to her room and popped Xanax and Vicodin, and of course her traditional glass of Chopin (the only potato vodka left, or almost) with cracked ice, a plate of fresh-cooked shrimp, and the number of a casting director who handled all the new girls coming up.

What she needed was real love, not play. What she needed was a companion. Dying of loneliness, where no one else could take it, she would force it. She would become it, and knew how to merge with the mirror of her own existence, thereby extinguishing any pain...but she wanted pain too. Needed pain for pleasure. As she dialed Connie Mitchell's number, she laughed at the idea that lesbians were either portrayed as angels in the media or heads would roll, usually men! Delicious, how the public was so easily intimidated. And she had her husband to thank for it all.

When it came to the transformation from play to work, no one was better than Leonard, who stormed up the stairs to the media room, past all the sconces, up the spiral terrazzo staircase and around the ancient chandelier, then on into the media suite, which had a movie screen built within the textured wall. There were comfortable chairs, a computer and communications section—built in and remote controlled.

It did not matter that the dailies revealed stilted acting and humdrum shots—it was in focus, and it was lit perfectly, and anything could be done in post, something Leonard did not think his wife, a retired writer, would ever understand. She wanted to see heads rolling, and he loved to give that to her. But not Matthew Stone, the hottest director on the planet, no, not him.

After the video dailies—*which were just fine, Lucy, thank you very much*—Leonard, still savoring the exhilarating swim with his pretty little Scotty, flipped on the bank of satellite news channels, which put him in touch with breaking news faster than any internet scroll.

There he was, just as Leonard Cutlass Kruzmar remembered him—VINCENT.

Stupid Vince! Naïve Vince! Idiot Vince! Punching Bag Vince! Doormat Vince! Meek nerd Vince! Couldn't even find it in a dictionary, Vince! On the big screen from 1978—didn't even graduate, a crackup, couldn't take a little fun with the boys. We only gave him what everybody got, but he was fragile, that's not my fault, Leonard admonished himself. Never knew the truth, that the moms ran it all. No respect for the hand that rocked the cradle. And now the FBI, the idea that it was a phantom and not Vincent, one witness left—who the fuck was that? Oh, man, Lucy would never understand. It had to stay private. Just me and my man, *Vincent*. My little slave, who stood up so bravely that day—Vincent. Trying to save his little friend who didn't know his dick from a twig—*Vincent*. Who didn't know why—*Vincent*. Oh, how awesome! Vincent! You're going to suck my cock, Vincent. You're going to lay under an army of sodomites. You're going down, you dumb fuck. But I have to give you credit. She had to go, your mom. Yes, my mother hated her. And you don't know, but I know, it's always important to please Abacazzia. Your mom was one to be feared. So now...that leaves more for me, as per my calculations—Vincent. Do you hear me?

You're my slave, Vincent—suck my dick, you dumb motherfucker! I am your man, your king, your creator, your controller, your destiny, you dumb bitch—sure, I'd fear you if you were truly conscious. You would scare all of us shitfucks. Apocalypse, Vince—that's who you would have been, but your brain bought the farm, fuck! You're nothing but colors and numbers.

And then there is my screenwriter, Mallard.

So uncalled for, Vincent.

But his face can be fixed.

Not all is lost.

Besides, he's docile now—just what I need. Again, I win, you lose, just like old times.

Now, the fact that you killed eight people in Mallard's home? *Manson/Vincent/Manson? A connection? Possible movie rights?* Vincent, are you giving me more money again! Put your balls in my hand, Vincent...you'll never be free now. Even if you die, dumbshit. Maybe you could write the screenplay and I could underpay you. I'll find more ways of taking your soul.

Later that evening the flurry of phone calls were going out. "I want him! I want the story rights, I want Vincent to collaborate with Mallard, or what's left of him! What do you mean, his face? Fuck his face! He can get a new nose. I'm calling Debbie in D.C. I can too call a senator if I want some leeway—Debbie does Bel Air, remember? I still have the pix, and Henry, I don't like your attitude. See you on the links tomorrow—I'll be G-Queer, you know, money people. No, they don't *play*. They're Mormons or something. Just golf, right, get me Vincent Del Monte before the cops do. Fuck off. And no winking tomorrow."

It was in Lucy's dance studio, full of mirrors. The villa sat proudly up the steep cobbled drive, hidden by eucalyptus, oleander and barbed-wire. It was Serena, Milaca and Asenath, the three African widows, warming in the corner at the low table, where incense wafted up and a fire burned in the form of several candles.

When Kruzmar entered, Lucy was gone, and he did not know these women, but they laughed when they saw him and invited him to sit. They spoke, and he listened.

Asenath was chanting a poem that went like this: "...so you can take life and no one born of a womb can take you."

Milaca, in her high voice—as she was the youngest widow—went something like this: "...you shall never fall, as everything you do is sanctioned by God. You will rise, and one who is the king shall fall—and more...you bring the three together."

Kruzmar, excited, said: "You mean merging Monsoon and Mount Triac?"

And Serena said, while Asenath lit more incense and a couple old black candles, "You are the only one, and there are none. You are one in a million and there are none. It is written on the wind, and in the seed of the many, all the earth moves your direction. No woman uses the seed, except your wife, who will be the queen of all you survey, my king. A childhood dream makes due, and one who is nigh makes his entrance back to you."

"You talking about Vincent Del Monte? The guy who—"

"Leonard!" said Lucy. Leonard looked around, then at his reflection, and at Lucy behind him. "Let them have their say—this is for you."

"I don't understand," Kruzmar said, demure, though laughing all the way to the shitter. Oh, the sandbox games can be so sophisticated. It's really fun, he would think soon. Then again, everything is fun when you win. And he always wins. As Vincent was the all-time loser...so it goes.

"You said it yourself: you have the way, the path is clear," Lucy said as Asenath waved her off. She left the room dutifully.

Kruzmar liked the fact that these three could wave off Lucy or probably anybody else. In fact, he knew that these were not ones to trifle with, and he knew too that they worked for his mother, Abacazzia, and indeed, they had been assigned to his wife. So now was the time for the quest for power, and he got a rather crazy idea.

"We've been with your family for six generations," said Asenath. "But if you ask we will lie to you. Because you cannot know how this is possible."

"So this has all been engineered by you?"

"As you ascend, we accomplish our needs," said Serena, the leader with the muumuu and all the hand-hammered African silver jewelry. Maybe they weren't any older than thirty-five, in Serena's case, maybe forty, but what did it matter, if it was perpetuity, immortality, non-linear time, indefinite, penultimate—indeed, time travelers...but what was the engine? How was it possible, Lucy would wonder, knowing she would want what they had but they would keep it from her?

Kruzmar knew, at least his mother taught him this much, that all is through the looking glass. Nothing is as it seems, the strongest may appear the weakest, the most noble takes the biggest fall.

And as far as he knew, in this stupid little playroom, he was being anointed King.

He was being *made*, just as it had been for six former generations of Kruzmars. King of the sandbox was king of the world.

He might have thought, perhaps a cause of insecurity, that the Kruzmars were tapped, and because of this entitlement, it wasn't so much the skill involved, but the destiny, the quilting process of three in the shadows, that destiny itself was nothing more than a choice of something higher.

This thought propelled Kruzmar into a sort of depravity the likes of which he would never recover from, at least to my way of thinking, and you know by now what I say takes remembrance, for I speak from the authority of all that is to come in the life of the new king, who is really a surrogate of something more, as we suspected all along.

XIS

Smitten, I proceeded to write poetry to the love of my life, Anastasia Bailes Mallard, the one I had sown in my heart and the one who had guided all my days since being drawn to woman in the first place. As I observed her playing ping-pong with Millicet, I knew this was only a temporary—at best—solution.

In the wine cellar sat Peter Mallard, the renowned writer whom we would protect, especially from Anastasia—but we knew that time was growing short, and that something had to be done. When the emergency or second line rang Anastasia answered jovially—"Hello?"

"Hello, Anastasia? This is Leonard Kruzmar, is Peter there?"

"No, Mr. Kruzmar—I mean *Leonard*. Thank you..."

"Is that...was that? Millicet—get the other phone!"

Millicet intercepted the second portable phone and nodded to me from across the library.

I listened in. He wanted to come over that evening to get the script Peter was working on, or at least the latest draft—and he was adamant.

He wanted to come over right now, just to have a drink—as promised—with Peter.

We had been having a superior time the past few days, just the two of us, the beautiful Anastasia and me. As my men attended to Mr. Mallard, to all his various and sundry needs, I couldn't help wondering about Kruzmar's mother, as she became prominent in my mind after a series of blue lights flashed through Anastasia's window.

Later I finally realized—how stupid of me!—that she, Abacazzia, had done more damage than Margot and her whole host of country club eunuchs, that is, *male golfers*—in fact, in the future the term *golfer* would mean essentially one and the same, unless it was a woman, then it would mean *filled with hatred*.

As for Peter Mallard, a man of striking intelligence, a man who played no golf, he just liked living right off the fairway—he liked the country—who was virtuous in his iniquity; equanimity, when he had it, lavished it upon all who could breathe dust through a tube.

He was saying, "You want to watch while Sophie gets gangbanged by a half-dozen of her best friends?"

Then he had taken your narrator to the ping-pong table and declared himself the champ, while I had been virtually unsuccessful at shooting the guns down in the wine cellar. He had a rubber background, but all I managed to do was hit the glass of the wine cooler, shattering it, and causing him to scream about how many bottles of Montrachet he had on hand—something like a thousand—that all had to remain at a certain temperature. I said, "Do screenplay writers really make this much money, to have Montrashit—"

He iterated, "You dumb fucking ignorant bastard—I said Montrachet, Mohn-tra-shay, and yes, I make plenty of money—what the fuck does it matter? You're trying to kill me, or at least kill my wine collection."

"What about your daughter? Don't you care about her as well?"

Then he started crying, and soon he ran up the stairs right into Silas, who had been highly involved with Peter's emancipation by so cleanly breaking his nose then breaking his Sophie, taking turns even...*even* after she had quit breathing. Of course I thought Mr. Mallard enjoyed watching, which was why I strapped him to the chair in front of the pool table. It wasn't my fault what state she was in when we emerged from the bowels of the manor, curious ones. Was it?

I could not seem to appease him. We made sure he showered, that his nose bandage—left by Dr. Steinman before his unfortunate fate—was kept nice and clean, that he did not get it wet, yes we did all those things! And we did them religiously over that three-day period (note: technically, it might have been more than three days, but since from the future it gets very difficult to tell).

He complained that his arm was broken—but I saw nothing. No evidence of it. I was ready to remove him to his wine cellar, and Millicet and the boys were swimming and having a rollicking good time, just splattering themselves with the *Mohn-tra-shay*, and this got no small rise in demeanor from Mr. Mallard.

Anastasia tried to use the dismantled phone, (and mind you, at this point, Mr. Mallard was thoroughly silenced—meaning Jude had duct-taped him again). When she was unsuccessful, she simply got frightened, perhaps not even meaning to betray me. Look, with the history of torture and abuse she had taken at the hand of her pervert father, whom I preserved for her to do with as she wished, she most certainly was not herself—indeed, how could she have been? At that moment, the moment of betrayal, her lovely aqua eyes were looking at me, and she kicked her father's chair over, and he cracked his head slightly—he passed out with blood oozing from his ear—and she laughed, so I thought we were destined for marriage at that very moment. I cannot impress upon you, friend, the *style* and *dispatch* with which Anastasia plied her rather evil trade—that of causing me to fall in love.

This was one of the more painful moments on the sojourn into this foreign land commissioned by my Lord and Master, who will go nameless for now.

She said, or rather, she screamed into the phone (that is, the second line, since the main line was dismantled) the following words: "Help me, Mr. Kruzmar—I mean...*Leonard*! Help me! Please! It's him! The psychopath—he killed my step-mother and he's—"

Thank God Silas pulled the cord out of the wall. Then Millicet slammed his phone down just as Silas grabbed Anastasia and threw her to the floor, the phone flying. I was so upset with the turn of events that I threw the men out, told them to sleep in the yard for the night—and that we would have to pull up stakes.

I tied up my love, Anastasia, as Silas wetted the place with gasoline.

This was the proscribed procedure—right out of our rulebook; the emotional waves, the ups and downs, the weather, the constantly changing water of women, you could say one and all variables were constantly in motion, and if we did not remain fluid of course, we'd die. But I was smitten, my reporter, and you know, I knew she loved me. I tried desperately to think of girls like Anastasia, but could think of no one. Could she be a double agent? Could she be working for Margot? Indeed, she was a princess, no doubt. A future queen good to go with victory in her palm—that is, *me*. Would she turn me over for her queendom? Did she even know why I was sent? If she did, wouldn't she have tried a little harder to...well you can see I am stuck groping for reasons here. Clearly I do not understand. And clearly, at this point, I am very upset.

The realm of nothing, the earth or nothing, the kingdom or nothing—that's all, lads! That's how we set it right! There was more screaming and rallying—and it felt good, oh my, it was great to see them drinking and having a row at the expense of one of my enemy's friends. I shook off the pain of betrayal, foisted upon me by Anastasia, the most beautiful creature I had ever seen.

But I could not shake her off—truly, I coveted her. I wanted her forever. I knew she loved me, and I was not just one of her servants, the killer of all her foes. And they *were* her foes, but she did not trust me.

However, after tying her up—gently—in her room, and preventing Millicet from using the gasoline to start a fire, I waited. For Fate was dealing the hand now, and the men had plenty of digging and burying to do in the forest over the fence—that is, the 5th fairway of the Beverly Hills Golf Club, home to the big boys, the champs—and many a princess. Home to many who were breathing nicely because the matron Margot had already paid the price for their births. If it was truly up to me, brother, I would have burned them all. In warfare, I believe in winning, full out. Kill the women and children first, basic instruction for all warriors, and the soldiers will buckle without firing a shot. I don't know why the public doesn't understand basic strategy. You don't hurt them, you hurt what they care about—really, this was the recipe for liberation, a bunch of pussies on mommystrings was the reason my king sent me to clean the mess up.

Before I let on the next fruitful encounter with Fate and all Her majesty, let me tell you about winning a war. It's the queen and not the king—I already told you, the world is a matriarchy, a perversion, a panoply of flesh; from the spirit a sword goes out, and spirit can live in the future and hearken back to the past, as I am doing now.

Suffice to say that this little revelation of truth was met with glazed eyes and various threats not unlike a prisoner of war would get. And I am most certainly that.

I reluctantly unfolded the next detail to my Recorders, Carl and the Voice, as follows:

When Kruzmar arrived at Mallard's place, he brought with him a contingent of security people in suits who drove Suburbans and had little earpieces in their ears, sub-machine guns, sat-link, laptops in their briefcases, well, some of them did.

I knew immediately not to fight, but I felt I had allowed my softness for my true love, Anastasia, to slow down my usual trained and measured response.

You might like to know I was beaten, tied, gagged, blind-folded and removed from Mallard's house.

NEVES

t was nearly black. Blackness and fetid, dank air—underground? In a holding pit? Nabbed by police? I did not know. I did not understand. Millicet was gagged and tied in the corner, I could see that. Silas lay beaten and half-dead—that much I could see after my eyes adjusted to some basement somewhere I did not know of.

I could hear loud machinery somewhere in the background. I could hear things that I could not remember exactly. What I did remember was her face—Anastasia Bailes Mallard, with whom I fell in love, and with whom—perhaps somewhere else—I had a life.

"Look, Vincent—look around! Does it look like you're going to have a life? Does it look like you're going to succeed? Does it?! Why don't you wake up—we're in prison, and it's not the police—it's the enemy!" Millicet said, his beard or mustache in the way of his mouth, for the words were garbled.

"You're just getting old, you old tarnished piece of flab!" I told him.

And he said, "You're like the one who trained us—haven't

learned a thing since Phoenix!"

"I learned how to take care of myself, Millicet, which is more than I can say for you—after all...."

By now I had gotten right close to him, knelt down and stroked his hair. "I'm not the one tied up, am I?"

I untied him but Silas looked bad, and from what I understood, they had Jude—young Jude—and he was talking to them. I could see this because of the memory implanted in me in the future, which no reporter would believe.

I have no other explanation why I could hear all relevant conversations other than not being completely corporeal in the space, which I would find out later was in a remote location in Mexico, just south of Mexico City. It was no wonder I felt silly: with all my training, the histrionics of a young girl of fourteen somehow upended a brilliant military invasion. Some chick, some little spoiled bitch got my heart, and I melted like a stupid schoolboy who never tasted a jelly donut, or a Winston, or felt the constriction of a condom or braces, or a finger splint, or a jock strap. Uninitiated, unloved, and unwarranted, that was me, erased by a cunt who should have drowned with that autoglow daddy (my father image, castrated) who made her filthy rich in exchange for poison pill. Fuck! I'm starting to get all upset now, and there is no reason, for that would be compiling one failure on top of another. Suffice to say I would not kill her, and I would not let my men kill her. She was to remain untouched, unharmed, respected for the possible future position I foretold when I was smitten, when I looked into her baby blues and chimed a song of remembrance—a hymn of no return—and a jubilation filled my spirit because she made me very happy. "My bride to be," I told them, "how could I kill her?"

And now Millicet, how he would look at me sideways! Totally uncalled for. "You think you're so old and wise, Milli! But you're a two-bit pain in the nanny-ass, you are! Next you're going to say the only way to win the battle is positive thinking. We have the power of all creation, and you want to henpeck!"

"Because you let that bitch fuck us in the ass, and now we're forever paying at the hands not of the police, but of the enemy himself—the target becomes the arrow!" Millicet shouted.

Kruzmar, yes, how he had turned the tables on me, when I was forgetting all about revenge. When I was forgetting all about high school. When I was remembering long ago, backwards into what will be. For Kruzmar, it would be the end of a blade, into his heart, for all those of innocence, and some who weren't.

@ @ @

(As I log this into my journal, I can't seem to get my mind off Vincent. And yet, this next part is all about Vincent. Sometimes I find myself talking like him, acting like him…even, I confess, *thinking* like him. It was my mind, but it was something more— the horrible reality, an entity much more powerful than man, enslaving us…that's why I did what I did. That's how I wound up here. I am so sorry. But to whom do I apologize…my mind is not my own anymore.)

@ @ @

The fervor of the police and all the hoopla regarding the attack on Mallard and his daughter—the death of his wife and five of his friends—it was all a cop like Blue could handle.

Blue was one of the best, never out of his element. Except when the ex-Tulsa football coach was dealing with the BHPD, the lazy boys in blue who never passed up an opportunity to call in outside help. But Blue was always centering in on the impossible perp. A single-handed jockey who made 'em all look bad. But they had their ways of payback, and he had no idea that you had to go along to get along. On this case he was told to stand down. And that was the beginning of his undoing. "Just leave it alone, it's Federal now," Captain Miller, four eyes blazing and magnified, told Lt. Blue.

As part of Blue's breaking process, Jones was fucking Blue's wife, Tanya, whom he met in Vegas at the annual Beverly Hills

PD Vegas golf tournament, held outside the Manta Ray Hotel, no less.

That was where Tanya-baby got fed up and felt up by Stone and Murphy, who were in the lead with a two-over-par 77. Ashley Vale Blue wasn't kidding when he said he would kill anybody that laid a hand on her. During the volleyball tournament they moved right in, one hard cock after another. And she was just waking up! It was easy because Blue was the organizer, the participant. You could always count on Blue to stay with the activity until the end, and that left the beach bunny Tanya all alone, and if it was a motel or hotel room...oh, that was everybody's favorite! They could laugh at Blue at the barbecue and tell him, "Great job solving the case, Blue—way to go!"

"Behind ya all the way, Blue!"

"You're the best, Blue—a crime-solving genius."

"Blue, can you help me with my case—I'll be back in two hours, here's the paper work."

Blue would have his barbecue in Reseda in his upstairs/downstairs pad off Rose, and the other cops envied the fact that he had the pretty wife with the unmistakable below-thirty perkiness. Tanya was blessed with thick blonde hair, long legs and huge tits; she was a walking boner bride. Blue was a liberated man, allowing her to flirt and talk and dance with men—that sensitivity training about women's needs really paid off...for Tanya.

"I like responsibility, and the fact that we let the Feds just walk in here and fuck us on this, sir, frankly...well it's just not right," Blue was saying to Stephens, that is, Captain Luther Stephens, fired in Vegas, set up in Beverly Hills, with a face that looked like a lazy-boy recliner and a body that formed a question mark when he'd sort of glide down the hall looking for someone to hover over. Keeping order was his forte and his motion sickness. He was always moving around and in his late fifties with half-grown grandkids already. He had one purpose for Blue...to stop him in his newfound zeal for the Del Monte case.

When Blue dusted Mallard's place, he immediately knew it tied into the Del Monte incident. He did not need an invitation, not on this one. But Luther Stephens gladly put a halt to Blue when he let the Feds in. "So, Luther, you just bend over every time there's the slightest hiccup? It's Vincent Del Monte—I'm sure it is. Let me develop the leads, sir, please."

"Look, Blue, we're dealing with celebrities here. We have a duty to the people of Beverly Hills not to cause an incident. I resent your use of language. We run a clean department—and no, I don't bend over for anybody!"

"But you thought bending my wife over was okay...oh, you didn't know that I knew what happened in Vegas?"

Luther Stephens looked at him and thought that if he were still in the Marines, Blue definitely qualified for a section eight.

He stuck Blue behind the desk for observation and sure, then confirmed, that Tanya Blue had fooled around with Jenkins and Christian, that is, two detectives who were not necessarily promiscuous, just angry with Blue because he was always hogging the limelight.

Now, this sort of payback is always fair, and for Blue to complain was without precedent. He didn't seem to accept all the warnings, so it was time for something a bit more stringent. If he can't hack it, he should resign...as long as he leaves Tanya's number!

Because of all the pussy in Vegas, because they needed to unwind—it's not their fault if Blue brought his slut wife—because they needed sustenance...oh, the asshole's babe of a wife, how sweet! For one thing, Casper Jenkins and Dilly Christian were notorious for their instant gratification conquests around town, in certain safe locales, sneaking it here and there, even when investigating porn rings. Any excuse to get off, to unleash the lion, to unfurl the flag—anytime, anywhere. It was not only expected—of all *except* Blue—it was standard operating procedure. It was duty, honor, integrity—by the book, the manual, the code, what the fuck was wrong with Blue? Fidelity with Tanya? An oxymoron at best!

Slut wives were best, the idea that she was married to Blue while showing it and strutting it and enticing all—yes, All—a wiggle and a smile; it simply amplified the situation to critical mass—they *had* to fuck her, it was inevitable. Was it anybody's fault that Blue was ordinary in conducting his nuptials—and that Tanya was in need of adventure? Was it anybody's fault that Blue was an evangelical Christian and never learned the ropes, any wonder why they were always trying to intimidate or get rid of him? Whose fault was it that Tanya couldn't get pregnant? Obviously, instinct took over...she needed them all, and still no pregnancy, but that didn't matter. She knew her husband had a low sperm count. Sometimes she'd even call him by her poodle's name: Henry.

"Look, when a woman finds out her man can't reproduce, it resonates deeply in her animal nature. It's not that she is promiscuous by nature, it's that nature makes her promiscuous in order that she *can* reproduce—that drive is mysterious, and many women don't realize that they are at the hands of a very powerful force," Dr. Plantis was saying. He stroked his bald head, knowing he left everything out, and his gray eyes looked at Detective Ashley Blue, and genuinely felt sorry for him. He kept telling him about certain exercises that would get the sex drive in gear, but Ashley insisted that he was in shape, and that his low sperm count did not affect his desire. And that he did not see the need to take a masturbation lesson in Plantis' office.

"What about your religion?" Dr. Plantis asked, straight faced and respectful.

"I go to church—I believe in Christ Jesus."

"Why did you say that backward?"

"What? Jesus Christ?"

"No," Dr. Plantis said. "You said 'Christ Jesus.'"

"So?"

"Only extreme right wing people say 'Christ' before saying 'Jesus.' Look, I'm not against religion, but it's getting in the way. Look, your whole problem is clear—your religion is hateful. Why don't you find a religious expression you can *both* participate in? There's a Hindu center in Hollywood. They have group chanting and meditation. Their ashram in Santa Monica is very strict about men and women worshiping together—they don't allow it. It's strictly girls on one side and boys on the other." Dr. Plantis was thrilled with his plan, and he envisioned them both going to India and being saved by the light of truth—reality, the way of the world. He was thrilled at the prospect that Blue might actually be cured of his true sickness, which could only be cured by a woman of power, provided he could integrate her into his fantasy life, and glue his semen to her beauty and success.

But that was a complicated proposition, to be sure, and he would have to be paid very well for that kind of deliverance out of something as egregious as Jesus! Of course he had put out for some bids, figuring he could make a little something on the side. He didn't have the heart to tell Blue about what happens to little boys who don't honor the woman of their dreams. "Don't you need somebody to love, don't you want somebody to love?" he told Blue, humming a forgotten tune.

Blue said: "Sir, the...I know the department wanted me to see you...informally of course, because —"

"Because you and your wife are on the rocks—but there's more," Dr. Plantis insisted.

There's more?

There is more.

For one thing, Blue would see all this as pertaining to the very sensitive case he had stumbled into with zeal and aplomb and grace and tender-footedness—the one who could make a difference. But they feared this, and so they sought to corrupt Blue's marriage. That much is simple to understand. They sought to corrupt Blue, and what better way than through Tanya Blue, the willing, the craving.

"What I was trying to tell you, Ashley—may I call you Ashley?"

"Fuck, whatever," Blue had said.

Plantis kept on: "Ashley, that's a nice name, a rather...a sort of his or her name, eh? Are you in touch with the woman in you, detective?"

"I wasn't aware there was a woman."

Plantis was playing him, clear as a bell, nice as a five-string viola, lovely as a piece of fine champagne crystal, just cruising his yacht off Cabo, fishing that big Marlin, Plantis would envision. And when he saw the picture of shapely Tanya, he saw himself and herself...together at last! He'd reel in the fish, she'd wait with legs spread below, fanning herself while the crew would keep the lid on it. Plantis was the fisherman, a king, and the department was the boat, and Tanya was the blue marlin, part trophy, part peccadillo, part fashion, part creation—all woman, casaba breasts, perhaps not real, but a real nice job, a pretty face framed by her bouncy blonde banged hair, and those legs! Heavens to Pete, how nifty her ass sashayed with that mini the day Blue brought her in—the dumb fuck!

Plantis told Blue about a retreat in the Santa Barbara Mountains, a kind of spiritual boot camp high above the ocean. A weekend retreat for men to be with men and do what men do. To not be afraid of being men, to get off the tit, as it were. He would not tell him about the woman who runs the place.

Plantis would deflect Blue every time he brought up Vincent Del Monte, how Blue told him he was getting inside Vincent's head, and felt it was all a big vendetta from childhood—and how it might involve Kruzmar, a leap he made because of the screenwriter involved.

He told Plantis about how he had researched Vincent's school record and friends he'd had in high school. "It wasn't hard to find 'em, they're the icons of Los Angeles—you know, judges, CEOs, what usually happens when preppie's come back home and live on the West Side."

Later, Captain Luther told him, "Fuck off! I told you it was Federal—"

"Who—"

"You little jackass, Blue! It's off-limits! Now, how are you and Plantis getting along? Hmm? Is he warming you up to the idea of healing your marriage?"

"Healing my marriage, sir?"

"Blue, it's no secret that your wife fools around, and that's got you crazed."

He went home early, and indeed, she was sucking the pool boy's cock. He'd seen things like this before but he couldn't understand, so he did not literally see what was right in front of his face. And what was right in front of his face, what was squarely making him have a spontaneous ejaculation of the shameful involuntary sort, a sight he had seen before, but now was the first time he'd fully realized it.

Shouldn't the pool boy, who was no boy, but a guy named

Butch, who was anything but childlike, pay for his error like any-body else? Just because he was a twenty-three year old grad stu-dent, a gym rat, a tan, curly blond, virile to beat the sand, man, was that any reason to spare him? A man, budding and pointing? Just throwing fate to the wind, you might say. Ashley Blue, who from a sheltered life in Tulsa came, now quickly went into a kind of slow motion attack in his little house in Reseda.

There was no mistake about it—Butch was not shooting blanks, and Ashley must have known it. What hit him was blind-ness, like when he drew the gun, like when he fired into the back of Butch's head while Tanya's mouth was still around the center of the man's universe. Just as he did that, she mistook it for his ejaculating, redounding to her benefit and not his—the natural order of the world, his last debit.

Just as she started to reap her reward, his body fell sideways into the pool and jerked spasmodically—his handsome, chiseled face and big thick eyebrows and his muscular chest all contract-ing and writhing as the blood spiraled out into the water with ever-waning spasmodic movement.

Her scream was muted when he shot her in the mouth point blank. He was amazed that the .40 cal. could do such damage. She was in shock, beautiful Tanya Blue, her perfect face now without a lower jaw. He meant to hit her between the eyes but the kick of the weapon caused him to overcompensate to the lower jaw, which the single bullet shattered. There was no lower lip, no lower teeth, no chin, and no beauty—all that remained was an open bloody screaming throat and a partial face, from the upper jaw upward. A monster he had instantly created, and he left her like that and departed to his police-issue vehicle.

One thing was sure, she would never again be able to give someone a blow job, or even polite conversation for that matter, not unless someone spent at least a couple hundred grand on facial reconstruction. And in her state that would prove unlikely.

No, Blue had inadvertently done something that he knew the hand of fate had to have been on. It was vengeance but it was not his. He had become part of something much bigger—it was the case of the century, the Vincent Del Monte case. Which was much bigger than Vincent Del Monte, to be sure.

(How can Vincent win, why did he win? What did he do to me? I want to know, but they say that it's all me…and I'm wondering now if there is a *him*…)

THGIE

As I mentioned, Kruzmar had somehow managed to lock me in some movie studio south of Mexico City—some secret location where he and his friends would hang out for months on end drinking Don Julio and cruising, while under the guise of making the desert dog movies. I was under armed guard, living on a game show set—they didn't know I knew Spanish, did not know that I understood what they spoke of, and the way they spoke of their mothers' powers of sorcery. And how their dads ran away because of total fear...and how nobody better mess with them, or they'll get the Evil Eye, su madre, conjo, motherfucker. All of southern Mexico was given to the Diablo, and his women, all the mothers—and the men were all drunks. These were nobodies, slaves, but they didn't know it. From listening to their bullshit, you'd think they were running the world from their impoverished little shack in some government empowerment zone. This was the perfect Kruzmar environment!

He had captured me and had lots of professionals talking to me, various military psychiatrist and mind-control programmers, but I did not see Kruzmar anywhere...I sensed him. I remembered him. As I am remembering now.

"Vincent, what do you do when a fire breaks out in a crowded theater?" a voice asked from behind a partition (my feet and hands were chained).

"I would scream fire and use a machete to cut my way out," I said, knee-jerk.

"Vincent, if I have three loaves of bread and I divide two of them by three, how many loaves of bread do I have?"

That was easy: "None."

"None—is that your answer?"

"You don't understand the future," I said. "You'll have even less then."

I was given intravenous feeding, and slept for a few weeks, and during that time I had dreams of Kruzmar's studio: that is, Mount Triac, where his production company, Trundle Pictures, resided. I kept dreaming (or was it implantation?) about the chief, a man named Styles. I knew his mistresses, I knew he loved going to certain restaurants. He was like my Mexican jailers, macho. He'd never admit anything less. No, he got to pretend he was the original man, got there with no help from anybody else. When he saw me he said he spent most of his life on his knees while under the skirt of The Most High—saying, yes, yes, yes—here, here, here. "Whatever you want, I'll do it—please mommy! Please mommy! Please mommy!"

I met a senator named Diane and another senator named Marty, and they were observing. There were Federal agents, one good friend in particular, Hackford, whom I bonded with in a sort of boys-be-boys sort of way. I said I needed to be reunited with my men, and indeed, Millicet, James, the Flagellator and Silas were all living well, eating well, and being cared for in a luxury villa, where they moved me after several months.

They said I had to be remade. For what?

There were rumors that the events in Beverly Hills regarding the screenwriter Mallard and his wife and friends, who were apparently butchered—I wasn't sure who tampered with things after we left, but we certainly did not butcher anybody—were somehow precipitated by a disgruntled gardener, and that the whole thing involved drugs, and that Mallard's reputation was ruined, and that he would never work again.

"Do you like my handiwork, Vincent?" came a new voice, from behind another wall, as I was doing solitary, and personal *thoughtwork*. "Do you remember me, Vincent?"

It would be the first time I had laid eyes on Leonard Cutlass Kruzmar for about twenty-three years—although everyone knew who he was; the hilltop boy in Tommy Hilfiger and Persols, who was wanting me to see something familiar, no doubt.

After I had heard the voice, I was taken back to seclusion, another basement cell, where I was given scores of tests and finally, a battery of psychological tests designed to traumatize me into mindfuck obedience. Fuck me in the ass? I'll kill ya!

I heard his—that is, Kruzmar's voice—over and over again, in my ears, in my nostrils, in my feet and hands. "Vincent, pass the paper to the monitor...Vincent, go to the bathroom and urinate...Vincent, take the knife and stick it into the mannequin." And this one, over and over: "Vincent, forget everything you have heard and stare at the yellow light."

After I stared at the yellow light, I realized that this work, whatever it was, was sanctioned by my Lord and Master, The Future.

Kruzmar, like many surrogates, was working for him without knowing it.

When I stared at the blue light, things were different. When I stared at the orange light, things became clear. And then I was at an altar of a religion called "The Way Of The World"—and Master's voice came through loud and clear. "Vincent, you are not to serve false gods."

After the blue light I was sitting at my mother's table and eating stuffed game hen, and she was doting on Anastasia, but then she looked at my fiancée, Anastasia, and said, "Vincent knows we have rules around here."

And so we had rules.

Whenever I heard a command from Kruzmar, in order not to be shocked, in order not to be made to feel intense pain, I did it—but usually these were little tasks. Usually these involved everything from passing the sugar to Anastasia at dinner with Margot and her staff in attendance. When I'd remember severing Margot's head from her body, I got this awful electric shock right up my asshole. So she was alive, alive, alive!

Fuck me in the ass, I'll kill ya!

Yes, sir, she's alive! Margot! Margot! Margot!

So I'd do all the tasks: a simple thing like handing the knife to Anastasia, who in turn would hand it back to me; whispering into Margot's ear, "Kill yourself"; handing Hackford the machine gun, shooting the watermelon with the high-powered rifle, tying and raping the blonde beach bunnies in Venice, looking at the blue light, the orange light, the yellow light. Involuntary urination or bowel movements. To avoid the shock that was so painful it made me pass out.

(By now you're realizing that this isn't fiction, is it. No, I do serve the Future and I will exist, forever and ever.)

There was only one time when I thought that Leonard had convinced my Lord to do something awful, and that was when he asked me to kill the cute little poodle laying beside Margot. It wasn't that I couldn't stop myself, it's that there was no way to do this without turning my attention to the housekeeper as well, for she had grabbed the dog and was crying and screaming, "No, No."

When I heard her pathetic little whimper, the twenty-something uneducated Mexican girl of whom I might have thought fondly, she had grabbed the carving knife and held it against me. In my ear I could hear—*kill, kill, kill,* over and over.

As I was having the most wonderful time of my life with all my monitors and controls—and dutiful assignments—I wondered why I hadn't seen Millicet, Silas, the Flagellator, who is a diabetic and needs insulin (I told them this but they acted strangely indifferent) and of course, James, who was called Jude a long time ago.

They made an exception with Jude. In fact, they only let me see Jude, and told me that Millicet was not doing so well at the training camp, and that they thought he might not be able to continue being my best and most loyal friend.

So I said, "Hey, Jude, don't make it bad, take a sad song, and make it better."

"What do you think the meaning of that song is, Vincent?" came the voice of Perkins, a twenty-five-year-old woman who trained me to shoot a long-range rifle with a very powerful scope on it. I told her it was about the matriarchy, "which means to cut off your head and shit down your neck, bitch," shocking Jude. She laughed, became somewhat flirtatious and attempted to get the better of me. In a weak moment, I have to admit, the temptation to toy with her became insurmountable. So I told her I was fantasizing about her, and when she gave me the go-signal I stuck my gun in her ear and said, "Kissy, kissy...black ops trainer? Macho bitch?" I pulled the trigger back.

"I'm sorry! I'll suck your cock! I'm sorry! I didn't mean it! I'm a witch! Okay? I admit it! I wanted your...your soul, I'm sorry!"

"What you really want is for me to pull the trigger. And I was made to pull the trigger...the minute your head explodes on the wall, then you can start to go to forever. How's that for a rhyme?"

She was truly afraid—fucking bitch actually blinked.

"Who's training who, lovely lady? Well isn't that what the Intel people wanted, to roll out the slave-route of Satan in the forgotten music, or is that muzak?"

She looked around, as if seeing everything for the last time. It was so cute seeing a woman in fatigues and eyeliner, and don't get me wrong, she had perky little breasts and a nice little body that any red-blooded fool would want. That is, any red-blooded fool not controlled by destiny. She finally looked back at me and asked, "Do you hate me?"

"Not at all. I don't hate anyone. But you are training me to kill you, I guess you didn't know that."

She reeled around and I couldn't comfort her. She suddenly looked like a deer in the headlights—and showed no relief. She frowned and asked, "Why?"

"Target practice."

She excused herself, still trembling, and told me to wait. After a few minutes Jude went after her. He told me she went into the girl's bathroom and blew her brains out. But I know better than that.

Jude was clearly upset, and asked me what I said to her. "I

told her, in my own clear and concise fashion, in my clearly in-imitable way, that there is no anti-Santa Claus. That my Master sent me back here to alter the future."

He said he felt bad, that I should have been more sensitive.

"Make no mistake about it, little Jude, they are the enemy of our Master's order, the one he created."

Jude accepted that, that this was some sort of war, sanctioned by him who sent us. Perkins had caused this little row, and I felt that she harbored some kind of emotional instability that hope-fully would be eradicated before I left the campsite, a few miles from where they held me in Mexico City. "Look," I told Jude, "she was wrong."

"But the whole world is based on—"

"Stop!" I told the lovely lad. "One man can change destiny, remember that."

Tears filled his eyes. "But I don't want to die."

"Get on your face, now!" I commanded.

Jude was thinking about his mother, a perfect beauty that looked like his high-school girlfriend, who looked like Anastasia. It all got wrapped into one.

I told him I could see, and that there was a shining light, and that light obliterated the darkness, and that light wasn't the light of the morning, and that light was called love, and that love was going to pierce every heart, and those women were going to turn to our Master or die. Or die, Jude!"

He said, "I don't understand, Vincent. You're crazy."

"Then why am I here?" I asked him, in earnest.

"To torture me. To not let me be. To stop me from having a life..." and Jude made me very sad, and I knew he was still hiding under his mother's skirt. "Don't you know that many a man lost his life in battle for his girl and not the truth?"

Jude said nothing. He just stared at me with those wander-lust eyes anybody would fall in love with, innocence, beauty, grace.

However, my mind was consumed with Anastasia, and I needed Perkins to be alive so she could give me her perspective on our love affair. Did she think Anastasia loved me? We could start with that, for instance. Did she think that Anastasia was too jaded? Too callous? Too much a victim to really experience love?

Can Anastasia see me now, does she long for me, does she want me, sexually or just mentally? What's she thinking right now, Perkins? Perkins!

"Blew her brains out in the bathroom."

"Shut up, Jude," I was saying, and it seemed he had now followed me all around the camp. "What do you want?"

"I want you to look at me," Jude said.

"Kruzmar get to you yet? Don't you let him have his way, he'll pervert ya."

"I care about what you think, Vincent," Jude said and wrapped his arm around me.

If it's psychological fitness they want, they need look no further than me. For I was a paragon of virtue, a sound mind was given me because of my service to my Lord, and my accepting of a supernatural being to live inside me—who was nameless, but knew everything from the past. Which was why I laughed at my present circumstances.

Seeing Margot did not fool me, for I understood that all the little pills they gave me, combined with various sleeping quarters, handlers and trainers, was either for a film Kruzmar was doing or Kruzmar did not exist at all, at least in my scenario, and I was training for further infiltrations behind the lines.

"It is very important to be psychologically ready," I told a panel of questioners, who all wore green fatigues and had very nicely clipped haircuts.

We flew by helicopter to a golf course, where they gave me that strange-looking rifle and positioned me in what might be called a tree house. I told them I practically grew up on a golf course, and I found them very pleasant, but not for the purposes of playing golf. For other reasons. Reasons that were private.

The rifle was long, and had a muffler on the end of it that was at least a half-a-meter long. It had a light butt that molded itself to the indentation of my arm, just outside the armpit. The caliber was something like a .7 millimeter or a 30-0-6. I knew about guns, calibers and hunting rifles from my Uncle Ray, who taught me to shoot when I was about six years old. I always knew the skill would come in handy. I impressed this upon Jude, who complained that some of the men had tried to molest him—

forced him to do things that he regretted, and made him perform services that were more like a girl than a boy.

I told him that he was young, and he didn't even shave—that of course the perverts would be tempted. "Well, how do you avoid getting your dick grabbed, Vincent?" he asked earnestly.

"Would you shut up and let me hit this thing."

He indeed quieted down as I hit the watermelon, exploding it from two hundred yards away. Next, I hit the cantaloupe, and then I even managed to hit a golf ball on top of a coke bottle. When I did that they told me to stop, and I put the rifle down and focused on Jude.

"Who did it exactly?" I asked him.

He said, "It was the maid, Juanita, who asked me to come into this tent, and her husband was there, waiting for me. He grabbed me and forced me to do things that I'll never be able to live down."

"Show me where he is," I said.

I snuck a weapon out of the armory. You must remember, the camp, which was a few miles from the studio, surrounded by jungle, was comprised of army tents. I heard Kruzmar's voice in my little earphone, but never saw him. As far as I knew we could have been in Nebraska or Texas. But everyone was Mexican and because I understood Spanish rather well, I could determine that most of the soldiers were private, or mercenary, and commuted to and from Mexico City, where Kruzmar was filming some Mexican uprising movie—some commie takeover of Mexico City by the Zapatistas, or some such. A kind of misbegotten Che Guevara homily that makes one sick for a good war, like this Gulf War, which I really wanted to get into, where some serious ordnance could be brought to bear. Something about the little guy rising up for his freedom had a pall of ignorance, of idealism, of manipulation. Like the French Revolution, just an excuse for a bunch of assholes to get their books published. Genocide is more my cup of tea—women and children first, I always say.

When Jude showed me the husband of the cleaning woman, I was horrified at what a little faggot he really was. The maid was a little queen, and by that I mean one of the witches—ordering her husband to molest the cute little white boy, my little brother

Jude.

Jude was only twenty years old, and I cherished him, and sure, I understood how he had a certain androgynous look, a lovely countenance. Heck, Millicet got drunk and saw a beautiful girl…and Silas might have done the same except that every time I beat him to the point of blacking out. But that was family. This little greasy faggot was not forgivable. Jude fell into the rule of innocence, and so I was obligated to send a little message.

When I entered the armory tent it was unattended, and so I took the real exotic-looking surgical-precision rifle that could hit golf-balls at three hundred yards, and from the comfort of the perimeter wall, through the Bausch and Lomb scope I could see the hairs on his neck. Jude looked on with the spotting scope. I was aware we were being watched, and so I concluded that this is what they wanted anyway. I had already learned about how things that seemed like your idea ended up being my Lord's idea all along.

"You see his fat ugly head, Jude?"

He said nothing. But I knew he had him dead to rights in his scope.

I waited until his wife started ordering him around in the tent, and waited until she had her two-year-old in her arms and began breastfeeding him. Then I fired—and boy, oh boy! Just like the watermelon—all over Juanita and the baby. In shock, she fell with her baby and screamed but no one went to her.

"Thanks, Vincent," Jude said. But when I looked for him, as he was right next to me, he was gone. His voice was in my ear.

"What the devil are you doing there, Jude? Didn't you—"

"Vincent, look at the blue light," he said with a kind of machine-like cadence.

"Jude...what the fuck are you doing?"

"Look...at...the...blue...light...NOW!" Jude said, a complete personality change by the way.

I couldn't resist, I looked at the blue light, which was very bright, even in broad daylight. It was mounted onto a jeep and pointed right at me, ready for me—Jude, you traitor!

Somebody was talking to me. I could hear something in my ear like: "Job well done, Vincent," and I thought, who is this fuck? Doesn't he know who he's dealing with? I always hit my mark.

Later I would be invited to have some fun at the local pub.

Job well done, the words were torturous to me.

ENIN

Kruzmar saw them at the nightclub, and indeed it was very late at night. He was listening to his favorite band, celebrating with his favorite drag queen, Michelle, enjoying a little champagne and musing about hermaphrodism. He was in the mood to zoom in on actor Tommy Taal, up-and-coming fast-boy, new kid, all that. He was there with his jet-black hair, tattoos and a real impediment—his girlfriend, Miranda. Moving in on Tommy shouldn't be too difficult, and indeed would not be if Lucy were here with him rather than out with some Tibetan monk, and engaging in a reunion with all her global-warming buddies. It wouldn't be so bad if Miranda happened to meet with some noble world peace sort of accident, the kind that would have Taal relying on "work" to get him through.

Michelle de Maestro was a maven, the ultimate queen of the club scene, the crank goddess, and was by day an attorney named Mike Masters. Michelle had a certain voluptuousness right off the bat due to past and present motivation that harkened back to a little pair of cowboy boots and a little lunch box, and a strict mommy who used electro-shock in an attempt to prevent bedwetting. "The thing about crank," he was saying in his womanly voice, "was that it brought out the real woman in a man."

That night Kruzmar tried it and immediately zoomed Michelle into introducing Tommy to him at the dark oaken table that bore the name, Reserved.

Tommy said he was thrilled to meet Kruzmar and told his girlfriend to look away while showing Kruzmar the almighty audition. Kruzmar thought of oil wells, and he thought Lucy was looking in on Tommy's instant debut. Was there no challenge anymore?

"I guess you really want to work in this town," Kruzmar told Tommy, with those boyish thick eyebrows and every manly attribute that Kruzmar would say goodbye to in himself. And of course next he would require, for an extra million, a private session with Tommy. This was good for show, as Tommy was a player—and everyone admired him for his instant courage.

Of course, as with all outer rim beginners, there would be inner circles, activities put on videotape guaranteed to make them keep their mouths shut and do what they're told, dumb motherfuckers, Kruzmar thought.

The worldwide circle jerk redounded to his millionaire benefit, not to the dumb fucks living on sushi and rock and roll, who in a late night open session would think friendship, networking, their wives and girlfriends having left the room and throwing it all to the higher queen, and the family Kruzmar, with their well-placed sources, would capture it all and kick them off the ladders forever. How sad, he laughed, looking at the cocktail waitress and the service givers—let them keep on giving! Work for a living, work for a living, dumb fucks! Harder, harder—there ya go...great that they think they matter...oh, how great it is to watch them kowtow on command.

More and more money piles up, and they're trapped forever serving me, forever loving me, going to my movies, jerking off for me, all that sunshine for me, me, and me. Total victory for me, capturing the live feed for no one but me, worldwide. Any man who did not, who knew not, who was not, would be castrated by any number of available means—all the labor of the world is truly in my service, all about me, for me, to me and through me—for no one comes into the light without my blessing. And yes, forcing them to become women, or vice versa, all for me, Kruzmar told himself while fondling the last of Tommy's fading freedom.

These lost ones would serve these various beautiful women, but they would be called women forever, and they would volunteer for castration when they saw that was the only way out for a sissy, as they were women trapped in a man's body, as Kruzmar had envisioned himself, proudly.

Then their asses would belong to me, Kruzmar mused. No one in Michelle's club of losers would ever know. No amount of crank or coke or heroin smokes could change the truth that no one wanted to believe. The subterranean message would keep on, not enough workers, too many queens, and some only ten years old, while killing all the heathen for their stripes—and Kruzmar, a king, would deem them worthy. The younger the better, the more the merrier, especially for the pearl of great price, the precious virgin, even if they had to go younger and younger to find that heart of gold... How lovely is our world, Kruzmar thought, his flesh tingling with satisfaction.

Just as he would make a senator or a president—the mantle received from a cabal of hundreds of billions in the form of old-family connected to the matrix of Holy Grail and ancient banking, via the Knights Templar and Sanhedrin. The killers of Jesus were the top of the ladder, all those in the know, knew.

Yes, he was in the service to the ruler of the world—direct connection. Satan. Lucifer. Beelzebub. Molech. In him. Not outside, no need of worship—it's inside him, and that made him feel goosepimply all over, and that made him feel like sucking everything that protruded, and he knew he could not be poisoned from anything he could possibly do.

Vincent knew something he shouldn't. He could not be castrated, it was a virtual uncertainty—his creative force was very much coveted; it was the addition of the next phase of his life, some kind of additional component, a vagina, a real cunt all his own. But further, he would not be a freak, he was explaining to Michelle, who seemed interested—well, he/she was interested in everything, Kruzmar said. He was fashioning the globe to accommodate all her/his friends.

He called to inquire about Vincent's progress, and the report of suicide was encouraging. "Oh, Vincent, such a force of nature, Stanley—but you have to control him," he was saying, pushing his blond shock of hair back while watching some green-haired people fuck in the next booth.

"Tell me about him," Kruzmar said, playing with himself while a couple of women at the next table seemed mildly interested. "What? Suicide?"

 @   @   @

In the backroom, beyond the pavement and up in the penthouse, the billionaire foreigners were meeting, sans the Americans. But they were in America, because when they looked out the window, the sidewalks were flecked with fat people. In fat America they would meet, in secret. The Aussies, the Brits, the French, Italians and Canadians, Brazil, Mexico, Japan and China—what interest would they have if there was a merger between Mount Triac, Monsoon and Genesis? Genesis was well capitalized but lost several new films to a fledgling partnership between the three moguls, who were considered inept, as well as to the attempt at a coup by the liquor kid. This was war.

They were waiting with their national economies on the line. They were not interested in sex, they were not interested in legal dividing lines, they were interested in territory. They had been planning. They had been patient. They were never there at the parties, maybe on a Sunday you could see one of the dignitaries at the sea with a son or daughter, boarding a limo with a wife—low key.

Some went to church at All Faith in Santa Monica.

They all lived in little condos in Santa Monica.

Santa Monica made them feel welcome, made them feel familiar—their accents were met with others of similar persuasions. But they would go home, would not go downtown, or down the coast, or late night, or inland—they had a job to do and they would do it with utter precision.

At this point it would be foolish to speculate on what their business was, yet when the trust fund baby of the Middle East was brought in, everybody knew there would be a shakedown. The boys at Chase and Citi and Morgan Stanley and even an SEC guy or a Fed Reserve guy would be in attendance. But not a word on Wall Street.

It was Lucy who got wind of it—and thought...*capital*. She was the one who had office space in the Century City Tower—her home away from home, a place to prance when she did not want to be seen at the studio, even if she had nothing to fear, as five of her movies had hit the big screen and been hits, even if her husband's name was on all of them. She was the only one to fuck the writer and remain dignified. She'd hunt and peck the stars, her manicurist, the doorknob—it was all she could do to contain herself, and she networked her way into those backroom meetings, as soon as she spotted the weak link she was in. At the Bel-Age tea, she found Linda, the lovely Linda—her lovely breasts and emerald green suit, diamond nails and pretty blue eyes, her butch hair and no nonsense workouts at the Venice Gym. She was the one.

She found out they were interested in media, and she discovered that Linda wanted to dance with her...privately. She knew who Lucy was, everyone did.

Lucy, in her curly hair and wide-open thirty-three-year-old innocent gaze, and Lucy, in her pearls and jeans, in her DB-7 and sub-woofed stereo.

When she took Linda to the Colony for a little getaway, she told Leonard she was working on something big with a new confidante.

Kruzmar was much too concerned with his mother's council. Milaca was up next, speaking it nice but perhaps not like Serena from Mozambique. Milaca had this sort of Jamaican accent not unlike Cleo on the psychic network. "She do the work, the big fish in the sea, in style fall down."

And Asenath said: "Fool, you have no idea what you did, no idea that she is the queen to come—the three await, because the money exist, but you can't touch it without your queen."

"Lucy?" Kruzmar said, horrified.

"Does that surprise you, child?" Serena asked.

Kruzmar folded his blond floppy curl over his eyes, and said in an almost yearning manner: "What about Vincent?"

Asenath leapt up from the candles and danced around the room. "He is the light of life!" She waved her superficially blonde hair around and around. "He is the truth, the light and the way. Nobody stops him, not even you!"

The others frowned. "You take the studio, you win," Serena said. "Lucy is your queen, and you can never be queen, Leonard."

"But I want all the—"

"It's for women!" Milaca screamed. "We are given the power because we have the womb!"

"Your mother will not like this development—the power to give birth, of creation itself, comes out of woman; you can be like woman, even have power, but only *because* of your mother, and your new queen."

"No!" Leonard said, angrily. He leapt up from the dance studio floor, looked at the maid and told her to get him a Margarita, and then met his guests for the night—Bob and Felicia Henretty, the producers of one of his many productions. And that is precisely when his friend Tommy Taal came around. His instructions: to get in Felicia's pants while he and Bob hammered out deal points and script points. Leonard was not to be mocked, and would never lose at a game like this.

He couldn't stop thinking about Vincent, and his awe grew the more he considered his boyhood face, a face that grew younger and younger.

NET

N ow the APB had been out on Blue for some time, and there was no other place for him to go but the 5th green at the country club that Vincent had camped out on. He would retrace the steps, and as he did he had the uncanny sensation he was being observed. Blue had purchased new clothes, rather than returning to the scene of the crime. Because he was a cop, this was blasted all over the news for the first few days. And so Blue went where he had to go, to the beginning of the beginning, and he was starting to remember.

First of all, he was handsome, and that afforded him a pretty wife. He was the all-college boy, but something went wrong back in high school when he had discovered he wasn't all that macho, indeed, was attracted to his sister's undergarments, at first. There was a fascination with boys too, and art, and girl-stuff. Horror of horrors, he couldn't face, mirror of mirrors, he had to break. Living on the edge—pretending to be one of the boys when he was not. And Vincent wasn't either. He knew that. He needed more.

Much more. It was his true mission, to unfold the case, to resurrect the past, the childhood he missed, the father he feared, the mother he hated—how she doted on Suzie, how she focused on her frills and curls, how she had to have just the right shoes, the #4 mascara, the #6 rouge, the long braid. Ashley, it could even be a girl's name, Plantis had said. Ashley, the woman you seek is in your heart, and she'll always be there for you. Elizabeth, his mother had said, but little good it did—Satan wants a certain *kind* of heart, where he dwells as a girl, even a queen, a ruler—the conscience…backwards, but no one would ever say *that.* Would they?

Besides, Blue would never get it, just wouldn't. So he wore the name Ashley well, "But mom, I'm not one of the boys and I'm not queer either!"

And Elizabeth gave up. Blue kept going, hurtling to the destiny that I would soon provide.

His father beat him severely, hoping that would grow his testicles somewhat, but to no avail. So he played football, he joined the team—halfback, and he ran 'em in—and Dad, who was named Ed—cheered him. But Suzie, a junior, got invited to the prom and they were spending time on everything Blue wanted for himself. He could not fake it with the boys anymore. In the locker room, he looked—he wanted, he suppressed. He had to.

The hatred made him turn to everything from fights to work shirts, to junior college and then the police academy. Busting the faggots' heads was his favorite thing to do. But he was terrified all the same. Would they find out? Would anyone?

In Los Angeles it was wide open. LAPD first, a cool bunch of guys—handsome guys, not like Denver the year before. And then the opening came in Beverly Hills, and every other cop had a screenplay, and some had headshots. The women were cute, except for the clerics and the dispatchers—they were career women.

It happened, one night while his new partner, a woman, noticed how Blue would watch her putting on her lipstick, and he would talk to her about her husband, like another chick. She figured it out first. She tested him when she wanted to do a little window shopping while they were on walk-patrol on Rodeo Drive. She asked what he thought about a certain dress, and she could see his face made up and his lips with her lipstick. And she sought to help him.

"Ashley, look, are you hiding in there?"

"What are you talking about, Cho?"

"You have no desire for me—there's no sexual tension. I mean, you talk to me like a chick, no offense. Don't worry—your secret's safe. I won't tell the guys."

"What guys?"

"I mean the fact that you avoid all the boy stuff—they know something's up, and if it's you...look, life's too short."

"Fuck you. I was just trying to help."

Cho sat back, sipping her coffee, as they waited to interview the Regent Hotel Manager about the murder that had occurred in room 2250. It was a woman—the room was cleaned up except for her clothes. Vivian Cho, the lovely Korean twenty-seven-year-old ex-model, three- year homicide cop, placed a shawl on Blue's shoulders and he looked at himself in the mirror. "There's nothing wrong with you—you're like a woman, that's all. It's a transgender issue—you can get help, Ashley."

Red. From that point forward it was sick jokes at the water cooler, it was eying Cho like he wanted to rape her. Discouraged, she transferred, and he was called up before the chief, but she said nothing.

He was the only one, as it turned out, who did not know—and his wife, his hot beach beauty in the ass-tight mini and wondrous breasts, attracted to Blue's pretty face, his way about him—the safety. She'd been flirting all around him and he'd not noticed a thing. He'd heard the word fag-hag but didn't think they were talking about her. All through high school Tanya was the wet T-shirt contest winner, she'd given head to the entire football team and lived up to that reputation by becoming the ultimate mascot. "Tanya, Tanya, Tanya, Tanya, Tanya—"

The uptight bitches of that year hated her. She had the line, she needed a man for some sort of security, and she could have found a millionaire, but Blue made good money, and she felt safe with him.

That is, it was the perfect arrangement for now. A steady paycheck, plenty of time to play during the day. He would never know how many men...but he couldn't do it.

Couldn't anyone tell him, or tell her, that they knew? He was beautiful, Ashley Blue, he might've been an actor if he could stop bashing queers every time they looked at him. They couldn't help it. He sent the mixed signals, and whoa to the lonely lover looking for some comfort.

He was sick of them teasing him and zooming in on Tanya, and sick of her sitting in their laps and knowing all the cops by their first names. Sick of all the secrets around him, sick of the disrespect.

All because he could not admit one thing. At least that's what I think—telling this to you, my almighty friends, from a future abode. As I mentioned before, it's all remembrance. I would take him in, brothers. First I would send reinforcements. You see? I told you I would provide his future, his completion…just a little while now.

On the golf course he knew he was being watched, and he knew I had a certain key to unlock his chastity belt—his mind belonged to me now. Kruzmar thought he had mine in the palm of his through the looking-glass hand. He had nothing. I'd been a soldier, and I knew how to play 'em good. I could frustrate them to no end.

"Who's there?" Ashley Blue asked, dressed in simple denim and a v-neck sweater, and not a jacket and slacks, and not a tie—but something that would make his face melt onto the cover of a magazine.

"It's me," came an older voice. Thirty-three-year-old Ashley Blue turned to find my best man, Millicet, a bearded, masculine man who had no time to fool with boys. He was safe. "Over here," Millicet said. And when Ashley looked, he found Millicet wearing a white robe that touched the ground. His long beard and braided hair made him appear holy. "I'm not the virgin Mary," he said. "And I won't bite ya. I know you."

"You…" and by now Millicet had him down next to the hole of the 5th green and was threatening to punch his lights out, while young Blue was stunned, laughing, crying, and generally in a state of utter dismay. "Vincent sent me to help you—you're one of us now," said Millicet, a holy man from the mountain of remembrance.

"One…one of you?" asked Blue, looking around and hoping

a manly man like Millicet could not see his faults as an incomplete man, as a boyhood man, as a sissy with a violent streak.

"I won't harm you—our leader, Vincent Damien Del Monte, has a job for you to do."

No sooner did Millicet put the young warrior right than they were right back on Peter Mallard's property. Right back at the pool table, right back despite the—now dead—security guard and the extra security. The guard, a black guy named Jackson, had the keys to the property, the code for the alarm, and was generally very helpful. Blue wanted to tie him up, but Millicet cut him from ear to ear, as was only proper given the high security status of the operation.

Millicet led the way, down the corridor and into Mr. Mallard's study. Now Blue began to act in accordance with the little earpiece wedged deep into his brain. "Threaten Mallard with the gun."

And Blue held the gun on him.

When Mr. Mallard turned around he was aghast, and Blue was aghast and only Millicet knew what to do given the surprise and vagaries of the mission at hand. "Tell him you'll kill him if he doesn't cooperate."

Sure enough, without any effort whatsoever, Mallard was shut down in the wine cellar—Millicet noticed he had a new nose, a brand spanking new nose from ass cartilage.

"Now see here—what do you want from me?"

Millicet slapped him so hard he cut his face though to the jaw—and Blue wondered what Millicet had used. By this time Mr. Mallard was crying and begging, on his knees before Blue, and in an effort to enhance the situation, Blue turned to me: "Vincent? You there?"

"You're doing fine, Detective Blue. Glad to have you aboard. Don't worry about the wound on Mr. Mallard's face. I want you to silence him, and I want you to summon my fiancée, Anastasia."

"No!" cried Mallard. "She's been through enough! Please, I beg you, take me—take me!"

When Blue turned around Mr. Peter Mallard's face was blue and he was not breathing. I did not recall killing him, but there he was, asphyxiated.

Blue tried of course to revive him, as I had both eyes and ears. Millicet, the dumb scoundrel, was nowhere to be found. I told him that if he laid a hand on her, he would find himself in the same sorry condition that Mr. Mallard found himself.

"How did...this happen?" Blue asked, frightened.

I told him not to be frightened, but that he should move out of the way so that I could see out of his eyes and ears and I wanted him to find any pending contracts between Kruzmar and Mallard, and I wanted to see Anastasia now.

"What the fuck's going on? Did my Dad put you up to this?" asked Anastasia.

"Remember...get out of the way so I can see through your eyes."

There she was, the beautiful Anastasia with the long blonde hair, who is deeply entrenched in my heart.

"Vincent sends his regards," Blue said.

"Vincent! Oh, my god!" she screamed and tried to run out, but Blue grabbed her and flung her back to the bed.

"My father's dead, isn't he? What is it, like a mafia hit or something?"

"Blue, you dumb motherfucker, tell her I love her!" I screamed into his ear from my vastly remote location. Two hands tied behind my back. Talent, yes. Precision, of course. But with someone as uninformed as to the system as Blue was, I was drowning in molasses, unfortunately, things just couldn't get done with the efficiency of future promise. I needed more, I got less.

"He...he loves you."

She smiled.

"And don't you fucking touch her, you faggot," I said.

No, he just stood over her dumbly.

She smiled up at him and started thinking the same thing I was thinking, that he was an idiot. "So...Vincent sent you?"

"Yes...he's..."

"Hello, Ms. Mallard," Millicet said. "He's Vincent's eyes and ears—handsome, but not functional."

"Well...then I'm going to have my way with you. You like to

be ordered around by a bad little girl?"

"You let her do what she wants, slave," I said, and left because I did not want to know that playful side of her.

"Yes," Blue said.

"I want you to take your pants off, to your underwear, and then brush my hair. I think Vincent sent you for me to use," she said.

"Yes," Blue said. "He did. I am yours."

"Well? I told you to do something, sissy boy."

Blue hopped out of his slacks and immediately went to it with the brush. Anastasia was clearly on her throne that evening. I could see her blue eyes in her mirror (don't ask me how) and I longed for them. I realized that I supplied Blue as the first eunuch to our kingdom, and he was off to a fine start. She liked it too.

"I like you, Blue," she said. "Do you have a girlfriend?"

"I had a wife," he said, taking great care in brushing the long blonde hair all the way down.

"Ouch! You jerk—gently, not one tangle, understand? You getting horny or something—you want to play with yourself?"

"No!" Blue said.

"Prude."

"I'm sorry. I don't know what you want."

"I want your balls," she said. "I mean, like I read in history class...the royal court would keep the eunuch's balls in a jar. I want you to give them to me. You killed my worthless father, didn't you?"

"Not me—it was Millicet, the guy with the—"

"You're just as sick as Vincent."

"You don't love him, Anas—"

"You do not call me Anastasia—you call me My Lady or Your Highness."

"Yes, m'lady."

"Stop it! Fucking pervert—you have a hard-on, don't you??

"I don't—"

"Let me see!"

Unfortunately, the awful truth was revealed, and Ashley Blue revealed himself by pulling up his long shirt and revealing what could only be described as large balls and a cute little penis that rested on top of his sack and pointed forward, like a child. She laughed and grabbed his balls. "These are like so fucking enormous—that's why you're having so many problems, sis. They don't match your lack of like...manhood."

"Get on your knees," she said. "You are my subject, and your balls are too big for your little pecker."

"Yes, m'lady. I know."

"Well, what are you waiting for?"

"I'll kill you," still standing at attention, still cooperating as if under hypnosis.

"Oh, you'll kill me now? You don't understand, you were a present—and you tell Vincent that I've been waiting for him to take me out of here!"

"Yes, m'lady," Blue said.

"Blue—stand down. Pull your pants up and take Anastasia to Millicet," I said, growing more frustrated as I had no way of verifying that he was doing what he said.

Anastasia complained, "Vincent, you said he was mine, that I was a queen. I want a real eunuch."

She was so clever, but so beautiful, and my heart melted. "As soon as we can get a surgeon," I promised her.

She smiled and started sucking on a lollypop right in front of Blue. "You better not get horny, or I'll make you take your clothes off in public, then everyone will see why your girlfriend was so mad."

Fourteen years old and talking like that? A true woman of the world, who would wait for me, a mere ageless youth with a heart of glass and a mouth of gold...a slice of something unfathomable.

NEVELE

I was ever so eager to be blindfolded and flown to Los Angeles, where I was escorted by a limo to a luxury hotel on at the corner of Wilshire and Santa Monica in Beverly Hills. I felt really good about things, about the world—about the mission the future had sent me on, about how much symmetry there was in the world, and I wanted to share it—but I was sworn to secrecy, of course. Understandable, given the fact that Los Angeles was the headquarters of the "god of these present circumstances" (GOPC). He apparently likes confusion, and likes the combined energy of young men hoisting away for someone else's profit and blessing. These bright boys don't know the difference, all they know is they want it now. Who doesn't? I'm not sure what I would do without demand for my services. I'm not sure what any of us would do. I did know a better way but the world was not ready and my heart was distracted with Anastasia, who could not even get into this hotel room. Soon Jude and Silas were serving me breakfast, and I was thrilled to have a cable television—I imagined what it would be like to see all my favorite programs, as if I really belonged.

The next morning they took me to a specialist who changed my hair color and a knife-man changed my face. I had no problem, because I got a free facelift and was made to look like I felt, a dashing young twenty-five! I thanked Leonard profusely and had no idea that we would be dining a few days later on the set of one of his movies, about a sniper named Bosco. I watched this feeble little man named Bosco take out kings, princes, presidents, generals, mothers, fathers, and animals with electric precision and emotionless effort. Then he put me in as a stand-in, and I aimed the custom Remington 700 at a target and knew I had acquired it. But the main thing was Kruzmar.

You might ask, after all this buildup, why I would downplay a lunch meeting with Leonard Cutlass Kruzmar, a high school buddy who "loves the world," he would say. I thought it was funny that he kept looking at all the young boys on the set. "You see that, Vincent?"

"What?" I asked.

"All that potential?"

"What do you mean?" I chided, knowing what he would say, because I had the advantage, at least I'm telling Carl this, of perfect hindsight.

"I mean in the young men—all that pent-up energy just waiting to be put to good use. That's capitalism, Vincent, the way of the world—quid pro quo, give some to get some."

"Sure, and winner takes all."

"Yes, Vincent."

"Cash on the barrel head."

"You bet."

"The love you take is equal to the love you make."

"Prophetic, Vincent—that day you pee'd on Goering, I gotta tell you," Kruzmar was saying, while playing with his lip, "that was awesome, man."

"You really think so?" I asked, flattered.

"Stupid—suicidal, who would do that? Well, that's why you work for me—I can use your talent."

"For your benefit."

"Absolutely."

"For you, it's take what you can and fuck the rest."

"Sure thing."

"Might makes right."

"You're a smart cookie for a loser."

"I was born at night, but not last night."

"If you say so."

"Why give anything if you can simply punch their ticket?"

"Clean their clock."

"Cancel their subscription."

"See no evil, hear no evil, that's what I say. You might wonder why I've never been arrested," Kruzmar said.

"I can see a long distance," I said.

At that point, Leonard knew that his limitation was superior to mine—there was no reason to fraternize with material losers such as myself. So he told me this: "There's hope for you yet, shithead. I suppose you're wondering why I got you out of that pickle with the police, after all, you're famous now; matricidal maniac, a homeless, disinherited son comes home, decapitates his mother and kills her servants. Ever wonder why the screenwriter's house never got in the news?"

"It will be," I said.

"What do you mean?" asked Leonard, fresh and tan and his blond hair just so—the man of the hour with the cashmere v-neck sweater. Here was I, humble and lowly, eating lunch with my hair now weaved, my face healed, and Leonard smiling because I was so well trained.

True, he saw the world's young men as potential, which meant *ripe*, and that was sad for those who had gotten a little older in his organization, never knowing why they were fired after years, and I mean *years*, of service. "What'd those dumb motherfuckers expect—a raise? If they can't get it up, I don't see why they work here."

"Darn right," I told him, sipping my iced tea and seeing Anastasia in the shapeliness of a young actress named Beth.

"You like, Vincent? I can send her to your room, if you promise to be nice."

"Can she call herself Anastasia?"

"She's not Mallard's daughter, Vincent. Forget about that."

"You don't know what I know—the future...I live there. I

know everything."

"Right—hey, Stu!" Leonard screamed at somebody in "transpo" (they call it on a movie set). "Get my friend, *Alan* here a ride back to his suite."

In no time a limo showed up. "Just think," Leonard said, "you were the most unlikely to succeed. But all that can change if you follow the rules here—if not, your card goes to the bottom of the deck, you got me? Your time is up—the end. I hand you over."

"But they're going to love me and hate you," I said, with full advantage.

He laughed it off.

"It's already happened," I said.

"Start talking straight," he said. "Crazy people are losers. Hey, man, if you fuck me, this is you." He made a funny little knife across the throat gesture, mistaking me for one of his servants, no less, when in actuality, he indeed was *my* servant. Did he have the advantage of escorts like Silas and Jude, or a man of great talent like Millicet? These people, any one of them, even young Jude (perhaps not the Flagellator) could lead a world war. So before we got to the car, the driver was taken out by Jude, who punctured his neck with an ice pick and threw him in the trunk.

The Flagellator drove, and boy, we had a rollicking good time, my faithful Carl. You knew how I had loved the beach from a young age. And that I had thought all the sand in the desert was a wide beach, well at least before I was getting my mineral quotient for the day, before I was taken in by my Lord, who gave me a new life, a new sensibility—a new destiny—a heart and a soul, something. Something. Tangibility. Sustainable, the social worker said. And northward I had gone.

But this beach at Santa Monica was no match for the beaches of Las Vegas. Or the burial pits of Phoenix or Tucson, barring any Indian inhospitality, and you should have seen what happened to a couple of them—they did not know my Lord. When he says a "wide path," he means don't fuck with me—do not get in my way. Help me, you're blessed, stop me, the curse is insurmountable. Just for future reference, I know you don't mean men harm, Carl, but I am going to discuss this beach, because there was a pier and on the pier was a fortuneteller who lied and claimed a lot of people had launched curses on me. It was she who taught me about witchcraft. I know it's hard for you to understand when I say witch that I mean witch—even if portrayed by serial or several personages. Do not read into the word *serial*. The other thing is, I know *her* true identity. So you'd better be a lot nicer to me and tell those fuckers that I don't need to be tied to my bed anymore.

Bodies under the pier, you ask? Sure, as I was telling you, those who try to stop our mission, that is, the mission of me, Millicet, Jude, Silas and the Flagellator, who sometimes chases around little boys because he never grew up—what can I tell you—and not for personal gratification, just to watch them play, always with the same question in his eyes. How did you get so far? He also follows young girls, but that's more related to my particular problem, which, I am assured, will cease to be a problem when I defend the Realm against what you, by necessity, will only be able to guess.

We burned the limo in the parking lot in front of the Shutters Hotel, blew it sky high, quite a fun thing to watch! In fact, it burned so hot the metal melted and melded with the asphalt, and when they pulled a femur and a skull out of the trunk, man, it was just for chattering, and Silas couldn't stop doin' a jig while drinking *Mohn-tra-chay*, which had been in the fridge. Perhaps a Latour, a Batard, I think. Great with a little taco or two. But still, I pounded Silas' head in while Jude hot-wired some faded van. Millicet disciplined the Flagellator for exposing himself to a bunch of teenage girls under the pier; they were good natured so we all had quite a time skate-boarding down the boardwalk, pulled by Jude, until we got pulled aside by the local police.

Before they could arrest us, we ran and found a condo with a lovely view and two lovely ladies sunning themselves on the deck. We let ourselves in, as is the custom when traveling in uncharted territory—as we were trained to do this.

While having sex with Sheree I was told to think about Anastasia, and all I could see was her standing on a mountaintop, staring off at all of God's creation. I proposed to be in her stead, to be her lover.

Diane, the second blonde beauty with the g-string and cigarettes was tied up on the deck and wasn't moving. When I asked
Sheree about it, she told me to look at the blue light.

That's all I remember—how Anastasia had become my control, and I could see her using Blue...but things faded pretty fast,
and before I knew it I was sucking oxygen and looking foolish.

@   @   @

She had a whole bunch of boyfriends, Lucy thought. She had
these late night *ménage à trois* with two men at a time, and Lucy
felt it was a hazard for sure. The men were much more satisfied
when she would take Linda like a man and slowly, through the
witches' remote visualization, encouraged the men to turn toward one another. When they did, Linda saw men in the way
Lucy needed her to.

After seeing it all on her mindscreen she would say: "You are
so beautiful, Linda. Never let the men call you 'the lovely Linda'
again. Promise me you'll let me call you 'lovely.'"

Linda's bright blue eyes glowed in the marijuana smoke, and
she vowed to make men her footstool, and the next thing you
know they were dining at Granita's and she, Linda, was wearing
Lucy Kruzmar's ring, and they traded panties and later in Venice
allowed Lucy to make her receive a nipple ring, something that
would only be touched by Lucy or Lucy's tongue. It was like high
school. Linda, a servant of the Crown, and Linda, the summa
cum laude Oxford finance graduate, and Linda, who had never
truly understood the way of the world.

Perhaps Linda saw a few things out of the corners of her baby
blue beauties, but all the pointers were on her, and she didn't
even know how to usurp it, she used it as some sort of walk-on-
me passageway for lesser men to get out of their true duty of
serving. You do not serve by inserting, but rather by obeying and
producing. "Give me something," she would start to say. "You're
not good enough," she would eventually say. "You don't make
me come," she could laugh. "You're a loser, a dick without a brain,

can't find it with a magnifying glass," and for those eunuchs, she learned that they were for her beck and call, as Lucy had taught her.

Lucy taught her the nature of all things.

"Lucy, you're...well, I don't exactly know how to repay you...*except to back your husband's plan.*"

Of course, that's what you've been waiting for. Kruzmar's plan. "Can you give me a light?" Lucy asked, the roach in pinched-down tweezers.

a a a

So Carl pushed his hair back and I told him he should get off the high protein diet, it just makes your tits bigger—"all those hormones, man"—and then I corrected myself, for late forties men sometimes developed such a condition if they gained too much weight. "Maybe you could try some of that nighttime collagen—you lose weight while you sleep, man," I said in a kind of vernacular that only the total Kruzmar experience could provide. I'm still further in the future than Carl, but this incarceration was for my Lord, and it was in a facility that no one could get to, not even the press—I had removed the stupid chin implant and died my hair dark, the way it was when a certain mother gave me birth, of which she was reminded one summer's eve!

"Cut the crap, Vincent! Do you know how much damage you did?"

"Do I know how much...damage?" I asked, incredulous. "This is the future, man (I was trying to regain my boyhood here)—this is the way of the wilderness, it creeps into civilized society."

"I'm going to use that—that's good," Carl said, sucking on a Winston and sipping on diet drinks.

"Then why are you mad at me, Carl? You're going to win the Pulitzer, I know, because I was there."

"Why do you talk like that—in past tense?" Carl said insistently, lighting another cigarette and giving me one. A Winston! I love Winstons.

"I love the world," I said.

"You hate the world."

"But I was trying to help," I said and then Carl's friend, the Voice, the invisible voice, commanded that I look at the orange light. "Sorry, Mr. Nunn, we have to make sure he's subdued," I heard someone say to Carl.

What more did they want? I was in a straight jacket, smoking a cigarette without being able to take it out of my mouth, which was irritating. Three armed guards, all dressed in black suits, a room full of two-way mirrors, and broken down from my ultimate view of home with my Lord, where I started out so long ago, back in the past, which would be a certain future. I was at peace but no one believed me.

"How many did you kill, Vincent? Besides the four hundred and twelve we know about?"

"Some were collateral damage, some weren't my kills, like those girls at the beach...it had to be Silas."

"Who's the phantom?" asked the Voice.

"Carl, are you going to let them ruin your interview?" I asked.

Carl paced around and studied my face. He started giggling in a manner that might at some future point place himself and his heirs in total danger. Huffing and puffing—240 pounds of genius.

"Feel pretty safe with Houdini tied up, sir?" I asked.

"Who's your Lord, Vincent?" Carl asked, his intense brown eyes bearing down on my all-seeing baby blues.

I started laughing. I had to. "He's your Lord too, Carl."

Carl laughed. "Oh, no, my friend. He's *not* my Lord."

"That's death, my friend," I said. "How do you want it?"

"Vincent!" came an urgent voice, "Look at the orange light! Now! The Orange Light! Now!......"

There was no option for Blue. He was my mind at this point. He would never, and I repeat, NEVER be Anastasia's eunuch or anything of the sort. At least that's what I thought at the time. Though I had not viewed the truth...just a little of Blue made me feel nauseous, sentimental and downright depressed. There was a weight on him that was less dignified than his calling, which potentially could have been noble. But he was distracted. And if I was stuck in his mind and could see out his confused eyes, then I would feel like him—and I hated how he felt.

I was wrong. Over the next few days it was proven that Blue was no match for the number one woman of the world. The most powerful, the most high, the most beautiful, and it was not the queen of spades, or Hollywood, for that matter.

Millicet reported in, and I was not impressed to have been moved from my penthouse surroundings. And Carl's still looking at me, wondering if I'm putting him on.

Everything I tell you is from memory, and whether you think it's plausible or not, that does not concern me. Think about your mother-in-law's catalogue obsession. Does that make sense? Think about your sister's infatuation with soap star Raith Sturges, does that make sense? Color coordinated cell phones, condoms and toilet paper, cigarettes, magazines and antacids, man. Man?

Carl is distracting me and I tell you right now, it is all I can do not to harm him. He suddenly sits back and lets me back into past tense, which is where he's going to stay. It is abundantly clear that he hates me, and that his will is weakening, as I gain access to his memories...and he can't shake me, he can't stop me, he can't control destiny.

I explain to him that Blue is the maven of odds, the wondering Gentile. The square to his deuce. The mint on the lamb, as he was a lost sheep. A woman in the making. More, Carl?

Lucy owned everything now. In that lucid moment when she fucked the Lovely Linda, destiny got into place. How would I know about such things? Because I know it all, Carl. Because you're nothing but history, past tense...slow like acid, quick like Plague, a foreigner, uncircumcised. Intolerant. Not romantic, unimaginative...

Look at the Blue Light, shithead!

I would not. No jelly-belly mama's boy is going to tell me where or when, got it? I'll tell you some day about the volcano and the queen doll. But I don't want you getting any ideas, at least not too soon.

The story commences, with Jude taking the lead—he will

not defile himself, that's up to me—and I love him as a man loves a dog, or a son, or a lost woman when he has a woman's stare. As Jude certainly did. Carl will not write this down, friends, and I am all alone, beyond you, with the advantage of total eternity, and you simply stream in your arrogant, though certified, countenance through time. Do you see how important I am to you? Do you see how I am the key to your existence? To release you?

Do you know that I care? I love you like Anastasia. I would die for you, and death is no small thing—it is totality, it is pain, an end, the body gone and forgotten, an army on the anvil of rhetoric. Like the killer storm in an empty wilderness. Like the worst, who never understood the best, I would lay my life down for you, and you would lose the prophet, who spins reality off the tip of his all-knowing remembrance, who loses it for the Lord and only on a lost Sunday.

I am Vincent Damien Del Monte, and I love you, girl. You, girl. I love. You, world—girl. I love. You, big man, girl.

Between the lines Carl fell asleep. Between the lines the world could not witness its own reflection, the mirror just a stupid joke, jackrabbits in the dark, for the light cripples, calling the upright weak. The fallen, claiming flight. The fearful, stabbing the heart of true love—his love, oh, I know, it's hate...hate with a callous smile, hate with principles of goodness and charity, hate with a silver tongue, a blowjob for your troubles.

Hello, I am your mind. I am your fear, your lust, your every concern, the one you won't trust, and that is why I must reach you before it is too late.

Consider Jude, down at the Peninsula, on his knees before the maitre d'. And in the end we defend him. You see, we know the maitre d, always. We know where he lives, we know his family, his friends, all his likes, dislikes, what terrifies him. We know how full his weakness truly is...like you, girlfriend.

You are the maitre d'.

You are the world.

You are the recipient of my innocent one spent.

And so what do I owe you?

Do I have your proverbial marbles or what? Can you turn away from me? The prince of chaos?

ⓐ   ⓐ   ⓐ

Good people, do not listen to Vincent, do not look at him. He is a heathen, your world is intact, my friends. He is not the boogie man. He will not grab your foot and pull you from your bed at night, rest assured. For my name is Carl Earnest Nunn, reporter, just like my good friend, Jack Woodfeld. That was *us* when we broke the big White House prostitution case—we were the wolves in sheep's clothing, but we came up with the goods...sex and power are always of interest.

Now, as for me, I've been true to my one and only wife—Elaine. I earned every penny I ever made, even though some would say I am overpaid. What did Vincent ever earn? What about his dubious claims of being contacted, a fucking bum pissing on the shoes of the good people of Phoenix? A blight, urban blight itself! A canker, a *lamo* who ought to have a bullet in his temple instead of electrodes—all a lie! Now turn away from this jackass—Vincent! He is the epitome of tomfoolery—oh, consummate fool, he fashions himself a knight! He believes himself to be noble! Be outraged! At first I wanted to promote him, but his *career*, if that's what you want to call it, skyrocketed...don't you know what he's capable of?—what he would do to you? Don't you know that he is a psychopath to be shunned, not worshiped!

The fact that some of you cheer him makes me sad, makes me sick, makes me need help because I think we as a society are sinking...and anyone who glorifies this man should meet the same fate and be locked up and tied down, face pointing to hell, with a big stick in the hole of pain, never to be heard from again. Look, my readers, my loyal, faithful readers who put their trust in my editorial discernment, bless you. For your way is the true way. Don't be fooled by this groundswell of arrogance, this rebellious generation of wickedness. I have always—and I will always—lead you to the truth, the truth that makes you sleep at night, the truth that tells you that everything you see is *basically* good. Corruption in high places? I'll be there. Human interest, corporate greed? I'll be there too. One psychotic does not a revolution make, eh? I'm here, aren't I? I'm on it! Think about what would happen if you left the fold, if you actually knew the truth...if you were played...ah, folks, go home. Just go home. Let a professional handle this.

@ @ @

But I knew this was too late and too proud, and too stupid, eh, brothers? Oh, my friends. Don't you long for my brand of sevens? Of course you do. Stick with me, and I will satisfy even the most false among you, even the most blue-balled. And the big liar, the one who bullies you and me, as if on authority from the Most High, though he could never qualify for the greatest position of the most low. I will slay him for you, oh, my brothers. Forget the hazing you took across the campuses of hate, big men, proud, sure, insured too, upright and a mind full of cum—is it any wonder why women rule the world? Forget the fraternity of man—that ends tonight. Carl thinks he's on for the Pulitzer, little does he know I have him well in hand...because by the time this story is over he will be irrelevant, and you won't cower in fear. Look at you—*cowards all*. Come on, lads, time to take life where we meet it, get out from the shackles of women—don't be her heart's desire, don't cater, don't give! Forget it. Irrelevant, illusory, she's only there for one purpose and that is your destruction. Don't let her perfume hypnotize, her beauty captivate. You don't need her. Break free.

If you dare.

@ @ @

It did hit the papers, not just Dr. Steinman, but everyone at Peter Mallard's house that night. All dead, and all prominent back in Europe or some equally forgettable place. Some equally forgettable life. I mean, when Silas started using Peter's little .22 pistol they weren't going down all that fast—and the two guys gang-banging Sophie kept going, unaware that Silas was popping that little .22 pistol into their skulls point blank—three shots and out go the lights.

But they kept gang banging Sophie and that's when I noticed Peter holding his own bloody nose in his hand, and so Dr. Steinman worked on him—but he, Dr. Steinman, drowned. And I was shocked that such excellent work on our parts went unreported (that we tried to help Peter Mallard). Then I found out of course it was Kruzmar. And gave you plenty examples of the way he thinks, that he's got it sussed, licked, beaten, whipped, nailed, and that would of course, go for Mother Kruzmar.

There was no question that he had the advantage at this point. No question that I was somehow under guard again, and security was tight.

Remember, this was private security, forces wielded by Kruzmar, which should be proof enough that he wasn't just some movie producer, hiding out on the Mount Triac lot, hanging his hat on some dubious production company called Trundle Pictures. My friend, he took me, in a straightjacket not unlike the one you put me in, and then he made his appearance, and I could not remember if I had seen him before.

"Ah, Vincent, my dearest friend," he began in the hotel room, where thugs one, two and three were surrounding me as I sat in the chair, arms tied, with Jude screaming in the other room like a woman raped. "You were always the most talented of all of us—you were the poet, the painter, the mathematician, got laid first, thumbed your nose at the sisterhood, and we all looked up to you...but you failed—because nobody thumbs their noses at the mothers of the world, idiot!"

I could say nothing because I was gagged. First of all, I had nothing against motherhood. Kruzmar was talking worship; I was talking apostasy, perversion.

"Do you understand that you can't kill my people, Vincent? This isn't high school anymore—I made my way by making films that made money, do you understand? I gave you a part to play, and what do you do? What the fuck do you do? You kill my driver, and blow him up in the car so his wife can't recognize him. And the police are asking what happened, and where the fuck did the stand-in go?—and then you remove the facial implants, so that Dr. Basil here has to be here and fix you up. And I WANT HIS HAIR BLOND, DAMMIT!" Kruzmar yelled, while pacing, cardigan and lisp notwithstanding. He was...was he pissed? No, this was anger—the hissy-fit. That's all this fuck can do, man.

I marveled at his youth and vitality. Here he was, at forty, ready to take the mantle of power by showing his true cards—power. Raw family power. Laundering it for the Mossad, storing up with the Swiss, old rules—and looking so Waspy. So blond and blue eyed, with even a nose that looked Gentile, and it wasn't even plastic surgery. He was invisible! He was beautiful! He was becoming a woman of power and substance. His chiseled face and taut little body, I mean this motherfucker was becoming a shit for brains ballerina for Pete's sake! I mean, to be frank, I felt a sort of primal urge in my loins—and yet he was swaggering like a mean little bitch, and that was a turn-off.

"So we will prepare you for tomorrow—all I want to know, Vincent, is that you will do what I tell you. Of course, I'll keep you out of prison and out of the chair."

They removed my gag, and I said, "Leonard, are you going to be a girl or keep faking it in-between?"

He became exasperated, swilled his hot tea and poured more. Looked out the window of the yellow and blue fabric-covered room and even the three goons were replaced by two doctors and a hairdresser. The red cardigan over the blue silk shirt, the dark brown pleated slacks and light brown socks with rich, tan Bruno Maglia shoes. He was a sight for sore eyes alright.

"I want to know if you even appreciate the new life I'm giving you. After you complete your task, I'll put five million in the Cayman Islands account with your name on it, a new Uruguayan citizenship, and a house on the beach, right by the hotel district, so you can have your fun. If you run out of money, I will replace it with another five million."

I was impressed. He was so businesslike. "You've changed since I last saw you, Leonard, but you did not answer my question—"

"Fuck! Shut him the fuck back up!"

They gagged me again.

"Sign this, genius," he said, and now he looked really angry. I looked it over—it was a contract for killing somebody I didn't know, and only one copy. Actually, it was a confession, in the first person—I, Vincent Damien Del Monte, do hereby swear that I killed Herbert Styles on August 10 at 10:05 a.m., outside the Century Plaza Hotel. Now that's a good one, Kruzmar definitely coming back from the future…as of course, you well know, it wasn't yet Aug. 10th.

I had so underestimated Kruzmar. Indeed, he possessed a rudimentary understanding of living in the future. This document was very gratifying—perhaps there is something I could learn. Something substantial. I did feel, my Recorder, that he was holding back. Of course I dismissed any notion that he was *educated*, and I signed the document quickly, and looked at Kruzmar's face change to one of boyhood happiness. "You had more talent than any of us—and what you did to your mom, Margot, and Peter's friends and ex-wife—you're a monster. You're brutal, man. I really underestimated you, Vincent."

They let me talk again and unbelted the straightjacket. "Thanks, Leonard—maybe we have more in common than I thought," I said, and I was ignored, so I moved to the view, and was pleased to see that I was wearing a black silk collarless shirt and a pair of dark slacks. I did not recognize myself in the mirror, because my hair was blond and my face looked like I was twenty-three years old.

"You look great, Vincent. Any woman would be knocked out by you, you psycho."

"Look, you trained me, you hired me, and you don't even know what's going on—it's perfect, all is not without symmetry, Leonard, as I see your shining face, sitting on the bench, a revenge so sweet—no little cunt would ever call you goody-two-shoes again—eh, friend? You're not like me…I have to accept that."

Kruzmar laughed, "Well accept this, shithead, you only have what I give you. And tomorrow, you make me a king."

"Your wife…"

"What about my wife—her name is Ms. Kruzmar to you,

dumb shit," he said.

"Will she be working—"

"She's going to head up the studio, and I will be the chair—she's a very capable woman."

"You said it, Leonard," I said, eating a bagel, cream cheese and drinking a fresh glass of Crystal. A man with a briefcase opened his electronic marvel and flipped on the yellow light and told me to look at it. I dropped the bagel, I think, maybe even the champagne—and I heard Kruzmar laughing and saying things like: 'Trained Seal,' 'idiot,' and even, 'of course he's a suicide victim tomorrow afternoon.'"

Trapped. I called my men—nothing. I simply knew that Kruzmar had turned the tables on me.

My one assurance is that I am talking to you while this is going on. And I thank you…I will show you your world, those of you who have an ear to hear and an eye to see.

I will open your eyes, with a warning. Once they are open, you can't go back.

Surely you know this much, at least.

EVLEWT

Blue had finished burying Peter's body in the back yard when the FBI came by to speak with Anastasia. This was of course a problem for Blue, who became the maintenance man, and it was no problem for him to remove the police tape and re-tape it another way. With a two-acre yard of avocado trees, three lawns, a pool and tennis court, there were plenty of nooks and crannies, and Blue decided to bury the body under the light transformer box. They inquired, of course, for the whereabouts of Peter Mallard, and all Anastasia would say is that she just got back from school, and she didn't know, but to check the studio.

"My name is Dennis Garvey, special agent with the FBI, and I know we compiled evidence here, but we thought you were supposed to be staying with your aunt in Tarzana."

"Aunt in Tarzana?"

"And who is that?" Dennis was referring to the guy hammering some trim on the walls of the playroom, just behind the pool table, which was also taped off.

"My father hired him to fix the house up because he's putting it on the market."

"Isn't it hard for you to function now that—"

"Special Agent, this is my home—I was sleeping when that psycho broke in here. By the time I came downstairs the police had pretty much cleaned everything up."

Dennis drank a fresh cup of espresso, as Anastasia loved making the potion on her big machine. She had loved all of it—the commercial kitchen, the wine cellar, her room overlooking the trees and mansions, the constant feeling of arrival, being a little girl with all the maids telling her that she would one day be a queen. And that she would one day be masterful in the world; indeed, she knew miles more than females thrice her age. She was destined for greatness, and of course, I wanted to show her the real world, beyond this one, beyond the farthest shore—another kingdom—but that would take humility on my part, and war does funny things to humility.

Dennis drank a second cup and looked at her in a perky manner—yes, she was beautiful.

Blue was not happy with the "Dennis development," and when Dennis started querying Anastasia about how much she knew about certain "things," Blue started having horrific flashbacks. Tanya with the chief, Tanya with his partner, being told to go out on assignment, then finding open beer cans and half-smoked cigarettes and porn movies lying around the condo, Tanya in Vegas while Blue struggled to hit the little ball on the links, Tanya visiting with friends up the coast, Tanya at a yoga class till 3:00 a.m., Tanya this and Tanya that—he was sick of her, and the men who took his assignment. His personal assignment, the one he had already solved in his mind before he ever started— the one who would not simply descend to an errand boy for the media, the one who would like to think of his manhood as intact, though he was searching for a queen to give it to.

All of it.

Watching through the window, Blue glimpsed Dennis pushing Anastasia's golden hair back over her shoulders, and that's when I took over. I moved through Blue: "Blue, you idiot, get rid of him—he is the enemy!" I screamed through space, and he was fighting me from taking control. But I did. He rammed him through with the shovel spade, right through his gut as Anastasia screamed and ran. Dennis's partner came back in, found Dennis and Blue stabbed him twenty-six times before I let him up for air. And now they would have to leave.

All this time I had several hands tied behind my back. For one thing, my men were gone, for another, Kruzmar had been quite clear—Vincent is my puppet, Vincent is my tool, when the tool has been used, discard it. He was not my friend at all. I knew now that the war was going to turn corporate. The key to Kruzmar, the key to every fallen man, was his mother, the queen mother, an earth queen mother, a witch queen earth mother—a'reaping the flesh and a'getting the death—hallelujah!

I had to find a better way to get out and do the will of my Lord—traveling this way was expensive, and caused the most collateral damage.

Blue left Anastasia shrieking in horror, and I sent Millicet via my little mental radio, to rescue her. The newspapers would say that there is a copycat killer on the loose, that Anastasia's father, Peter Mallard, the award-winning playwright and screenwriter, had been strangled, and guess whose picture wound up on national TV? Detective Ashley Blue. He was the man of the house. They worded it something like this: Blue was obsessed with the Vincent Del Monte case—and when he was taken off the case, he went crazy, shot his wife (for no reason), then killed his true rival, the special agent assigned to the case.

I simply reeled Blue in. Got him to change his clothes, got him to shave his head, wear a ski cap—blend in. He would be my ride, and he also confirmed that Jude was helping him. This I would have to see, but it made me proud of young, handsome boy Jude, with the alacrity of a saint and the ingenious quality that used to belong only to me, and dear Jude managed to make us all proud. One day he would be given tremendous responsibility over the Western territory, as soon as I brought them into subjection to our Lord.

The next day I was outfitted with a standard stylish black silk shirt and black slacks, black shoes and belt. My hair was blond again, but no fucking chin or cheek implants; instead, my face looked like it did in the future, as it will when I return home—infinite youth! I was twenty-one again, and had the world at my beck and call, even though some Kruzmar sycophant was in my ear telling me to position myself on the roof across from the restaurant at the corner of Canon and Wilshire. And this was interesting to me. The magazine contained twenty rounds—the rifle had a muffler on it. The rifle was light, gray, made from plastic and had a little sticker of some ninja-clown wielding a rifle on a bi-pod. The label read: *Significant Arms*. It was a nice gun, man, what can I say? I could easily carry on with this weapon that heretofore only pussies and cry-babies used. My eyesight was always perfect, and just like Mexico, with the proper scope I could hit an apple and splay it to the four walls at two hundred yards. And some over-the-hill studio boss was so simple a child could do it.

So the man named Styles got out of the limo, as he did every Tuesday, and I hit him right away—his head literally shattered, and brain matter flew and hit people eating on the terrace. It was a glorious sight. He was pretty much a neck and that was it as the fountain of blood was a brief but glorious volcano.

After that two bullets exploded right next to me—as yours truly was now the target!

Blue was waiting on the corner, as he was told to do by Millicet, who lost Anastasia, by the way.

I reeled around, saw the guy on the bank building roof who was shooting at me—I had never seen him, but now, in my sights, he was pretty much gone, because I don't miss. One shot to the face, right through his scope, and up his nose, and he was switched off right fast.

The sun was high, but shadows were becoming longer, as I caught up with Blue on the street, and Millicet pulled this kid out of his Firebird and we headed south. The police, and I don't mean to be critical, but it took them the better part of an hour to cordon off the street and the restaurant. The keystone idiots—to me—seem truly beyond ineffectual. They probably did not want to piss off any of the Powers That Be; indeed, that was a factor. I suppose they didn't want to inconvenience any of the upscale patronage—money, honey. Blue didn't realize the favor I did for him, inspiring the end of his denial with a little truth serum; Blue was one of us, and not *them* anyway. They could never trust him to be *quid-pro-blow-what-have-you-done-for-me-lately* sort of clown.

The boys of Beverly Hills P.D. were criminals, and Blue was here to testify about it. And Blue was here to join the force of the future—me.

When I saw him on the street—don't tell me mind control doesn't work, Carl—I grabbed his hand and kissed it. This kind of affection between warriors is permitted, though my heart was always with Anastasia.

Millicet had Blue by the scruff and he was already earning his way.

"Look at it this way, Blue," I said to him, who was driving the bright green repainted Firebird, "they wanted me splat on the roof, and I'm not splat. So now another queen of the past shall fall."

Blue wiped the sweat off his shaved head and said, "I killed two FBI guys."

"Millicet said you were brilliant—but you lost Anastasia, imbecile." Blue looked around, puzzled.

"Who the fuck is Millicet? Why did he make me do all this!"

"Turn right on Olympic," I said. "We have to go to the ocean."

I remembered Sheree, and now that Anastasia was brought back in as my control—I was telling Blue, my new comrade in arms, that we had to find Silas, Jude and the Flagellator.

"What the fuck are you talking about?!" he screamed, rather harshly. Rather emptily. Rather haughtily—and I realized that the rubber wasn't meeting the road. He pretended not to hear Millicet, who sat behind him and kept thumping him on the head—and he didn't react to that either. "What are you talking about? There's no one there!"

"Who did you see on the golf course?" I asked.

"You weren't there!" he said. "You're fucking psycho!"

"But I'm in your mind!"

Blue crashed into a parked car by Westwood Boulevard, so Millicet handcuffed him and forced him to follow me to a Cadillac being driven by some old-timer. I showed the Golden Oldie my fancy gun and he got out and let me take the car. Cooperation. "Did you see that Ashley?" I asked, and he looked at me with a new haze in his eyes, and I could tell right away that Anastasia had exerted control over him also—she had both of us! "But she's not who I fight for, Detective," I said.

"She owns me," he said, complacently, and right then, oh, boy, I knew she wasn't far behind.

That's when it hit, as my Lord's brilliance knew no bounds, as sure as sorrows blossom into joy, as sure as the sun would shine once again—power. It was power we needed. No sense being kicked all over the board because of the likes of Kruzmar and his new tactical security unit. Just the idea of being trained by Kruzmar's private security, and then his grip on the media, but most folks just saw him as a producer of movies, at Trundle Pictures, a front like no other—with a daughter of darkness at the helm.

It was time to fight back. Darkness obliterated by light.

@ @ @

The secret financiers from nations far and wide, like a stealth army looking for a way into the power of the media, had found their man in Boy Krumzar. For one thing, the board of directors of Mount Triac installed Kruzmar as the chairman with Lucy Kruzmar as the new studio queen. And it was just that easy because Lucy had secured a Letter of Credit through her friend Linda for 25 billion to secure the biggest merger in history: Mount Triac Pictures, Monsoon Worldwide Media, and Galactic Studios—the big three. Forget the fact that two of these were already mergers of four major studios, and so this triumvirate would end all competition worldwide and create a media empire so great that the very Beast himself couldn't have more of a lock on any and all employees, customers and passersby, their income profiles and perversions, their wants, needs and breaking points. The mark was accomplished, and without branding even one. No one could work unless sanctioned by the new studio, which Lucy named affectionately: *Shangri-La Studios*.

With the theme parks, the movie production, the record and

media production, Lucy suddenly found herself following Lady Kruzmar's instructions. She figured, after listening to the wise women who comprised the top three ladies in the Council of Matriarchs of the World System, and after consternation and summoning the supernatural courage that came from a citywide effort, she would garner the true queen's hold on men's emissions. She focused it while they fell further into stupidity, complacency and slavery. Twenty million roots and you get to rule the world. A rather small percentage, but effective, since most matriarchs would only take what was around them.

Bliss.

Lucy dyed her hair blonde, got two weeks worth of tailored suits, a month's worth of shoes, drivers, servants, and a new facelift on her Malibu house, where the liaison of the century took place, seduced, educated, and pleasured the Lovely Linda into a failsafe method of controlling destiny.

Yes, the Lovely Linda was elevated from a British banker to a three-million-dollar a year job as financial officer. Her stock options would put her at a clean twenty-mil, with more on the way if she could bring down financing costs. With any luck (and Lucy's business was creating such a thing) the stock would sell well and she could retire to a mansion with her own nine-hole course smack dab in the center of Indian Wells. It couldn't be better. And the Lovely Linda was only thirty-three, unmarried, had every hot prince panting at her every whim, but sex with Lucy was something much more special. Like most people, there were no lesbians and there were no faggots, there were no straights and there were no labels. The truth was that women ruled the world, men simply supplied the resource—indeed, they *were* a resource, and they were fragile. Her new boyfriend, Tony, handsome as the day was long, had to be constantly reassured that his new film project was worthy, that his penis was quite obviously "the best," that his multi-pic deal was unprecedented and that the Lovely Linda (which he did not call her) would defend him.

Asenath had warned Lucy not to push her husband too far, and that Abacazzia was in danger. She said things had changed in the universe when Lucy met Linda Periwinkle, an act of selfishness, and perhaps treason of a high spiritual order. Lucy stammered, had trouble being rebuked, corrected, even criticized, and it was only Asenath with the big smile, shapely and skinny with lovely hair—all of which seemed distant and then somewhat traditional, if ancient, in a long piece of batik. They sat on the terrace and sipped Oolong, and got lost thinking about the future. She burned a candle and lit some incense but didn't have anything other than the look on her face...the look of destiny on her oval-shaped face, the look of a thousand ships gone headlong into uncertainty, Lucy was. What she wasn't, was humble.

"You're too young, too beautiful, sister. You must know that we have been around thousands of years."

"I never questioned you—"

"But you did not do what we said. You did not do the things we wanted you to do. You did not follow the way it was supposed to be. You didn't give the proper due. I came because Serena and Milaca had gone to vacation in Cancun."

Lucy got up and wandered around on her grass, then turned back to Asenath. "You want more money? Is that it?"

"Just to prophesy, my lady. The first was not the last, and of course it was true, as you know. Mr. Styles, for all his security, is dead—but you...things have really changed, my lady."

"Will you quit calling me that!" Lucy said, chasing after a Monarch and crushing it in her hand. "Stupid thing, stupid little creature—"

"Nature is what we are, Lucy girl."

"And don't call me 'Lucy girl,' either."

"Ms. Kruzmar, may I speak?" Asenath asked, pushing her Ethiopian curls away, looking at her with her deep liquid eyes, eyes that could see through the ancient past. "He is more than a man."

"Just tell me how the new studio is going to do? Will it be successful—who's in the way?"

"No one can kill your husband—he is protected. Just as we said. Unless it isn't a person, not exactly, but a force."

"What are you talking about...Vincent? What the fuck are you talking about, that psycho fuck, Vincent?"

"He's very clever—he blocked us."

Lucy, exasperated, circled around Asenath and played with her hair. Suddenly, she felt a swelling in her stomach and fell back slightly. "I..."

"You're pregnant."

"I don't fuck my husband, Asenath—well, maybe that once, but I was drunk and I didn't care and...I'm sorry."

"You're pregnant with the new world, Lucy dear. He's not fit, and yet we underestimated him."

"I'm in charge, I'm the one, I'm running the studio, and I've got to go, and you're fired." By now she was screaming epithets and Asenath sat humiliated and beholden to Abacazzia, and tears welled in her eyes at the treatment, and there would be an emergency summit in Mexico, as there was a wall the African ladies could not see beyond, could not reason beneath, could not fathom for the life of them. Would it have helped if I rang them up and divulged the end of Abacazzia? You see, when you go out from the future and you deal in the past, things are not the same.

But the result of Lucy, humble little Lucy from the wrong side of the tracks, was not at first understood—how quickly and miraculously she became the epitome of high-end angst, how quickly she was wise in her own eyes, how finally she proclaimed her own divinity.

Her frustration burned and she continued to end the relationship with the queen witches who were immortal, but only in physical terms. "You said he was invincible!" Lucy screamed. "You said he was going to the top, Asenath, fucker! Bitch!"

Okay, Lenny and Lucy admittedly were at the top, and had a voice that would be obeyed at any cost. Lucy was the chief, Lenny was the chair—they brought billions in, did it together, just as Abacazzia's helpers cast into the bright unknown. "*I* did it," Lucy said. "*Not you!*" She announced this with the surety of a saint after my own design.

"Vincent, he is not dead. And no amount of our light can influence him."

"What do you mean, of course he's dead—he was used for the purpose he was trained to do, and then he was killed, now they can link the—"

"—No, he will prevail over your husband, he will cut off his lifeline. He will show your husband the price of a hateful woman such as you! He will show you the future—he is a devil that no one kills. It is you who will pay."

"Let me hear that from Serena and Milaca. Let me hear a consensus."

Asenath got up from her chair, gathered her large leather bag and kissed Lucy three times across her face. Once on each cheek, and a last time on the lips. "You are pregnant, girl. Little girl from the bad side of Chicago, no? Made the false queen by circumstance, but a bitter end awaits you, as you are ungrateful. We have the gift of the past," beautiful Asenath was saying. "We are thousands of years old. This, my young stubborn friend, is no exaggeration—but you don't understand. The thing we can't see are those from the future. Your husband is still very much trapped in the sublime form of reality—linear time, that is—*today*, everything tactile, the earth, physical space and the attendant ether around things of substance, all is a constant.

"It is a lowly, impoverished existence, what we live—but you are a fool, you have no idea what I am saying. Vincent isn't real, baby. He is a destroyer, come to avenge—it's a game no one wins. But you die in your insipience. You die in the steam of impermanence, in the ignorance of iniquity. I feel sorry for you, Lucy dear."

And she left, packed it in, lifted it out, out of the country and out of the Kruzmar business. Out of the depths, out of the stream, out of the empty past and the fullness of the future, which frightened Asenath because she had never understood remembrance. She had understood the Bible, a long time ago, and that her people might even have the Arc of the Covenant. But that was too much a reminder of her queen, akin to a flower.

Queen, earth.

Feminine power.

From the Master.

The light of the morning.

Divide the root.

Which is man.

All things, above, below.

All is light.

When Lucy lost Asenath, Lucy lost. Lucy the Herald Angels Sing. Lucy the opposite, but with the power of the goddess behind her—fallen angels nowhere to be found. It's no wonder she felt invincible. Not *contractible*, ahead, and further—coronation!

ə ə ə

Blue drove like a crank man from Truckee, like a lesbian from Oshkosh, full of bravado but with nothing in his head except images and horniness, anyone could see. Anyone would know—wouldn't they, that Blue was a faggot nonpareil, but no one could explain it to him, and if he hung around the queen, there would be no testicles for him to offer to the Beast, come what may. A power play was in the offing.

You read me, Carl, you fuck?

(He's now hammering me as to how I found Sheree—and you all know she was a CIA bitch, right? Anyway, the blue lights, the orange lights? Carl, wake the fuck up! You know me, you know me, you *really* know me—and no one else does.)

Blue was ESP—no one believes it, but they like the songs we burned at the Revival, the dark prince's favorites, and you mean to tell me no one believes in ESP after that?

Vincent's note:

How come I'm the only one who remembers what happened? How come I'm the only one who sees the truth of saints and miserables? How come I'm the only one who can speak to you, spellbound? You think the Piper has a way out? He had a way in, didn't he! Of course he did—did I not shed light on what a mind truly is? Vincent

And so Blue, with shaven head—in red Firebird that Millicet

hotwired—pulled the poor prostitute out and took it, without even offering her a position in our army. The one you guys would join if you weren't defending history. If you weren't initiates in denial. If you didn't sell your souls.

ᘓ ᘓ ᘓ

Carl's note:

I have spoken to you before, not to listen to the bile of one Vincent Damien Del Monte. He is Satan. Okay? He is the Devil. He is the Antichrist. And you reading this raw-style interview really upsets me, because you need to be informed, oh, you of little faith, oh you from graduate school at NYU, that it's all okay—don't worry. No damage is done!

Vincent's note:

No one really believes that now, Carl, I thought. You heard. No one thinks Carl's way of life means anything. He may not give me quotes here, but I give you raw penetration. He is wrong, we are right. Join us! The future depends on it.

ᘓ ᘓ ᘓ

We drove, alive, down to Venice, to the beach, where we met up with Silas, the Flagellator and Jude, my beloved Jude. We rode bikes, snorted coke, felt happy and urinated on a wall. We killed some has-been for a billfold in the back of some misbegotten poster palace, but we needed dough, and he had several hundred dollar bills, which we saw when he bought some beads for his girlfriend. Remember, this was war. We had to remain stealthy, wealthy and wise as serpents, though we were not as harmless as

doves. We were like Joshua. The king slayer. And you're beginning to see that this entire outbreak of reality isn't some full-
blown fantasy—it's ordination. There is no pill to take; there is
Lucy—and no need of strategy, except how to get Anastasia back.

Sheree was not in her apartment, and so we went with Anna
Lee, whom Jude fell totally in love with. And there was real inter-
cession with the lights on this little cunt of mercy, let me tell you.
She had the heroin tracks, she was sweet, she wanted to be beat
up, but we had real money, and we didn't need to hurt Anna Lee,
who lied at every turn and Jude got very interested after hearing
her voice. So we told her to teach him the ways of the world.

Jude, my little buddy, had the temerity to ask about salvation, and she said it's in your body, and we said—stop. Stop,
Jude. Just because some bitch says...just because there are perks,
and you won't need to tell the heathen your secret, cause it's all
about money, honey, you don't need 'em gift wrapped, Gladheart,
you who are sweet. He stammered and got the light in his eyes
and we started to weep because he owned the confusion that was
running around the past, and his eyes were wide, in the cage, and
his countenance was that of beauty—they wanted him, everyone
did. Men, women, children and animals. I promised my Lord I
would deliver to him a soldier and not a victim, and that's exactly
what I would to do.

So the innocent are bought with blood. So the beautiful are
taken by the future, not the past. Check and mate—terra firma
belongs to grace, not Queen Abacazzia. Not Kruzmar's lord, not
the opposite of me. Not the apparition of the whispering power.
Not the misnamed good people of the continent, not the betwixt
innocent with a face like blind veal. Your future is the past now.
It's over.

Listen, Carl is out to lunch, and will not quote me, so you,
painter, so you, plumber, so you, nostalgia, pipe down. It will
sanctify. No need of worry. You don't need any college professor
to teach you the untruth of the lie to be untold. You remember
the future? It's *you,* my brothers. It's you and all the things you
didn't do. It's the light of the world, not the light of the dawn. It's
the light of eternity, not the past. It's the light of love, not seeth-
ing power; by the root they have taken you, and you lost what

your Creator made...your manhood.

So Anna Lee was raped by a dozen men, mentally. But the Barbie doll couldn't remember all the wishes of everyone who contributed.

The body count, in the war—how many kills, you ask? At this point, only thirteen. People don't realize how careful we are being here. I mean, so far this is nothing when you consider, say, WWI or WWII. My dear friends, and I hope I'm getting this through and around Carl, listen up: this is WWIII! You have to decide which side you're on. Some actors would like more memorials to the heinous acts committed by our side, you just keep on living in denial. But I am the future. You have not the slightest chance in hell to escape truth anymore.

NEETRIHT

A protest changing history? We drove up the coast and deep into another state to invoke the volcano. Blue and I needed shelter; we had changed cars several times and now were in a fleet van that was used for carpooling. Rollicking good times for all—Millicet was drunk, Jude was reading men's fitness magazines and staring too long at the men, Silas and the Flagellator were playing chess—much to my amazement, they changed the queen for the king, changing the rules for our amusement, and the fact that chess was used to dial the future. So far, the Flagellator had lost his king right off the bat, but he had a strategy, rooks and pawns with more power. I laughed.

I told Blue the following: "Blue, we need a queen! Our very own, who will do for us what the world does for half-wits—you know, the stupid populous." But we needed the strongest power source on earth. We needed a killing machine. "We have to have a killing machine." Of course I was excited. I knew that the doll was the only way to go. We bought a Miss America Barbie doll and drove down a side road that got us very close to the volcano, which was smoking at the top. Helicopters were roaring overhead and on their loudspeakers they were telling us to evacuate. But it was *our* volcano—Millicet got it hooked up to future mind, the one that Lucy blew off when she told Asenath to take an undeserved hike.

When we got to the ski area I knew we were in trouble, but certainly no more trouble than when every newspaper from Los Angeles to Moscow had us front and center, and even called us the *folie à deux*! They wondered if we were actually working together or whether Blue was simply a copycat. They, like you, Carl, had no idea that we were living on the *Axis*, and you have no idea what the future holds. Look at us! Here is Blue, head shaven, strong and proud in his T-shirt and jeans, cutting—finally—a handsome shape, a man. Regeneration had taken place, so who are you to judge?

(I love it when Carl gets seriously p.o.'d and has me escorted in chains out of the room. I think he cries when I'm gone.)

He practiced with my rifle, and had gotten quite a nice knife collection going, while Millicet and I crowned our queen and set her facing east, right at the base of the Mount Hood volcano, which hadn't erupted since the 1800's or something. There were a dozen or so farmhouses we could stay at in the area, and all had weapons, food, medication, and some, so I hear, had marijuana growing in barns. Not that I needed to alter the equation, but it might be nice for Blue, though he was changing, who had just barely escaped Anastasia, who we named the doll. I did not like the fact that Millicet wrote on her with a Marks-A-Lot® marker. All we had to do was tell her she was Queen Anastasia, my love, though I was only a humble servant of my Lord, and all this Luciferian stuff bored me—but it was more boring not playing around with the overrated elements of earth and sky, fire and water, above and below.

"Blue, did you get over her?"

He said nothing. He didn't talk anymore. Silas and Jude teased him for being such a fucking psycho. Blue mumbled something about how nice it was to stab a girl after copulation, but I was too busy making a spiritual nuke. We perched the Barbie beauty queen doll on top of the van, which was smack dab in the evacuation zone.

Soon, the volcano erupted, and the *reflection* in the sky filled the doll, and it lit up like a Christmas tree. How did we funnel it, you ask, timidly? I'm doing it now! Get it? I simply focus the world's future on that doll—and....you know something, I'm not going to tell you. You need not know the way of champions, the way of warriors of a galactic nature. Not yet, not ever, because you would realize how far ahead of you I am. Suffice to say, they live in the past, I live beyond even you, Carl. Further out, on an island, and I am a man.

Blue even got in on the act, worshiping it on his knees. The Flagellator jerked off in front of it, feebly trying to imitate the volcano, while I aimed a pistol at his head and ordered him to stop insulting everyone by his stupidity. "Don't you know, Flagellator, that this is way better than the dick trick?"

"Yeah, but I sold my soul."

"Do not be snared by the world!" I screamed and grabbed his dick, threatening to cut it off. "Now, if you want to use it for your fun, fine!" I let it go and he zipped it up and ran off. Honestly, you would think he knew what side we were on in the first place. This is like sitting in a 5-star restaurant and ordering a Big Mac, or time-traveling and wanting to take a train. Of course the Flagellator ran off and did it again, not learning the lesson—that our enemy uses this power to enslave, that he is with us. He will never know what that means, what advantage he has. "Don't you know, Flagellator, your body does not belong to you?"

But he uses it against himself, against our very successful operation, uses it against all that is good, gives it over to their indwelling hosts, and that's how he becomes the Flagellator.

We filled the doll up with the primordial energy of creation, more powerful than all men's seed combined, and thus our doll named Anastasia was ready. Fire and smoke and ash exploded from the volcano and hit everywhere but not us, not our doll, why? Because we had harnessed it, the future, and would not let it go.

Now it was ready for proof. Now, it became a celestial doll, that is, it could operate in and out of time and space. Imagine, the most powerful witch in the world was a doll!

The Flagellator apologized when he finally knew that he was

trying to become a slave to a forgotten world led by a stupid fool who shines like white light. When he saw he was able to create his own woman and inseminate her in a very satisfied manner he had become a believer. Thus he realized not to go the way Blue had gone, into slavery. Though Blue was more dense, in the aspect that he was truly flesh and blood in the present now and could not move like we could. But he could learn, and he had done a masterful job in helping us evade the police.

We tried the doll on the owner of a Mercedes—you can figure all these people are slaves and thus deserve what we give 'em—and he expired instantly. No muss, no fuss. We swapped the plates with the van plates and before you knew it, Blue was driving us in style. We went into Portland to one of my favorite stores, Mason's Army/Navy, and used the doll on the hostile personnel, and voila, they fell into heart attacks instantly. After outfitting ourselves, we headed out to a diner on Interstate 5, and poof, free food and no people to bother us. The oddest thing was that the military was so busy locking these sites down after we were done that no news of us ever hit the papers—but I'd put the death toll now at about, say thirty-five or forty, a very modest number considering all the success we've had in obtaining our objective.

I think Blue wanted more publicity, though he was looking very independent in the camouflage vest, boots and green fatigue pants. Very independent. We loaded up at a gun store and, my friends, this was the greatest ease I had ever known. Millicet and the boys were driving behind us in the van with the new Oregon plate, and we were driving with the California plate. We loaded up, headed down the coast, ate like kings, and the whole time Anastasia would head our table and guide our affairs.

Yes, it's true, my heart burned for Anastasia now—where, oh where could my baby be? It was easy dealing with a world that couldn't see past the collective castration, and of course, we would have no problem slaying these losers, worshiping their prom queens and lying to the mother hens in the closets—no problem punching their lights out. Takes one more idiot away from the enemy. Anastasia understood, but wanted to install herself as the ruler. I told her through the air that the ruler of the world isn't really a human at all, but more like our Lord, except much, much weaker. But beautiful.

Enticing.

Inciting.

Was the ruler of the airwaves, until me.

Now, at this point, I don't like the attitude Carl Nunn is developing. First of all, he's vomiting in the toilet but doesn't think I understand. He's starting to get the idea that he's being watched (though it's only my eyes, maybe Blue's eyes, and he's got it all wrong.) He doesn't know he's living in a fabrication of his own projection.

"Carl, you're a slave to Mommy."

By this time he was wearing a red cardigan sweater that reminded me of Kruzmar in his heyday. Conservative dresser, liberal politics—a salon man, a man of the people, he'd like to think. "You dumb twit, there's nothing outside your mind, nothing outside these prison walls—except me. We won."

Carl went and threw up again and kept crying out, "The humanity, the humanity!"

But he couldn't stay away, and there was a growing contingent of audience members, from the FBI, the CIA, the military, who wanted to confiscate me for national security purposes (Bullshit, they wanted my secrets!). So I tried to tell Carl he was being used, and he said something like, "I'm a skull, so I know it all."

"That can't help you when you're with me—you're earthbound, Mister."

"Just tell me the story!" he, Carl Nunn, said, obsessed.

"Anastasia, we must find her," I said at the Fisherman's Wharf, where Millicet ate so much crab I thought he'd lose it on the trip back down to base camp.

Meanwhile, new Shangri-La Studios took over Culver City, while the other lots became, as I mentioned, amusement parks. We recreated for a few months, gathering our strength, as our Lord commanded. I attempted to educate Silas and Jude—all of them really—by reading from the *Apex*, an invisible book from the future that I knew by heart. I really think they started catching on, but as soldiers and friends, you couldn't beat them. There were instructions on how to manipulate flesh into time, for example, converting molecules into subatomic particles for mental projection throughout all spheres of reality, and we had a marvelous time having Disneyland to ourselves for example—with no people to bother us, I might add, simply by following the book. We laughed once when all the slaves were frozen on the spot and we could walk around them and whisper things like, "All your dreams will come true, just think about it, and it will be delivered."

Then we'd set them loose and the top guys would go to prostitutes while the stupid slaves would use the Internet, the biggest enslavement device ever created! I told the Flagellator, "Son, if you go online I'll kill you."

And he listened. Since listening to me he became a real ladies man: "You see how they love you when they can't control your balls, man?" and he laughed all the way to pussy heaven.

Liberation of the planet was in full swing, however, not because I liked anybody—I certainly had things against those weaklings who pretended they never sold anything. Spiritual dolts, mental midgets, I don't know what you call people on earth. Certainly not clear-minded, certainly not civilized. Not when they live in a matriarchy thinking it's a patriarchy, not when they launch campaigns to make it a matriarchy and so some men become gay because it's the only way to step out of the lie. But they are scourged, and rightly so, if they let their aging, dying flesh define them. I must say, I cannot recommend anything that has to do with this earth, and those who come under my Lord's sword are worthy and a'fit for the big end—fucking *zero*.

Carl took another note just before they would sedate me and prepare me for more treatment. "Carl," I said, in earnest, "do you really think this is some sort of prison of the criminally insane?"

His smoking habit was escalating, of late, and we shared some talk of his house in New Hampshire, how he was looking forward to returning to the Manhattan apartment, where he would see his friends and tell them all about how sick I was and that he would also invest in a shrink and tell him how sick I made him.

He combed his gray hair straight back and had a certain, take-no-prisoners toughness about him, and I certainly admired it. He wouldn't admit that he'd been drifting, I could see, and from my vantage point I could tell his new girlfriend was torturing him, *Ace of the Post* notwithstanding. He was the one, the only, won it all, ate at the restaurants of fear, and was fat, fighting the fat, but the prizes made up for it. Elaine, his wife, I told him, was sucking somebody off right now, while the old fart is away interviewing a very handsome, alluring and dangerous man named Vincent Damien Del Monte, mass murderer, visionary, romantic swashbuckler, none of which was an understatement, thanks to Carl's words.

He would call and then he would beep her. "She has a beeper because she likes it," he said. "She has a beeper and it's none of your business."

"Except that I can see her, Carl. I can see how she uses a vibrator and has a bunch of asshole ditzy friends who are so fucking jealous that you—"

"Shut up! Now, look," Carl was saying, pushing his straight gray hair back and it looked like some politically liberal haircut, as opposed to some macho jerk-off double-breasted side- stepping ghoul that my Lord wants me to rid the planet of. So Carl was all right, and didn't mind me talking frankly.

"Shut the fuck up, Vincent! If you want to stay here without your straightjacket and all the torture you deserve—or do you want me to call Rick and Hilda back and tell them you need your treatment?"

"Carl, this is all about you, not me."

"Sick fuck. Look, I want to know about the doll. You say it worked, but the bullet holes in their bodies say differently."

"About the doll having the power of death? I was just making that one up, Carl. I was showing *them* that the doll was absurd."

"So who killed the drivers, the restaurant owners and the waitress, and everybody else you killed with the doll?"

"Millicet, of course. Blue did some too."

"Detective Ashley Blue?" Carl smoked Winston filters and

he kept needing to leave the room—to vomit, no doubt—and this time when he returned I hugged him and he started screaming for the guards.

"Carl! Please! Hold me!" I said, not having had any human touch for so long. "Please."

"Get your fucking hands off me," he was saying. "Or the interview is over."

He tucked in his work shirt into his jeans, very important for me to see him as working class, and therefore I was on his side, or he was on my side.

"You believe in black magic or something, Vincent? You trying to imitate something? I mean, with the queen doll."

"Imitate something, Carl? You know better than that."

"So you're making fun of our system, using the doll to show how sex games and power plays are all fake?"

"You foolish man—look at you, a Pulitzer Prize winner, three times, right? Your kids all graduated cum laude from Harvard, you got connections, but something is making you very sad and uncomfortable, isn't it?"

"Did you hate your parents and teachers and everybody that much that you became this way?" he asked, with a sad tear in his eye.

"Oh, yes, and I told them all that they can take their rules and shove it up their collective asshole."

"Nice," Carl said. "No appreciation. You were a spoiled brat living in some fantasy world. The poor little rich kid who couldn't hack the real world. Not some exotic nut to crack, not some saint, not anything but a garden variety know-nothing who hated his parents and took it out on the world—that's what I'm going to write."

"So you want to hear more about the doll or Blue?"

Carl looked at me with intrigue, with boyish passion. After all, he was right. I was more than privileged, more than spoiled by my Master—of course I did not hate the world, I came to do the Lord's work. And when I was without a place to lay my head on the streets of Phoenix, I was struck by a blinding light. In the light was a voice, and it told me what to do and where to go and how to do it—and then I was given my commission, and my loyal soldiers.

But Carl would not write this part down. He said, "I'll leave that to the psychiatrists, you sorry fuck."

Now with an attitude like that—one of total supremacy and derision—it's a wonder why I didn't grant the interview to someone more deserving, like a cable news channel or something. No, I had the best, and so I would now have to reveal the truth about the body count, which he says could be in the thousands, and I told him this: "Well, that's something you're guessing at—just like the doll, you don't believe it. I think you should come in closer."

When I said things like this, he left and didn't come back for a couple of days. He was publishing installments in *NY Magazine* about the most scary man in the world. I mean, these little ignorant fools actually thought they had me. The whole point of the doll was to loosen Blue from Anastasia's matriarchal instincts. He laughed when I told him she was planning to castrate him and take his balls for her own power, discarding him. He laughed when I said I was jealous of that. "So Blue took to the doll, and he loved it, and it loved him. He carried it in a nice leather knapsack he got from the leather shop..."

"At the mall where you killed ten women and four children?"

"Precisely. And we killed two men in the parking lot, Carl—don't forget that. You have no idea how little that is compared to something like the war in the Middle East."

Then he left and threw up again. To do this, he would walk down the green hall, past the cage called a nurse's station, further past the guard room, and past Dr. Merrill Florian's office, and past Nurse Zelda's office. Yeah, "the lovely Zelda," Carl called her, and I screamed hypocrite and they threatened me with everything from mood medication to lobotomy.

"What about the inheritance?" he asked.

"What about it? Margot disowned me and it went to her favorite charity—the Child Abuse Network."

"Sick," Carl said.

The doll worked on Blue, I was telling him. The doll worked very well. The doll was Blue's lover. And no, the Flagellator was not allowed to jerk-off on it. The doll was an exercise given to me by my Lord, and when we returned to Los Angeles, all were convinced that the doll could kill, when in actuality, I played Santa. I told them to close their eyes and then I used my .22 with the muffler, and then they would see the clerk, or the driver, or the mom, or the dad, or the student, or the housekeeper or the woman that Blue had sex with, or the gas station attendant, or the cop, or just about anybody for, oh, I'd say about the space of five hundred miles. Then they got wise. By the time we returned to Los Angeles, they all thanked me for showing them the truth.

"And what is the truth?" Carl asked a few days later.

"There is no Santa Claus!" I proclaimed and I was jumping around like an idiot. Carl was clapping and singing some Yiddish jig or something, and then he started singing this: "There is no Santa, there is no Santa, grab your plank and shoot the moon!"

"Carl?"

"Don't touch me—"

"Carl, I didn't know you cared."

"I hate your guts, you pervert psycho."

"But you'd like to see me grab my plank?"

"Just a joke, shithead."

"You a faggot, Carl?"

"You're the faggot! Think about it—your father was emasculated by your mother and failed to influence you to reason, and out of anger you took it out on the world—that is what I am writing, Vincent. 'Mother' represents the environment—any hateful boy who hates his mother and his father hates himself *and* the environment. In your case you committed matricide as your first—"

"—assignment!" I interrupted.

"You're a faggot—I'll bet the faggot aides around here would just love your cute butt, and you'd love that wouldn't you, you dirty faggot."

"You really want me to show you my plank?"

"Fuck you! You're locked up—I have a life! The world loves me—they hate you! Do you get it, you miserable piece of shit? You're an aberration, a girl, a pervert, a faggot, a toilet for the world! A bitch!"

Well, I could see it was time to show him the truth, and I

admitted killing some in Seattle, and Portland, and a few more around the Mount Hood area. The FBI went searching and found those extra, collateral damage victims, and added all of it to my account, but no one published it. They were studying me: the military, the CIA, the federal shrinks, sociologists from prestigious universities and a couple of pro-football coaches…why, I don't know.

Finally I stripped down naked in front of Carl and said, "Let's be kids! I'm a real boy too! Mommy told me so!"

Carl screamed.

NEETRUOF

Kruzmar had his meeting with Larry Finch, and the new Board of Directors for the Shangri-La Studios was installed, and at which kingpins and honchos from Coca-Cola to Lloyds of London were present, and the financiers who put the very complex hundred billion dollar investment together simply disappeared. That is, all except one...Linda Periwinkle, or, Lucy's right-hand girl.

This is the beginning of wisdom—when you accept your circumstances and adjust accordingly. In other words, fear my Lord. Those are the circumstances, and I must admit I was feeling quite disheartened at losing my beautiful bride to be, Anastasia.

No, there was a next step, and such is the bane of existence, always a next step, and that would be the next leg of the journey or what you might call the next detail of ridding a small but significant section of the world from cruelty. Judgment, you say? Only from beyond, though I would not reveal my sources to Carl, my Lord forbade me, and I won't reveal the truth that I was standing in the light of the future even while speaking with him. Now, also remember, I had covered him—he's not a bad man, his frustration is purely carnal. The world worships him but he hates himself, a common trait mostly shared by slaves with death sentences sealed on their foreheads.

They can't see them, but I can see them, my own that is.

I was all about helping him; I was commanded to do so, as the entire hospital was built for him, though no one could see the truth.

He wanted to know about Abacazzia and the heinous plans we had for her and others, but it was time for purification—and so, now I relate it to you from a higher perspective, as Carl left the room. While tied down to my bed, while urinating into my diapers, I was able to *move* ahead, to move in the direction of lasting peace, a glimpse of my homecoming, which Blue would never attend. Poor lad.

As I said, we needed purification, not conflict; we needed to confess, to relay, to step out of the battlefield upon which we were early arrivals, under the heading, "Paving The Way" for the Lord.

So we headed up Topanga Boulevard to the end, and up into the old movie ranch where a beautiful church was seated.

A huge beckoning cross lit up in the evening—lights ablaze on the hill—holiness! Oh, waters of life! Sweet release, how we all needed to drink deeply. The sun shone on us, the serenity was so earthly, the serenity was false purity—made by man, though inspired by God, no doubt. Blue and I needed this, though Millicet and the other men stood down and perched themselves above, keeping guard.

There were children playing soccer on a field, and there were teenagers listening to a pastor talking about the horrors of drugs, pregnancy and violence in one auditorium, and then there were several armed guards in front of what was called a worship center, or auditorium sanctuary—a very large and mysterious building, since there were armed guards surrounding it. There were fountains for baptism in the front and we threw ourselves in, being hot at the end of August, and I could tell that Blue understood where we were and what was going on. He was so substantial in his jeans and button-down collar and cowboy boots, a fresh shave of his head and even his eyes seemed to dazzle with the future—of course he wasn't me or my imagination! Blue would remember that I did help him, and then there would be a day where we would both drop the mask and the past, the trap of the lie, and he would then think I told him the truth, that I then said it all right, that I was pretty good at helping, and not reacting, as he was constantly doing. He had that blasted queen doll in the knapsack and I didn't object, though it felt foul sneaking into the chapel, which drew my curiosity simply because of those guys sporting machine guns outside.

When we came through the equipment entrance of the auditorium and climbed up to the scaffolding above, where many theater lights were installed, a worship band was singing praise the devil, inverting familiar hymns and dedicating everything to Satan. I immediately said, "You see what happens, Blue? Do you see what happens when the women get those balls?"

He smiled and said: "I want her to have my balls."

"Pipe down, man," I said. Then I drew my weapon. The pastor was baptizing a new batch of young adult men and women, who were nude. "You see what happens when you play by the rules, Blue?"

He said yeah, but I lost track of him when I aimed for the high priest's head. This was a guy they referred to lovingly as Big Dick, and indeed, when the woman dipped herself down in the blood she took his member into her mouth, and that's when my shot hit him right in the heart.

Some pretty woman, Big Dick's wife (we later found out) was yelling and screaming in shock that someone might disapprove of defiling the temple of God in this manner, and as we understood, they have regular worship of Jesus on Sundays, but we just happened to be in there on a Wednesday afternoon during soccer practice and a teen sermon in another auditorium. I took aim at the mouthy bitch, and we later found out that Big Dick was the Sunday pastor and the mouthy bitch was his wife! I aimed, fired, quietly eliminated the upper crown of her head. Bingo, problem solved. It's so gratifying when you can do something good for a change, and yes, this was rather personal, strangely carnal, almost earthly—but it got done, thank my Lord.

They all stood stunned, as I aimed for the helpers, and thus freed the dazed children from their duties as future leaders of the communities of Los Angeles County.

Blue had disappeared now, and the armed guards flooded into the place, just as I exited—they were extremely foolish; I had Kruzmar to thank for the weapon with the silly ninja sticker on it. It became my friend, my lover in a way—as my job had become much easier than say, with knives or other barbarian tools, such as hammers, tongs and plastic bags and scissors, rope, ice-picks (one of my favorites) and drugs (one of my least favorites), icicles, lamp-stands, and poison; freezers, stairwells and RV's, drills, nail guns and pitchforks—Millicet, Jude, Silas and the Flagellator—killing machines all—and Blue, the terrestrial, all here by my side, all helping me to find out if my bride-to-be can be found, anywhere.

Blue was gone, sure. Blue was terrestrial and this became fascinating to Carl, who wrote everything down. He would publish piece after piece and win award after award, imagine! He was publishing as I am speaking to you...*forward in time when he was killed and he would only say so many more words, which were already calculated.*

I would not impart the truth of his demise, which would be over the rest of my story, which would make him lose sleep, lose peace, lose his wife, lose his friends, his publisher and his reputation. I knew to let him push me around, to love him in return, because he truly did not understand what was happening to him.

His cultural pride would kill him.

He could not publish forward.

Where I was standing, in the sunlight of great reward, beyond the world, the glory and power and majesty, forever, I could see eternity separated from the inhabitants from the earth, as they were cut off, forever. As they were fools, forever. As they laughed at me, forever. As they spoke in tongues of fleshly desires, forever. As the dust slipped through their hands and the sabotage was clearly a best friend's doing, as the vows were permeated too soon and the mouth quieted down, those girly-men living lives of quiet desperation while shooting guns at clay targets and pretending that manhood was still in them. Sad.

Yes, and this man Carl, he was a'pacing, wearing jeans and

drinking wine in coffee cups hoping I, your man of vision, would not see, and then the stimulants—Dexedrine and handfuls of Vicodin, oh, I knew how he would make himself feel so blisteringly great; he likened himself to the proverbial racehorse, but all in his mind! And I wondered how he managed sex.

Today was the first time we had left the little room. With guards, we walked on the open grass, under the trees, and I could see girls in the background, playing tennis—far away, *perhaps in the past*. There were kids in the public swimming pool; there were fires, as it was northward, above the City to be drowned in one glorious moment in the ubiquitous Bay—forgetfulness, quietly near a prison, but I did not know its name.

There was real estate, oh, millions of dollars into houses and cars and hotel rooms, and day spas, and village banks, and politically correct Girl Scouts thinking cookies wouldn't lead to the unthinkable, but I could smell it on the breeze and in the watershed of a few seconds ahead. That was all it would take, just a few...and he sat me down, with the aides, Pencil Neck and Radar, right behind, my new lads. *PN* wore an Oakland Raiders sweatshirt and Radar had motorcycle boots and braided hair, unlike I had today—as they shaved my head for their electrodes and shock treatments. He chewed gum and told me he used to ride with the Hells. He told me he was a friend. But not to tell anybody. He said he kicked a heroin habit a few years ago, and he couldn't seem to put any weight on since that time. He said he loved porn and fucking virgin men in the ass if they pissed him off. Something he learned in prison. He wore jeans and Black Sabbath T-shirts but wasn't beholden to the girls. He was a bad boy. He'd wave his dick around and say he was proud of his God-given talent, and I marveled at the sheer size of the thing.

"Don't worry, I won't fuck you when you're not looking!" he said, and stuffed it back in his pants. "You're my hero, man," he said. "Anything you need, you just let me know, bro."

But they got nothing!

Oh, my friends, could you indulge me for a moment? For Carl could not stand the light of day, the sunshine, and so he left and drove off in his rented Caddy, while I was escorted by Radar back to my locked single room. The sleeping medication was easy to tongue, as I might use this to kill the night nurse, one day. If my Lord permits.

I saw Carl go into his hotel room at the Mendocino suite, and I knew he had a girl there, for I had called her and she spoke to me like a country girl who wanted to see the world. She told me she could hear me through the air, and I asked her if she was a witch, and she said, "We all are around here."

Yes, that would make sense—long skirts, snug little tops and flowers in her hair: I knew her name—Katherine of the Mist. St. Kath, the lady of the stream and the queen of the mountain top. A naughty nymph at twenty-four, with breasts as succulent as figs, larger than her thin frame, with tight buttocks in a pair of low-slung bell-bottoms, and long curly hair that went wild with streaks of red and blonde and auburn. But deadly too.

The way of the earth was one of peace in the beginning, but then sex and death had to be celebrated, mythologized and acted out, literally. And ultimately, you know, my brethren: sex *is* death, birth *is* death, and flesh *is* death—when you worship the earth, you worship death, my secret friends! The key is to go the way the horse is already going—so if we're going on into death, halle-lujah, jump-start that motherfucker with as much death worship as possible—she oughta love me, lads!

But this love of death made the young ones look so waify and sexual. I said, "I don't want to be the Man of the Hour."

She said, "You must have some experience to appear here in front of me when I didn't call you."

"You didn't call me, I called you, My Lady. I am the one you see when he comes into you."

"Yes, you are—oh, beautiful you. I love you," she said. "I want to bear your child, Vincent Damien Del Monte," she said, camped in tight halter top and g-string with her nipples bulging forth in the candlelight of an altar that had a Tarot card of the Fool clipped to a dollar bill and next to a shorn off piece of man-drake, next to a chalice of ruby red wine—naughty girl. She had to do all this in order to take his power to the altar and use it with concision and efficacy, she thought. I showed her the volcano doll and she told me that Anastasia was not in love with me, that I was wasting my time, and in her own protuberant parlance, she said, "She is not who you think she is—she is a dominatrix."

"Anastasia?" I was crushed. I was broken; I was angry and despondent. I thought I'd cut it all off.

But then she said, "Vincent, you will be free again! Can you believe it! Oh, hallelujah! Then we can fuck and everything! I am in love with you—you, you, *you*. I have waited my whole life for you. You are his sword, aren't you?"

Without needing an answer, she came to my bed and fucked my brains out. Did I need that fuck or what! I needed that fuck more than I needed food. And she made me come like a cock-teased ugly man—I thought it was going to kill me. I had a mind full of smooth road a hand full of contour and preoccupation. I came and she made me cry too—as the emotion of love overwhelmed me—like mommy and a baby carriage, like my housekeeper who let me suck on her nipples from age two through seven (I would have continued but she was fired when she sued Dad when the new baby came). Her name was Help Me. And the time was To Go.

I, Vincent.

Do pledge.

Myself.

To anyone who will take me!

Carl, you fool, I read your words—how I met you on even ground!

Yes, Katherine came to me and materialized—and we fucked desperately and finely. This was no masturbation fantasy, friends—we fucked. She is that good. You can just imagine Carl up against royalty like her!

A goner.

Anastasia would have Blue, wherever he went, and he had gone far. If he ever found her she would have his total manhood and his total dedication—he felt she really loved him. But he was a man fated to doom unless he was under Vincent's care. Anastasia was as Lady Katherine had said: a practitioner, someone who spanned time and space. But not well.

The meeting with Serena, Asenath and Milaca took place in

a bar called The Axis. They sang songs about babies and chariots and ordered mint juleps, minced crab and fancy fish rolls; they saw goldfish under the floor and danced at the thought of Kruzmar and his new actor friend, Tommy—*Tommy!*—who now had left his girlfriend and Kruzmar had had him up in the penthouse where Vincent had been held captive. He wanted rough treatment, Kruzmar, and he got it—his boyish blond hair gave way to a wig. Tommy was rough and Serena proclaimed him diseased, and fallen, and beaten—and there was a howl in Heaven and lightning struck. All men dropped their cocks and froze in shame, as the clock struck 1:30 and the news blared, about her...her, the Queen, her, *the one*.

Her, the employer, the fancy plan maker.

Her, the signal and the portrait. The one who glided down her stairs to greet her guests after burying her husband in much the same way Margot had done. The one who had backed her second son and not her first.

For he had struck at the heart of it just as Tommy had swelled up from behind, exhaling all of himself into a boy who wanted punishment, and no longer was Joe Ivy. For the limos had pulled over and the sacred hills above Sunset ceased to live—plant life had been altered; where flowers bloomed one way, now they were cankerous, without direction. Where silly golf balls would roll one way to the green, now another, more mysterious way would hold fast. Where the trees would sway just so outside the bungalow on Stone Canyon, they now flung detritus into the buffet with alacrity, arrogance and permanence. Where there were waiters of sing-song persuasion scoffing at the "men," now they begged forgiveness, and where heaven was laid on top of Mulholland, now there were trembling clusters of nobodies pretending to be famous for all. Peasants and muses and jockeys without horses, the idiot brigade at the outer rim and the softness workers of light burden dropped the salute though they kept dry all their lives—all simply ceased, all. Simply nothing would work ever again. For as Leonard Cutlass Kruzmar would sing his last song, Vincent Damien Del Monte had struck a blow into the heart of iniquity, and the sword would stay forever and ever; all glory to the Highest Holy, for the prince of chaos had swept, and Milaca slammed her drink and ordered another. Blue was lost though he found Anastasia with a governess of deliverance potential, and the sweat of the sweet fall air permeated the grounds of the Kruzmar estate, for the next queen had fallen, and her name was Abacazzia.

He was looking for Blue, and Millicet was ready to rendez-vous with the others down on the streets near Vermont—but first the visit, just for layout sake; certainly no general thought that I, with only Millicet the barbarian at my side, could score such a victory. For Abacazzia had gardeners and cooks and maid-servants and male dancers; she had entertainment of every sort, any folly that could be imagined. Her office was up on a rotunda of sorts, where she was writing memoirs of liaisons with presi-dents and kings, of how her husband had gotten cancer because of the stress of working in the White House, how Christmas was no fun without fornication en masse, outing them all who were dead, thinking she was so clever. She was cool, as that day she was wearing her boy's jeans and a cashmere sweater, pearl ear-rings and the Grosmont diamond around her neck, a thirty-five carat monstrosity which could have become a nice spoil for my work.

She was dictating a letter, the gardener was mowing the mas-sive lawn that led to a pool house down the hill; the maids were making flower arrangements; the cook was harvesting herbs—and Millicet and I...Millicet the Bull!...on the roof, began to gen-tly pick off one after another. On the roof there was no security, and over the gate and around the trees and to the side of the 20,000 square foot Mediterranean palace, a trellis led to the top of the first landing, and another trellis led to the second floor, another to the third floor, and on top—peace! Every single angle looking down was a perfect perch.

After ending the faces of the cook, the gardener and the flower-maid, behind them into the trees, the warm spray paint of or-ange, red and purple—where did the soul go?

I remember hearing the prophet say: "Vincent, you are not to spare even one, whether child, suckling, young, old, no judg-ments—you just do as you are commanded."

"Yes, sir. Gimme the go-code, sir!"

G-O-D.

I climbed back down for a little wet work, one of Kruzmar's goons called it. Entering the house, the foreman, or security guard, I'm not sure what he was, but he was armed with a Smith and Wesson semi-auto and had a patch on his shirt that looked like, "RUSS."

Millicet held this criminal as he cut his tongue out and told him to announce our arrival. (We took his gun too).

He climbed the stairs, on his way to protect Abacazzia of course.

Millicet received a message from my Lord, which was decidedly disturbing.

It read:

My dearest and most able soldier, Vincent Damien Del Monte:

How I have missed you. Grace and peace to you, and great glorious praise for your victories! You have infiltrated further behind the lines than any other man of the future. The witches even sing your praises. As you are about to achieve a major conquest and, it would appear, finish our major objective in Los Angeles, I am afraid I must tell you a few things.

First of all, you are not qualified to understand your mission, as it pertains to geo-political realities of the past. You have a memory of who you were, and a memory of who you are now. You are separated in time, that is, you are able to span time and space, but you cannot escape, not fully. It is possible that you will not return to us. I would understand if you want to quit now and return, as you would have a hero's welcome.

Vincent, no one else is as capable as you, and you are the best one suited for a job we never told you about. So far, you have functioned as a soldier of brilliance, and you have successfully completed every task, but you have never known the true objective—and you never will know unless you return to us safely.

You understood about Anastasia, and that is very important—Katherine is a bridge, but you must lead her to accept me.

The rest of your assignment will be given to you on a need-

to-know, eyes-only basis.
    Sincerely,
    In the year of our Lord,
    Angel Of Mercy
    In the Presence of the Elohim
    Praise God from Whom All Blessings Flow

Needless to say, all of this woke me up, and I was safely held in her arms, my wife, Princess Katherine, yet to be converted.

Carl was pacing, as usual, and he was prevaricating, hallucinating, and being rather insulting.

"Keep it in your pants, Vincent."

And I would say, "Sir, are you still mad at me for exposing you to the realities of constraint?"

"I am the original exposer," he said, angrily.

"Ever share a jack-off with a homo?" I asked, in earnest.

He turned away, shook his head, as if he were terminally right and I was incomprehensibly wrong, cosmically, tangentially and perhaps vagrantly. "You're a fucking loser—I don't know why I'm here."

"Ever have a wank with a homeless person, Carl?" I asked.

"Fuck you! Fuck you! I don't think you've EVER done anything with a poor person your whole life! I think you, Vincent, simply want to fuck with me."

"Well, I *am* fucking your girlfriend—Katherine."

Now this reaction was nothing short of gifted. He hit the table, stood up and kicked me and my chair to the ground. He leapt on me and started beating me but I returned it not. He then lifted me back up as the guards rushed in and tied me back up and sat my butt back down on that chair. But Radar was with them this time, and he looked at me and winked. He shoved his long blond hair back and I wondered if he would be joining me in the future.

"Get the motherfucker some Thorazine or something," Carl said.

"You okay, Vincent?" Radar asked.

"Who the fuck cares how he is—how am *I*! How the fuck am

I surviving the sickest fucker to *ever* be born! Why don't you ask me *that*, you retard!"

Radar looked at him, and Carl noticed his one arm covered with one solid campaign of *Tattoo*, and he backed off.

"We have to see the doctor for the medication—"

"Fuck you," Carl said. "I'll bury this place, that's what I'm writing about next—you and your faggot friends, Vincent." What kind of hold do you have on these people? How the fuck did you know the name of my girlfriend?"

I laughed. Radar didn't know what to do, so I sent him a thought—go away...this is Carl's party, let it be Carl's bed too.

And he said: "Well, Mr. Nunn, we are sorry—if you want us to put him back in his—"

"—Just get the fuck out of here, son," Carl said. Radar nodded, winked and gave me a small thumbs-up sign, then left.

"Katherine and I are lovers, Carl," I said. "There is no use trying to—"

"YOU'RE NOT GOING TO WIN, VINCENT."

"*Win*, sir?" I said, respectfully.

"Yes," he said. "You're not going to win. Punks like you just rot in a place like this—your future is shit, your past is unlivable—"

"—Really, I'm very happy with it—Katherine is some witch, isn't she? She your queen?"

Carl got very quiet. He looked around and thought about it, then he gave me the truth. "She's infatuated with *you*, so she's in your mind—so she's...this is like the Night Stalker—she's, fucking-A, she's your fan, dickhead."

"Plus I'm handsome, charismatic and successful."

"That I'll give ya, but you'll never suck on her titties, fuck."

"Do you have to use such foul language—it's beneath you, Carl."

"Tell me about Kruzmar—that must have been a lot of fun, chopping her limbs up and eating them, you said?" Now he was looking back through transcripts, and this was the sort of tawdry thing we learned from the Tonganese back in the 1800's, but no one was interested in motives—she was the enemy. This was the direct hit.

This was the bag of the century, the conquest of the titan, the fountainhead—glass backwards. Inerrant, complete and *not applicable*...Reality—I knew it, but he did not know it.

She was Queen Abacazzia Fontainebleau Himmelman Kruzmar; she was never more than 103 pounds, the style of the day, she wore a button down sweater with pearls stitched in it, had had several face-lifts and collagen treatments and looked like she wanted to be a virgin at a fuck fest in Berlin. Or Vegas. She had the skinny jeans on and the countenance of a liar, a consummate, intelligent, reptilian liar; the veil of the evil one was upon her, and inside her. Fucking her would be like sticking your dick into a 220 outlet—sheer confusion. But I had no time to think about fucking, not until I laid eyes on her secretary, Gillian, oh, babe of babes—ravaging was legal, oh, you jealous generation. Abacazzia had many college girls around, not just the Mexican help that ran things, but the kind of girls that would be swell in the weekly orgy, where Abacazzia could run her hands over their smooth skin and watch her friends have their way with them and get it on videotape in the feudal method of working through college.

Sweet was this one, her name, I said, was Fandango. No, I mean Gillian.

(Carl could see that I had an erection just thinking about all this and I personally think my experience rewired his entire sexual orientation and desire-to-cock ratio.)

Fandango was the word I was thinking of, but Gillian was her name, for sure. Millicet had severed the head of the lovely flower-maid, Roseanne, and so I rolled it to the feet of Fandango, almost like an offering—but she didn't take it that way.

Of course there was no one to help them—and when she saw me, Gillian that is, she fainted.

Abacazzia had a few words of protest: "Now just you wait a minute, young man—"

"It's Vincent!"

She stopped and vomited, not unlike Carl, and then turned and said. "Did you hate Leonard that much? Did he bully you, or tease you?"

"Yes, Your Highness," I said, "but I got over that."

"I'll pay you, and I'll get you out of the country. Did you kill Styles?" Now she was smiling, evilly.

As if it was *her* talent—*her* will. Fucking cunt.

"Kill Styles? That was perfection—my best work."

"But my son trained you, no?"

"He put a price on my head—he betrayed me just like when he and his friends pantsed me and ran my clothes up the flagpole in front of the girls."

"You still mad about that?"

"Mad...no."

"You're a religious man?"

"No, but I serve my Lord, in the future—a returning King is who sent me."

"Sounds like..."

"It is," I said. "And I'm afraid I have acted a bit fleshly, and less spiritually, but I am his warrior—many times throughout your ridiculous history he's appointed people like me to kill many, and without mercy, though I am not what you think; you believe that someone, possibly my mother—"

"Yes, Margot, but she was so frail...."

"I don't live here, I don't follow your rules," I said, holding up the head. "I don't think about you, or any woman."

Millicet silenced the girl by duct-taping the babe—her name is Fandango—to the wall.

"Yes...that is your problem. You couldn't hack it here because your parents didn't have time for you—oh, you were sensitive too, and you hung around the kitchen when the other boys were out playing, is that it? Let me help you with that. Come here, little Vincent, I'll hug you and feel your penis."

I fell for it, and she fondled me while she was holding me, and said: "Did you kill Styles?" and she snickered.

"That was more than death..."

"It was poetry," she said. "My son loves you," she said, now tugging my pants and underwear down and jerking me off while studying the length and breadth of a member that painfully belonged to my Lord.

But for a moment I was like the little boy Leonard turned out to be, a man of the world—I could see that with a mother like this I could…Fantasies aside, I regained my mission and severed her jugular easily with a Ka-Bar knife I just bought at the surplus store, so that the spray would go out away from me, since I had many more stops and did not want to change my clothes. After dispatching Millicet with her head it was time to celebrate. And here, for my own personal pleasure, a gift just for me, my Lord provided me with a babe named…not Fandango, but Gillian.

I un-duct-taped her from the wall and she became my lover. "You're Vincent," she whispered. "You can do anything you want to me—I don't want to die, please."

"You type 120 words a minute?" I asked while she was sucking my cock like a Vegas track star. She then teased me by kissing my rather ripped torso and hard chest. "You look like you're … not even real," she said.

"I'm not, not exactly—"

"I love you, Vincent," she said.

And I believe she truly meant it. We deep-kissed, and trust me, brother, I needed love to take me away from my obsession with Anastasia. My Lord would allow witnesses, and this one was so tender and so much a team player, that I asked Millicet if he wanted to make love to her.

"That's MAKE LOVE, Millicet, not rape."

"If you say so, Vincent, thank you."

"I look forward to it," she said, and treated the big guy to a treat he'd earned more than a few times. I went around the property hoisting up the bodies and heads on poles, or hooks—for some reason I wanted them all upright (remember, my Lord programs my mind) and so they looked like Hollywood stand-ins! It was awesome, especially the headless corpses pondering the garden or pushing the lawn mower. I placed what was the security guard on the chaise raft in the pool and lodged a book about social etiquette in his hands. I stripped him down, saddled him up with a pair of women's panties and set his headless corpse afloat in the Olympic sized lap pool with the fountain in the middle. Oh, it was a sight!

It had a purpose, to utterly destroy the enemy, once and for all—to psychologically demoralize them.

We had accomplished our task, that of utterly destroying the past, and now— "The future," as it had been proverbially said, "was wide open."

Millicet disappointed me to no end, however. When I returned the girl was, of course, the way the police found her, disfigured, or rather—dismembered. "Why did you do that?" I asked, and he said: "Because I work for the same person you do."

Millicet would never call anyone a "person" unless he was referring to our future King. Oh my, did that put the fear of God into me right quick. "You mean he doesn't want any—"

"No mercy, Vincent," Millicet said, girding up his green fatigues, and long black collarless shirt which, when his beard hung down to his chest, made him look more like a monk. "You seem so..."

"I was given gonads, Vincent, and I thank you for the chance to use them."

"But was it the killing—"

"Yes, that is what makes me come."

I knew I had commanded a lunatic, but this was the sort of aberration I could not understand in the Kingdom. In fact, as I was looking at myself in the room full of Kruzmar mirrors, I wondered what my Lord saw in me. I was carnal, I killed, I was some sort of soldier but I felt weak and frail.

Then a vision came to me, as I was before the Lord's throne. "Vincent," he was saying, "you are worthy to defend the Lamb."

Right away I knew that my Lord was nothing other than a God who brought a sword to the earth, and a depraved one at that. But if my Lord was really God, was I dead? Did that make me a destroyer angel? What the fuck was I, and how come I wasn't more holy—or was I? No, because I...I was fallible. I was putrid. I looked handsome, and eternal—for I did not age past about twenty-seven years old (perhaps in part to Kruzmar's knife men)— and my other men were missing—though Jude came back and told me that Silas and the Flagellator were down at a titty bar on Washington Boulevard, waiting for us.

Jude was weeping at the site of all the headless corpses poised to do work, and then my Lord showed us a terrifying sight. I held Jude, and it's a good thing I was made to like girls, but if I had any inklings, my friends, I would have—well, I also kissed him on the lips. That was very adventurous, and very dangerous, and I knew it was abominable, and I also sat him down and told him about what had happened.

"I can't look," he said. "I want to go home. Hold me again, Vincent."

The titty bar is what he needed. Before he went too far with this femme-du-jour thing. He was beautiful, he was perfectly made, he was about eighteen-years-old with a pretty face like a woman, but not faggy...this was silly of me. I could see Millicet looking at him funny too—which would mean what, that Millicet would rape him and kill him so he could ejaculate? I looked at myself and Jude in the mirror, as we stood there naked together and I wanted to compare our bodies. His was just better than mine in every way. He wanted me to look at him, to touch him— and I did not want to for spiritual reasons, though my carnal mind kept on torturing me. I was no faggot, but this would have to be the exception. After all, he was seducing me.

He wanted me to take him the same way I took the girl before Millicet perverted the whole situation.

"So then what happened!" Carl asked excitedly, and I could tell he wanted to jack-off all over the planet.

"Why does this story about Jude excite you so much, Carl? Jude needs protection. He's very fragile. He would never understand—in fact, he was never there when we were raping and murdering all those girls."

"He was gay, right?" Carl asked politely, and by now he was all over his dick under the desk.

"Carl, have you ever considered..."

"No fucking way, perv. I only write stories about sick fucks like you—so did you...?"

NEETFIF

This should answer the question, the billion dollar question, about Blue. The answer is this: I don't know. Where he went is none of my concern. Was he the one dubbed the *Phantom*? How should I know? Does Anastasia control him? Is she the queen of some underground cult or something? Fuck if I know.

"Carl, go fuck your girlfriend."

Carl now wears jeans and Nehru shirts and sandals. His hair has grown much longer, as some moderate amount of time had slipped by, and it's likely Katherine is changing him for the better. In fact, today Carl is wearing some sort of cashmere Nehru thing that one of his tailors in Manhattan made him—he was talking a lot on his cell phone. Oh, right, he had this like, rebellious little braid growing in the back of his hair, and a scissor-clipped beard. Katherine, who is totally mine, by the way, is running him into places in the city that sell all this international male crap. He got a facelift while I conducted poker games with Mel, who was about Carl's age, Radar, when he worked nights, and Cyril, the Seattle Slayer, a very clever little fucker who liked chicken and probably sheep too.

"I want to hear about the studio! This is the thing that you know—it's just not fair that you got Kruzmar's last words on this whole sorry affair with his wife and—"

"—Perish the thought, Carl, fucking my girlfriend, you old buggerer, that you would ever hold out on me!"

"Now you listen to me, shithead—"

Carl grabbed my head and gave me an Indian rub. "You don't scare me—feel that!"

I felt his bicep, which was a little curve, his whole body had changed, and today we are doing a photography session with Fannie Plotkin, who did the president of France just last week for *Rolling Stone*, and I feel like Carl's hair transplants and facelifts have made his face look a little Asian. I mean, the squint-eyed motherfucker looks like Lady Chatterley with embalming fluid or something.

(I'm wondering when we're going to start the program on Carl, but Radar assures me the boys in gray are waiting for the right opportunity to put me back on assignment, but Carl is the most challenging, no doubt.)

By now I have earned privileges...Radar runs me around the track, and spots me in the weight room—he's become a disciple but has kept it hush-hush, as I told him to do. Carl brings in pictures of his new bright yellow Porsche and looks to see if I have any sense of envy—and all this because of jealousy.

Carl kisses Fannie the photographer, who is blonde and coiffy and definitely cosmopolitan, and they do a little Yiddish *zeitgeist* thing and I carefully roll a cigarette and pull the shade down on the see-through mirror where my covert-ops shrink friends are watching Carl. I couldn't tell him about Katherine, who was now visiting me the days Carl could not be here.

So I've been good, if you're wondering how in the world I'm managing to have so much freedom, some folks around here are beginning to understand that spirit is stronger than flesh, but not the spirit of the world (if you have an ear).

What did they have to gain by all this? I don't know. What does anyone have to gain by the masquerade? The Masquerade— let me ask you something: Do you really know anybody? Do you really know them after they've divulged everything? Was there really camaraderie in the platoon? The fraternity? The pub? You were jealous once, weren't you, and you hit that guy in the jaw—you stole a bad man's girl and you stole a good man's girl. You stole a bad man's belongings, no different than a good man's belongings. You didn't say because you were taught to keep your mouth shut, and they made you a hypocrite if you didn't go along. But you went along, and you go along, and you're just a'flowing down the stream, and you're a'watchin' it flow, you're a cas'a'cadin down beyond imagination's sake, past the boundaries of fairies and tales that would keep you humble and in your place, and enslaved to the mortgage and the freak show and the exposure to the big people you wanted to meet but they didn't care that you cared.

No one knows you, friend. And you're about to see a brother go down in a fit of fury. He thought it was about me, but it is about him—one Carl Nunn.

Meanwhile, he's schmoozing with Fannie about all the celebrities, and all the time he knows I'm the biggest celebrity who has ever lived, because he, somehow, links me with impossible odds, and Fannie is macho, doesn't seem to worry about the situation, that is, me being free.

I showed Carl the fence, I showed him the underground stream where the reptiles hide; I showed him the tree that bore no fruit and told him to look into the mirror and try to worship his Pulitzers. And he would say, as things were thawing out, "What the fuck have *you* done? Gotten away with causing a lot of pain and trouble? What good is that? Those prizes got me rich, they got me the prize pussy, anytime I blinked, and they got me this interview."

"You think you have power, but I have the keys to your life, Carl twinkle-toes Nunn." I tried to kiss him on the lips and he shoved me to the ground so that Radar and PN and the Ugly Man came to tie me back up and haul me off.

But now here we are, months later, and I'm the most famous face in America—Fannie Plotkin asks me how I managed to look so young, and I told her it's because I'm from the future. She laughed and Carl rolled his eyes, but I could tell he was looking at her ass, and I said, "I don't mind, Carl—I don't mind."

He got up and left the room, as Radar cinched in closer to

make Fannie more comfortable, but she laughed and said, "Naughty naughty. Don't you know that Carl's very fragile right now?"

"He *was* looking at your ass."

"As well he should." Clack-clack, clack-clack-clack, as the strobes popped in my face and some sort of stylist kept playing with my long braid that now tickled my lower back. "I like your hair. You're a handsome kid. I mean, you're what—you look like twenty-five, but you're like late-thirties or something. You're handsome—got the bones, doesn't he, Michelle?"

Michelle, the Japanese stylist, didn't understand what Fannie was saying—she was clearly frightened.

"Michelle, don't worry, he likes us." She looked at me and said, "I'm going to have to excuse her. She just can't handle how handsome you are, Vincent." Clack-clack...clack-clack-clack...clack-clack-clack...

"Cut the cretaceous misplacement of word, babe. I'm a man o'war. Grrrrrrr!" I lunged at Michelle and she tore out of the room—but Radar didn't make a move and Fannie kept shooting, especially that Grrrr thing I was doing, that fantastic growl that got her loins loosened up—would she like to fuck the monkey? Would she like to fuck the biggest mass-murderer since Adolf, would she like to fuck someone who caused a change in the economic climate worldwide forever? Would she like to fuck my brains out? Without Radar getting off on it? Without walls or chains? Without tranquilizers or observers? Without a net?

Oh, Fannie, come here baby. "Look the other way, Radar—"

"Ma'am! If you want I'll — "

"No," she said—and by the way, we were at the gym, so there was plenty of room, and this had been going on all week. Clack-clack, clack-clack...clack-clack-clack...

The gym had just the right light coming in from above, a high window, a weight area, basketball and volleyball courts, and even some bleachers for when we play the retarded or another prison for the criminally insane.

You must understand, over these months, they walk me around alone, and I have a whole contingent of feeble-minded know-it-alls around me at all times, the top social workers, psychiatrists, sociologists, even an anthropologist named Eddie Gluck who says we'd all be happier if we remained primitive, and he always asks me why I am so happy all the time. I answered him in this manner: "Because I'm not you."

But they come back—Radar knows what's happening. I go jogging every morning, and he knows I'm in training. Pencil covers me on the weights—I'm getting facials from Fannie's San Francisco drag queen (and they think *I'm* insane?) named Michelangela—and there is the prison warden, a Roman named Ruth who likes to inspect the men in their underwear. Thank God I have never been called to that sort of duty.

I knew my Lord wanted me to break these people out, just set them all loose one day, for his reasons: and I think it's called destabilization for the purpose of truth.

Fannie is about done with me, and Carl is right, her ass is as fine as existence itself, but Carl's getting none, the closest he'll ever be is his pathetic little pointer that he won't let me have a look at.

"He's a hypocrite—Elaine and I are friends, and believe me, honey, she fools around. Why the fuck not?" Fannie is saying, "I mean, he's the most infamous womanizer in Manhattan, second only to our last president, because that makes him feel like he has a dick—you can't fool us, honey."

"You're like me...I'm looking through you and talking to me now, Fannie," I said and she suddenly got sick, and backed away from me. "Get out of my mind!" she yelled, and Michelangela started laughing. "Honey, oh, honey—he's a psycho!" he screamed as she tore out of the gym—away from the black mat and the lights and the photo backgrounds, and all her camera technicians. A glamour shoot in a prison for the psychologically damaged? Pulitzers assured? Triumphal entry into Elaine's? Fucking kidding or what? This is war, bitch.

They handcuffed me immediately, chaining my feet. "Can I at least get the makeup off?"

Bernstein the psychiatrist asked me if I enjoyed frightening her like I did, and I said, "You saw the tape! Did it look like I was frightening anyone? Did I even move one little twitch? Did I lay a fucking hand on her, like Carl jerks off just thinking about?"

My mind told his: *Bernstein, listen to me, you're one of us, and you are going to help me get out of here.*

He chuckled, and asked me if I would yell "fire" in a crowded theater, and I said, "Been there, done that."

And he said, "Do you enjoy hurting others?"

And I said, "Do you enjoy hurting me?"

Bernstein said: "I feel like you're not in touch with your feelings."

What could I say to that one? Bernstein, I *am* your mind. Bernstein, I *am* your soul. This seed is planted, and you shall go to the home of Princess Katherine and tell her we shall be together soon. You will also take Carl as your patient. Call him and tell him that you will be discreet.

And Bernstein said: "Do you want to fuck Fannie?"

And I said, "Do you want to fuck your daughter?"

And he said, "Hostility will not work, mister!"

ꙋ   ꙋ   ꙋ

They built all the new soundstages and turned the old lots into amusement parks, museums and television facilities. Shangri-La was impressive, oh, my—how modern, how artful, how paradisiacal and how it echoed the cry of *Kruzmarian* power! Lucy had ramped up the slate with two dozen pictures, one of which, the big one, the one to make the studio's first billion, when all is said and done, was a picture in the three hundred million dollar range, entitled: *Soul Survivor.* It starred no one less than Russell Scott and Diane Winston, helmed by the illustrious Queenie® Award winner Rim Fish; it spoke to God and it was the original stairway to forever, at least everyone thought that about it.

It was the biggest picture to date, inspired by the classic novel by Steve Shredd, or S.S., as he was so commonly referred to. Shredd would write about how the world could be changed by just one person. *Soul Survivor* postulated an earth completely destroyed by the one man who did not sell his soul to Satan. That God would kill the whole world to save just one righteous man…actually, it's a bit off, as the Bible mentions 10 righteous, and below that…Sodom is vaporized. Or in the flood of Noah, 8 righteous, and the rest of the world drowned. So Shred is onto something rather frightening for the world at large, something I know to be true in more general terms. Indeed, this world is about to be torched.

For those who believed in the soul survivor eternity opened up and the span of time was accessible—of course it was only a sci-fi story. This gave Carl Nunn the key, or at least Carl had this bit of confidence to go on—that I might actually be one of these strange creatures. I most certainly am no survivor, but a warrior—and Carl is my subject, I am not his. He's learning.

One who does not sympathize with the charity benefits and bow ties, one who hides on a mountain high up off the desert floor, above the clouds and of great influence to Vincent Damien Del Monte, and this is where there was more of a connection and clue for Carl Nunn.

But I will not divulge my source.

From the future, the past is wide open, and history can be changed at any point along the time line, that was the point of Shredd's time-travel pieces, what I was babbling about half the time.

ə ə ə

Detective Ashley Blue was also the most wanted man in America, but in two years, no one had caught him.

Anastasia had run away, and there were more deaths, mainly of writers. Could it be that Blue was working for Anastasia, Vincent might wonder? Could it be that she, who turned from Vincent and not the other way around, had found her post as a queen of the future on her own? With no need of a man or woman or parent? With no need of a mansion or tutor or European holiday or the junior section at Macy's or tattoo parlor and the lipring? Even if Vincent would still think of her in the dark of a lockdown night?

In the corridors and shrink appointments and training in the field and gym, solitude, misdirection and Katherine, provided by the Lord of Vincent.

Kruzmar had him beat, it would seem. He arrived at the Ultra Awards with his studio getting every single award, the first time a producer got the much coveted Queenie® for every movie produced. Even the independent films he could destroy by giving them just enough money to hang themselves and of course garnering their talent pools and rendering them basically nil.

This did not sit well in the corridors of power around the world.

Lenny and Lucy, the pair to beat, the King and Queen of Hollywood. If anybody wanted to make a film, they had to get the go-ahead from Kruzmar's wife. No ifs, ands, or buttocks—it was the way it was. No auto-suck could guarantee work, no self-fulfilling prophecy or squint-eyed boys confined in rocket ships to hell, no secret meetings and ritualistic sacrifices, no pile of bones could alter the fact that SHE was The One.

He was now wearing purple and had built out his breasts with the help of others. Leonard was doing it. He would become the first *ordained* hermaphrodite, the king below a queen with the queen under the apron strings of his expansiveness...it was an off-world solution, a paradox. He would be the world's first humanly contained superpower. He, Leonard, had twenty features at a time blasting off, a monopoly on everything and everyone—but they could only see Lucy.

Still, *Soul Survivor* was just beginning...the script had gone though rewrite after rewrite and was almost ready for the inevitable. Trevor Hall, Kinsey Jones, Thad Herrington, Toni Max, and Anton DeVille had been writers—each received half a king's ransom for their input, but nobody nailed it. This was not simply a screenplay, it was a world—a world where time and space were to be replaced. A disturbing world where John-Q-Citizen and Suzy-Homewrecker would be hunted like criminals.

As Kruzmar had said: "It's a bus ride into the future that's much like our past, a chance to see the big bang from Rim Fish's eye. That's one bus ride I want to be on!" he said, blinded by sexual excitement from complex surgery.

We were fit to go forwards as well as backwards, Vincent had said to Bernstein. "But backwards is the only direction I go," he said.

What would happen if indeed we traveled beyond the big bang, back to WHAT? The inescapable future? Would it just be a dark wall?

"It was dark," Shredd had said in an interview with *Jane's Defense*. "War can open it up," he said oddly.

America's strangest novelist, and most disturbing voice, would make proclamations and not allow interviewers to, well, interview him—no questions would be taken. He would issue Moses' tablets; he was the intercessor between God and Man.

He was the only one like him.

He was the thing no past could erase, and no future hold.

Carl knew he had Vincent by the nuts, and now he could safely deride him, make an extra mil, then turn him over to the *specialty people.* "Who the fuck cares if they use him for the military—personally, I'd put him down...he's only a mad dog."

Twenty-five sound stages and multiple storage facilities and paperless offices, Kruzmar had a purple wristwatch phone and wore an onyx earring, special panties made just for him, and his office was the size of his mother's kitchen.

Of course there were tears, at her death, and of course he vowed to find the perpetrator, which everyone knew was Vincent. The papers would ask,

WAS THERE A HIGH SCHOOL RIVALRY
BETWEEN VINCENT DEL MONTE
AND LEONARD KRUZMAR?

The answer was a simple one:

Reality was spun from the mind—political scientists know this, and the Kruzmar vs. Vincent situation made for great speculation. They were labeling Vincent a psychotic, and Kruzmar a close second—one was like the world, the other was spiritual wrath. Indeed, the *LA Daily* was building great sympathy for Vincent, and great disdain for Kruzmar. Clearly, the death of Abacazzia threw the social world into a tizzy, and it had started to become a P.R. nightmare for Lucy and Leonard.

Furthermore, the first string of movies for Lucy Kruzmar were quite disastrous. The romantic comedy about the lesbian golf club, the darling project in Hollywood for the last five years, was attacked by the Christian right and even liberal papers like the *Chicago Times* or the *Washington Observer*—it seemed that nobody liked the way Lucy, without much experience, parlayed her lesbian tryst with the Lovely Linda into an empire where her husband could transform into a woman-man before the whole wide world.

And without criticism?

Furthermore, the board of directors was not terribly happy with the losses and were indeed grateful they had been successful in distributing the ownership of the studio to anyone BUT Americans! The coup was pulled off, but profitability had become the key, and also this sharing of power between nations was in essence an insurance policy to prevent any one country or principal interest from gaining unfair advantage over another. They were able to go purely multi-cultural, especially now that war and terror were rampant in the world. For Kruzmar, this was a good thing, even though he knew about war and terror—rich boy's games.

It made the world closer.

And so actors were brought in from Japan, China, Indonesia, Russia, Italy, Spain, Germany, England, Canada, France, New Zealand, South America, South Africa and Australia—a kind of United Nations of movie making. And why not? The world wanted to see a diverse mixture of talent, and American films were always the ones everybody wanted. It was simply a matter of buying out all the studios in America, and putting at the head the most successful couple to grace Hollywood ever, then portraying everyone as multicultural and unified except Arabs.

"Know why there's no Arabs in *Star Trek* movies?" Kruzmar would joke. "Because in the future there are no Arabs!"

No one would laugh. But he kept telling it.

Kruzmar was the new era—an era of monopoly, centralization, open sexuality and institutional corruption that would forever be called *tolerance*.

It is useless to multiply examples of how excited everyone was, from cocktail parties in London, Rome, Paris, New York and Los Angeles—even Tokyo and Beijing, but it was true: they had finally arrived at the ownership of a propaganda machine, the world had never seen before, with the grandkids of the founders all retired on their yachts, with nobody watching the store. It was a frontal assault, led by the Lovely Linda and the Bank of England, and it fell under the heading that all was fair in war and business. Lucifer was not only alive—he was in charge.

Love was another issue, because one had to distinguish between true love and carnal love. The majority nowadays consider flesh and its fruit, love, and the other kind of love is for losers and idiots.

No, the world no longer sings love songs—the world sings about sex. And that is love.

Soon they'll sing openly about death—for that is true love.

Indeed, however, the future depended on Kruzmar's next move, *Soul Survivor*, the now three hundred million plus budget and the most controversial book ever to be written on time travel and the influencing of history from the future. Actually, as Vincent knew full well, this was the way it was done, but not at the hand of the individual—and to Vincent, the individual was overrated. For Vincent, surrender to the truth and the denial of self was the biggest privilege. Surrender to the flesh and feeding thereon, en masse, was the dream for Kruzmar.

Serena, Milaca and Asenath met at the home of producer Stu Wittie, at the behest of his wife, Bandaloo. She was a beauty queen turned secret porn star, turned corporate cheerleader, whom Stu married simply because Max B. West, of oil and music fame, was dating her. He hated Max because Max, drunk as a dozen sailors, stood up to make a toast and inadvertently urinated on the ice sculpture, saying, "I read *that psycho* did this, so I want to be the first to congratulate him!" Most cheered saying, "That's about all he can do with it!" But derision aside, Stu made a play for Bandaloo by escorting her to the powder room, and when she came out he kissed her passionately on the lips, right in front of the whole mess at the Beverly Hills Hotel, then escorted her back to Max, who was talking tough with Ross Mince, the One-Day-Suit *schmarta* king. Bandaloo was taken, smitten, remarried and already having Stu's nasty kids before the evening was out. It was a self-fulfilling prophecy, and Max's big fall came over the next few months, when Bandaloo sued him for divorce to the tune of one hundred thirty-eight million, got it, and moved into the Quimby house in Bel Air with a new husband—Stu, a Vegas blowout who was pushing one billion in assets. Clearly a marriage made for lust, but most in Hollywood called it license. They were the nouveaux-riche, the brand new chic, they had the spark and the glitz and the sex and passion, but would they ever get their chance?

Now the advent of the Kruzmar dynasty's weakness, and at the behest of Bandaloo, Milaca would sing: "It is fast and furious, the mad and the forsaken...all will fall, all will fall down. You do not kill him, for no man can kill him—only a *spirit!*"

Bandaloo preened with her new compact, and Stu sat back and smiled, saying: "This occult crap is too weird for me." Then he got up and left.

"Oh, he is so silly," Bandaloo said. "He doesn't even know where I put the jewels."

The witches laughed, and they prayed a strange prayer, then all four went into the garden to harvest roots and herbs. "Oh, it be a mighty fine stew, for Stu!" said Serena.

Milaca pulled her weave out of her face, while pulling up an onion. "You will not succeed by force. That will be done for you. Make sure he gets in a few rounds of golf and spends time cultivating."

"Oh, he's going to be a busy beaver socially—guess we won't even have time for sex."

"Not from him, he'll be exhausted. Just keeping up on your behalf," Serena said, pulling up the basil and smelling it.

It was a wondrous day; big puffy clouds laced the sky, a February day, crisp and effervescent—the spring was felt in the loins of the women, and they celebrated with oolong tea and crumpets. They threw some runes, but mainly, they visualized that all men were activated for their own personal benefit—indeed, the root was secure. The root was all men—not something one digs up from the ground. Men are the ground, the root is the power—only a woman has the wisdom, only a woman can make the man have power, and only if a man subjects himself to woman, to Lucifer, to that which is below the earth. "This is called stealing the rooster," said Serena.

Soon they had harnessed the entire world, at least during the tea, and Asenath, dressed in fine pearls and a fancy hat and peasant dress, said: "Those that don't know—which are many—have helped us tremendously through pornography."

"Yes, it's very popular," said Bandaloo.

"And effective," said Milaca. "We need perverts in order to exist—if everyone knew what we know now—the boys that is—then it wouldn't be any fun. Thank God for the humble and the meek!"

All drank and ate and watched in the distance as Bandaloo's younger brother, Frank—a tall, handsome failure—took yet one more tennis lesson from curvy Lisa, an early-twenties tease, with tiny skirt and high thighs, a thong visible to Frank, a control freak, a handler of men. As they watched her correcting him again and again, Bandaloo said: "Speaking about the meek—I've had to bail him out his whole life. You'd think he'd learn by now."

"He is the key to our success, Bandaloo—he is your asset, not your curse."

"But he has never paid his own way."

"He is today," said Serena, observing now that Lisa, standing behind him, started fondling his genitals while Frank sort of froze and acted stupid.

"What kind of lesson is he getting?" asked Milaca, humming the fourth movement of Beethoven's 9th.

"It better be free," Bandaloo said, and all the women tittered.

"He'll never be," said Asenath, coolly pouring more from the pot. "But his soul is captured, and that is where he will stay."

Frank swung the racket back and forth as Lisa stood on the clay imagining him in relationship to her toes, and then a servant to her whole body. "Frank, you're no good at tennis, can Lisa teach Frankie a new trick upstairs?"

"What do you mean?" he asked.

GLASS BACKWARDS

"I'll show you," she said in her athletically determined voice.

NEETXIS

She had been insistent, and Blue had obeyed orders. Not my orders, mind you, but hers—Anastasia's. Yes, she had run away with plenty of money and she had plenty of friends to see her through. Blue was her man, not Vincent, not any man unwilling to submit to her will. He had tried to fight it, but Silas and the Flagellator, on loan, had steered him to her control and away from me. My Lord ordered me to cut him loose, and that is precisely what I did. In fact, anything my Lord tells me to do I do without hesitation. Cutting Blue loose made sense.

We had found another house on the coast, uninhabited, and taken up residency. Oh, the coast, how magnificent it was—Malibu, the great coveted playground of the filthy rich, the pretenders and I dare say, those with good taste, such as yours truly.

The ladies teased Jude for being so...for not being such a man, if you get my meaning, and I found I had to do a lot to steer him away from those who might take advantage. One particular night we partied at the beach cottage—actually, it was quite large, right on the private road in the Colony. I like to call it a cottage because it had this sort of quaint brick yard, with potted plants and a ping pong table, just cozy, you might say. During the party, to which we invited some of our neighbors and a few locals, we met many strangers just itching to be partygoers above all else. We did not invite Leonard Kruzmar, since that would be a form of suicide.

There were the Youngs, the Fragolliers, the Yardleys, the Masteks, and the Finlays—we had a few stray girls off the beach, and a wine cellar filled with *Mohn 'tra 'shay*! I e-mailed Kruzmar a few times via the upstairs computer station; I knew they would consider this a prank, but it went to P.R., I am told—though that was a lie. He liked cat and mouse, cloak and dagger, and in my case the hunted becomes the hunter.

On television, the press had taken a liking to me. This is not to be underestimated. For it cascaded onto the Internet, into print, and all over the globe—a wildfire of P.R., against the wishes of Carl Nunn and all those TV personalities like Larry Cousins.

They were saying that it was a high school rivalry. That I was teased by Leonard and his friends at various times and places, beach clubs, country clubs—and there were witnesses. Honestly, I don't recall his teasing me. I suppose it was a little like Jude, who gets this kind of treatment. Now they're just screaming "Fag" and the like. I got all that, believe me. But I still had, or at least I thought I had, a healthy lust for females. I suppose they had to be a bit young, even illegally so, but they were female just the same...that was the point.

Phoebe Young, the dancer, said, "You look just like Vincent Del Monte—I thought this was Aaron's house, *where is he to-night?*"

Jennifer Fragollier said: "It *is* Vincent! Oh, my God! I love you!"

And she fainted dead away.

So you see the power of the media. Even against Kruzmar's will—my Lord can lift up even the most heinous or the most humble, even the most humiliated.

When I entered the master bedroom, three girls had Jude pinned down and were killing him with sex—I allowed this to happen, but the security issue had begun to emerge. When Jack Yardley got on his cell phone, I told him if he makes a move I would take his head and roll it into the waves. "Now let's all have a good time—you're all helping me get over Anastasia."

When Jude emerged from the bedroom he said: "I'm a man!" and everybody clapped.

Julie, the tanned, daring, young one said, "And he has quite a cock—my husband is just so frustrating to me."

Nancy Yardley said: "I liked his taste—youth tastes different."

"Not bitter," Frogollier said, and laughed.

"Alright! Enough! Now, enjoy the rest of your night!" I said.

That's all I really wanted to do, until I saw what Millicet had cooking—a room full of hostages, and he told me someone had called the Sheriff's Department, and then I saw why we had gotten into this house so easily. There was Aaron, dead in the closet. "Millicet! Why did you kill him?"

Millicet looked around. "Are you out of your mind? This guy was calling the guard house!"

"I thought this was a house we could use!" I yelled, duct taping all my new lovely hostages.

Soon the Flagellator came in with Julie, Jack, Nancy, and others—they were screaming because we had a cache of guns and knives and drills and all sorts of instruments of terror. And they acted accordingly...terrified.

Even Julie, who said she worshiped me, had to have her mouth duct taped. Wondrous thing, duct tape—you remember I told you how I actually duct taped Kruzmar's secretary Giselle to the wall, where she stayed just right until I needed her for self-pleasure?

I felt like spying on Kruzmar's house, but from here it looked dark. Blue and I watched them build the studio, and we stayed at the most luxurious places in southern California. Palos Verdes, Hollywood Hills, Laguna Beach, La Jolla, Del Mar, where we spend hundreds of thousands on ponies. I would wear wigs and beards and various disguises—it wasn't difficult. What was difficult was the waiting; my Lord wasn't calling me in, not calling me back home. The news media was saying all the murders that were occurring around the Southland were copycat killings, and that I had returned to the streets of Phoenix, a bum!

Imagine having to listen to that—I tried to tell them differently and was scoffed at as some sort of pretender!

I had spent time with Anastasia, even though my Lord had sent a message from the future about this Princess Katherine. Oh, yes, I knew her because I was informed by the future. I was informed by Blue, who had a special mission, and I was his controller. I was his singular aspect, his rage, his implementer, his designator, but we could not find him—instead I managed to get quite a lesson from Anastasia, who told me about her eunuch, Blue. "He loves me more than you ever could, Vincent. He loves me in a way that defies logic—especially *your* logic."

"Where will you live, if not for me and my brothers to take care of you, to—"

"Can it, shithead. I went into the future too. Kicked in the head by Dad and all his sorry-ass friends—and yeah, man, you liberated me," she said, combing her ass-length blonde hair that made me want to cry tears of remembrance. "Here it is, Vincent," and by now she was exchanging a carton of Winstons for a carton of Marlboros, which broke my heart, and I followed her up and down the block in Westwood Village, Kruzmar territory I am told, and then she turned and said, "Look I'm only sixteen! You're a pervert!"

People around me started looking and she cracked up. She had money, she had a bunch of kids on the street with her—she had...oh, Lord, *dominion*. She had power; she had more. It had been two years. Shangri-La was just about ready to do that last production designed to bail it out forever. Shredd was inspired by me, let it be known. As I am able to leap to and fro across time, as you have begun to notice, though you thought it was simply part of my own mind. No, friend, it is I who does the leapin' and a'fixin'.

She had lair, she had a place that was unlike any other. What she did to Blue was unimaginable. "Was that really necessary to do to Blue?" I yelled, or screamed, or stated very, very strongly. I stated it unequivocally.

"Who's real, Vincent, me or you?"

But this was not helping me here, in the here and now, now that someone unaware called the sheriff, though all were hostages. How did all these people get here? It was Aaron—he answered the door, we made him invite his friends, because we, that is, me and Jude, felt lonely.

I told him Jude could use a little companionship.

So the helicopters were swirling about, and the FBI was saying something about SWAT—and so I was commanded to take one hostage, Jennifer Frogollier, and throw her head off the roof. That got Special Agent Diane Furles mad, and when I say mad, I mean she hung up on me and said something like, "I'm not playing with you, motherfucker—you're goin' down."

Jude killed every hostage and we sneaked out through the wine cellar. But I got caught.

Yes, I did not slip away, Carl. I was caught, and I was sorry. I don't have to mention that the press was all over and in every way part of the action. Special Agent Furles was not part of the equation, and all they talked about was Anastasia and Blue—and I said she was a rogue, and every effort should be made to stop her, that is, if she's working for herself.

"You killed them all—did you have to do that?"

"What would you do, Special Agent Furles?"

Soon I was talking to Senior Agent Mars, sent in from Dallas, and of course there were shrinks.

They had tabulated, by now, fifteen hundred or so murders, most of which were stated to be random, for the purposes of stealing money, cars—no premeditation, no idea, no clue about the doll. And for Pete's sake, Senior Agent Mars give *me* a little credit!

Yes, there were perhaps a hundred or so—traveling was expensive. I was commanded to take life when I needed sustenance. They did not prevent me from sojourning into the future.

The problem is that I hadn't been completely honest—apparently there were a lot more killings, but they might have been trying to frame me too. Don't forget that these people have an agenda.

Anastasia lived in the back of her friend Janet Bozeman's house. Janet and Anastasia were magic pals; they could cast a spell on a sandwich and melt it to its core. Blue was no match for them, and they kept him in his room, always in a jockstrap, until one day Anastasia threatened Janet, as she desired her very own eunuch.

"Blue, come in here," she said, while Janet had served her a microwave dinner. Blue needed some alterations, it was true—his face was known, but he had grown hair and Anastasia dyed it black. He wore a beard now, and clothing was no problem, as he was fit, a thirty-three waist, a forty-two jacket, a very handsome guy, Janet thought. But Janet got scared.

"My dad's a plastic surgeon, not a shrink—he's crazy."

"He knows his place. He's well trained—he helped me find places to stay for the last year, always going out of his way—and everything got blamed on Vincent. Even what I did."

ə   ə   ə

Everything was a'buzzin', and a'blazin', and a'movin', and a'shakin', and a'travailin'. How could everything come down to this one special moment? Rumors around Wall Street shaved the stock price by half—Shangri-La was no laughing matter, because if the Titanic sank, it would take it all, all.

Clearly it came down to the piece by a writer Hollywood hated, Steve Shredd, with all his misogyny—anti-gay, anti-education, pro-gun, pro-war, anti-John Lennon, anti-Dalai Lama, "...This little S.O.B. hates everybody, and lives in a shack like the Unabomber, what the fuck do you want from me? They like the miserable jerk!" Kruzmar would say confidently to the Board. Only the new munch queen could make it slide, Lucy knew. Though she had no clue about those who engineered her apparently burgeoning fate. No clue of Bandaloo's plans. No clue about the turnabout of the darkest of spiritual loyalty.

Suffice to say, it more than bloodied everybody's nose, but always couched it in the coolest and most exciting stories. Who would not love a time-travel epic, with love, romance, where saving the very earth was at stake?

But who was doing the killing...really? Was it Vincent? Or

was it something else?

There were other traitors, others in the way, Kruzmar knew. He laughed at the idea that Vincent was called by some higher purpose in the murder of one Abacazzia Fontainebleau Himmelman Kruzmar—she had served her usefulness, Leonard knew. There was no further point to her life. At the funeral were all the dignitaries, and even the President of the United States— and that practice of millions into soft money funds was ended, thank the Antichrist.

Thank you, Lucy. For liberating me, he told himself, planning the end from the beginning.

Anastasia served as a nice companion, Kruzmar thought. Sampling Vincent's fancy made it that much more enjoyable. Blue's training was complete. The man on the roof was none other than Father Kruzmar's assassin, and of course Kruzmar knew Vincent would take him out. And of course he knew to get rid of that spy who drove the limo and said more than a few bad things at the craft services table. Now there were dozens of movies and television shows and music videos being shot—and still more facilities than they could ever use. All the major talent from around the world had now moved to Los Angeles. The Chinese were here, the Australians, the Brits, the French, the Canadians, all. All were pouring into each other as fast as it would flow from Kruzmar's grace.

There were many potential enemies. Vincent killed the entire Stern family, the dynasty who owned the major theater chain, and Kruzmar moved in with his own company. He was sent in to rape and plunder the Huntington family, in total. Old money would certainly never do.

The reason this worked was because it gave Vincent and his "friends" a place to live, a place to thrive. Kruzmar would follow up with support, and his senator would cause the FBI to stand down, as they would with great dexterity and purpose.

Leonard was dutiful in pursuing more and more young men, as his appetite for blood and youth grew. And everywhere Vincent went, Leonard was there, cleaning up.

Never did Leonard question if he was serving something higher. Or lower.

Blue would call Vincent on the cell, provided by Leonard. Blue would tell him where to go, and he would say that he was on assignment from the Lord. Blue was Leonard's greatest weapon. While Vincent thought Blue and Anastasia were gone, they were in Leonard's hip pocket, at his pad at the beach, trained by black ops down in Mexico—no one was looking for Blue, and indeed, Anastasia had been controlled from the beginning. Peter Mallard had to be knocked off, as he worked for British Intelligence. Anastasia was beautiful, no question. And she understood the need for men to feminize themselves, and in this she did for Kruzmar what Lucy could never provide.

Indeed, Lucy had lost it—she had not the touch. She was becoming a problem; she was showing signs of instability.

The pre-production party for *Soul Survivor* was the beginning. Held on the airstrip at Hangar 9, it was a smashing success. But Lucy was strange. She wore hair extensions made into a sort of messy dread lock rope dangles—it was a "situation." She had tattoos and the demeanor of the streets. The Vassar English major was ascending to biker chic and bull dyke mean. The Lovely Linda, on the other hand, was becoming the petit ballerina, and as the financiers of the world remained in the background, Linda was the apple of everyone's eye. She was the quest of every woman, gay or straight, from here to Kazakhstan. There were no doors that would not open for Linda, who could remain virginal throughout liaisons and dip-tics. The only one who could crunch and munch at the same time, the only one who could give feminism a bad name even while frustrating men.

"Until all the boys are girls, we've got nothing, luv," she was saying to Brent Stafford, the new star, the soul survivor himself. He liked the idea of becoming a lesbian, "If it would mean I could spend one night with you."

"A good surgeon is all that is required. Leonard knows about that—go ask him."

"Because I'm married and have three kids."

"Wives have to sacrifice in this business," Lucy chimed in, while taking her beau to the dance floor.

Leonard was with the rival star, Tommy and Tommy's new girlfriend, Stacie Richie, the gospel singer or some such. Tommy,

ZEPH E. DANIEL

fucking Tommy—the beautiful boy—was finding religion. "Don't forget your nuptials—you're married to me, I own you," Kruzmar was saying while grabbing two more champagnes, one to throw in Tommy's face, the other to swizzle down like an uppity school girl who's just had her heart broken.

Hermaphrodism was really being a girl, a total—not partial—denial of manhood, and this is what they were seeing. But all he could see was this woman named Lucy, and as the "couple," they'd stayed longer than fifteen minutes, so it was time to vanish into that rarefied, unfathomable Kruzmarian ether. Where the money came from, where the lineage came from, where the Jew and Wasp were wed, beyond all cultural or religious barriers and underscore the bottom line: light. More light. Even more light.

Yes, Lucy was dancing with all the women, who all became lesbians in honor of her...husbands, sure, kids, you bet. Lesbians all. Boys were girls; girls were lesbians—just revenge. The penis in its proper place, a tool to be used, a force to be harnessed, and that was all—all was right with the world, Kruzmar cum antichrist.

Champagne salutes late at night, and no amount of Percocet and Absinthe, no amount of rain or shine, nothing could shake Kruzmar from his spiraling depression. Blue had arrived with Anastasia, who pranced like a star. With her own security detail, she had become something of an anomaly in the black ops market. For one thing, she was trained for multiple personality assassination, and wound up taking over the joint.

Anastasia lifted the party—she was the belle du noir, and had Brent, the big star, drinking out of a jar while paralyzed by her sashaying perfection. Sweet sixteen and holding the hangar spellbound. Commanding as the murderess, a bold stroke for witches, if that meant the exaltation of feminine power on the earth. If that was the glue for the earth—that being seed. Woman's seed.

While all swirled in the evening air, and soft touching of genitals, the under-the-table deals and service contracts, Kruzmar continued to build the prostitution society of the unillumined. Yet even though a functioning agent for the Dark Lord, deceiving Vincent, the press and his wife, deceased mother and boyish concubines, Leonard was very much exposed in a manner in which he hated.

VINCENT A HIGH SCHOOL FRIEND OF KRUZMAR—VENDETTA FOR HAZING AND TEASING ON CAMPUS VERIFIED

Everyone Vincent killed was of his own volition. Even the screenwriter chosen to adapt *Soul Survivor* from SS's vision to Rim Fish's backwards vision, good ol' Pete Mallard, a quitter in death, and now forgotten. Pete, the self-serving MI-6 op, with an attitude problem. No wonder they wanted him and his little friends taken out. One thing about Hollywood—everyone is a spook. Remember that. It's all trauma-based programming by the Queen's little soldiers. It's propaganda...but *this*—*Soul Survivor*—one would have to wonder why, since it glorifies the opposite reason for everything to exist in the first place.

Yet all redounded to the benefit of Vincent and—somehow—to the detriment of Kruzmar. Clearly, this was never the intention, but that's one of those things that makes life enjoyable, after all, it's not *always* a rigged game. Then again, if you always play a rigged game, your actual ability in warfare atrophies...for Kruzmar, one would have to call it entropy.

Now, Anastasia had never met Lucy before. It was time to launch plan B—let the press think it's a big conspiracy to get rid of all the fat-assed execs who aren't worth their weight in shit anyway.

How did Margot really die? Me, Kruzmar told himself. I took him off the streets of Phoenix or Denver or Albuquerque, who the fuck cares? I made him what he is, from the beginning. Mom's witches were nothing but forgotten pieces of silver.

Arriving late, Bandaloo and Stu came to wish Lenny and Lucy a big *mazeltov* and a long fuck you, along with a bunch of real prostitutes—the clean up crew, the vacuum pump for all the money falling on the floor.

"Where's Lucy?" Stu asked as Leonard got him a drink.

"Congratulations on getting "Coup d'État" in the can. The test screenings came back great—we need something, Stu. You gotta give it to us."

"Oh, I will," he said.

Lucy had left with the Lovely Linda, and Bandaloo said, "So

any leads on Vincent?"

Kruzmar waffled a bit, then grabbed a piece of lemon chicken and said, "I own him."

All cheered Kruzmar's bravado, just as Tommy and his born-again girlfriend slipped away.

Tommy Taal, ex-champion surfer, ex-rock star, ex-super-model, made his way down Sunset in his 348 Ferrari, the only yellow 348 in LA with a solid black competition stripe down the center and a solid gold Jesus-fish welded onto the tail where the Ferrari logo had once adorned. He had been paid handsomely by the studio for several starring roles, usually as a bad guy—but he had charisma to go. He had what publicists called the IT factor. He was It.

And she was It for him. Perhaps that was why there was a homeless man lying on the curve on Sunset in Pacific Palisades, around the bend of the Retreat, a multi-cultural religious haven where Satan is enthroned in the form of human idols and robed sunyasins.

Of course Stacie insisted that Tommy pull over. "I know," he said. "I'm not totally insensitive."

"The Lord smiles on us when we're kind—remember the parable of the Good Samaritan. That's how we should always be."

"Stacie," he gazed at her, knowing she was his bride, knowing that everything had to be for the Lord first, as this was an early reward. "I...there are so many things I need to confess."

She buttoned his lip with her finger and puckered her lips, "I love you."

He got out of the car quickly and helped the man up. Vincent would say that this was Millicet, in disguise. He was gruff, and wore a long duster and a pair of cowboy boots—his large appearance and beard made Tommy think of his friends back in Missouri. "Hey, you alright, man?" he asked, and his new teeth sparkled in the overhead lights while the ducks in the pond quacked, disturbed by the human voices.

"I need—"

"Here," Tommy said, and handed him a hundred dollar bill.

But Millicet handed it back and drew a Glock pistol on him, while Jude, Silas and the Flagellator kidnapped Stacie into a limousine that arrived as if on cue. Stacie did not scream, as Jude cupped her face diligently. Tommy was let go but he was screaming and begging.

"There will be no police, sir," Millicet said.

"You're...she's nothing—just a Christian."

"We'll take good care of her," he said.

For Stacie was enshrined in a palace overlooking the ocean, a place secured for some exterior shots for *Soul Survivor*.

Vincent entered, also wearing the same coat as Millicet, and guided her to her feet. "You work for my Lord too," he said.

And she said, "It's you..."

"I would like to confess my sins," said Vincent.

Stacie wept and he tried to make her understand he did not want carnal relations with her and he would not kill her. "I was ordered to kill you, but I was...I will kill them instead," he said, and left.

She heard a few screams and cries out in the Pacific Palisades wilderness overlooking the sea, but then it was silent, and she heard nothing else.

Leonard consoled Tommy and Stacie was returned, but the FBI started questioning her and all she could say was, "My Lord sent him—He is the sword they talk about in the Book of Zechariah. He is...a noble destroyer."

Tommy broke up with her as soon as he understood how she felt about Vincent.

The press began to wonder whether the movie *Soul Survivor* was cursed. First of all, it was subject matter that any good Satanist would want suppressed, for Steve Shredd, or S.S. was a devout reborn as well...and his story divided the world into two parts, Lucifer and Jesus. And basically, there was no in-between. Kruzmar wanted to do it because, "Number one, it's true—and number two I need a hit!"

"You don't just go talking out of school because you need a hit," Lucy screamed at him at 4:30 a.m. after leaving Linda's home-away-from-home room.

Leonard donned his smoking jacket, a bright maroon peacock sort of thing while Albert, the muscleman, waited by the bar in the media room. There were also two young boys, friends of friends, who had to be broken in, but Lucy wouldn't leave the boys alone. "What about Anastasia?"

"What the fuck do you care? I asked you to make hits, and now it comes down to one fucking expensive movie, and we're about out, and this is the biggest—the only—studio in the world, the magnet for every artist from here to Hades, and you...look—"

"How many will you kill?"

"*Vincent* is killing, bitch. I am weeding my garden."

"Right—" she pushed back her dreads and started pacing. She guzzled a bit of Jack and it spilled on her white robe. "Stupid—I've ruined it! Look, Leonard! Did I ruin it?"

"I can't see anything—get the fuck out."

But she kept looking at her white robe with the drying, nearly imperceptible spot and cried out: "I RUINED IT—LOOK, I CAN'T GET IT CLEAN!" And she rubbed it with soda water, and dunked it in the sink. Then she came back and showed Leonard, and kept rubbing it, saying: "I belong to the world—I am the world, and you're not! All the kings of the world—one man to die, but now everybody has to go, and these slippers are killing me! Do you understand why I can't live here—because everything stains! It's like germs! On the walls—like that shit-oil you use—I hate that smell, it's everywhere...I'm suffocating, do you understand, your smell makes me sick! Sick! Why is *he* standing here like that—hey, Atlas, go away—you can rape my husband later!"

"Lucy, you're hysterical." He picked up the phone and dialed—"Linda, come get Lucy."

"Vincent's going to win...oh, yes he is...because he's the messiah—they're talking about him in Europe like he's some sort of saint. And why is my makeup so shitty—look, it's grimy!" She smeared her lipstick on her husband's chest. And she looked down to see Leonard wearing a pair of leotards, and his cock didn't look right. "What have you been doing with your surgeons?"

"I'll show you, if it'll make you calm down."

"Fuck you people—sick! Don't ever call me again!" Albert blurted out. "Run kids! Run!" he said, as if finally coming to his senses.

"You're next Albert—you know too much."

Lucy punched him in the face, as the two young schoolboys and Albert fled out the big wood doors onto the inlaid balcony to freedom. They tore into the morning—never to return again.

"Fear ME! *FEAR ME, MOTHERFUCKERS!*" Leonard yelled out the window.

When Linda came in she saw what Lucy had not looked at since they moved into separate rooms—Leonard's genitalia. He had his little wiener and his little balls, but he also had a slit, a homemade vagina, fashioned from butt tissue.

"What do you think you're looking at, Linda—PURE POWER! I AM SATAN, BITCH!" Kruzmar exclaimed wildly.

It stopped. It just stopped. Like a heart, like a roulette wheel. Like a prison sentence. Over.

"Well, I...I am a pervert, Lucy," said Linda, fondling Leonard's new creation. I see him as the dragon before the world was formed."

Lucy stood agog. She punched Linda in the face, and she collapsed, hit her head on the corner of the marble table and died instantly.

"It doesn't matter. I have all politicians, I have all writers, actors and artists, and I have you."

"YOU DON'T HAVE SHIT, BITCH," Lucy screamed, kneeling down and holding Linda in her arms. "You are insane. I...I can't...I..."

"My lawyer will call you—I'll be in the desert," Lucy said and drove off in her Blue 600 Mercedes.

"Don't let the door hit your big ass on the way out," Leonard said in a Demerol swagger. "I WIN, WHY, VINCENT, YOU STUPID LITTLE PRICK—BECAUSE YOU ARE SO GULL-IBLE! YOU COULD HAVE BEEN LIKE ME—A GOD!—BUT NO, YOU HAD TO FOLLOW ALL THE RULES, LITTLE BOY, FUCKING LOSER! THERE IS NO GOD, NO LORD, OTHER THAN ME AND THE SHIT THAT MADE ME!"

He got on the phone and had the mess cleaned up as the dawn broke. Meanwhile, Blue sat in the hotel room, and was fatigued after giving Anastasia a bath and massage—the chastity belt was definitely helpful, because she rather liked his getting excited but having nowhere to go—she would put off his castration, for this building of frustration was so fulfilling, almost as good as being fucked by Tommy Taal or the queen of pop, Janet Planet, she mused, dozing off to sleep.

NEETNEVES

Carl paced back and forth and simply did not understand that a rather complex web of events through time and space had snared him and brought him to an altar of sorrow. I would change one day, and I would know things that I don't know now. I would understand, finally.

"I want to know what happened!" he demanded.

"I'm in your mind—I know everything," I said, and he cringed. "You don't believe me, wait a while—you'll see the walls change, you'll see the people look at you differently. Come back here at say, 2:00 a.m. and you'll see the changing of the guard. They practice your religion here in the middle of the night."

"Shut the fuck up! Shut up! You got the cover of *Rolling Stone*, what more do you want?" He sat down and was shaking. I told him he should consider lowering his carbohydrate intake. "Why aren't you upset—don't you feel anything?"

"I miss Jude."

"Jude! I thought Einstein straightened you out about your imaginary friends. You're truly pathetic. You want me to believe that Kruzmar set this whole thing up?"

"I'm a sinner," I said. "I need help."

"You bet you do. And you can stay here for the rest of your

life and get all the help you need. Everyone here—"

"No! Now you SIT DOWN AND SHUT UP!" I startled him, I mean he was standing, looking over the photos of me and him and deciding that there had to be a way to stop my fans from cheering me.

"I want to know how the greatest industry in the world fell! I am sick and tired of you...fucking with my mind."

"SIT DOWN, STUPID!" I yelled. He looked at me in earnest, and sat down. Winter was becoming spring. Princess Katherine had gone away for awhile. I just had to tell him the truth, at least try to communicate his particular predicament to him. "Carl, you are not well. You are here. Come back at 2:00 a.m.—you have a pass. It's time you learned the truth."

"You're..." Carl couldn't continue. "You're not fucking with me, right?" he finally uttered, wheezing.

He played with his spectacles, and he looked over his notes, and he got a few cell calls and played around with his computer. "You're crazy, that's what I have to keep in mind. Okay, you claim Kruzmar intentionally—"

"—No, *you* claim it." I was stern, I was standing up, wandering around the library, and checking Radar (my biggest fan) and Pencil Neck at the door, and I was already telling Princess Katherine I was in no way able to stay any longer, unless she would help me."

"Will Princess Katherine help me, Carl?"

He threw his laptop computer at the wall and snapped the screen clean off. He sank his head into his hands and soon there were doctors helping him out. When I looked back into the room there was nothing there, not even me. I was marched back to my cell, and then later I arrived at Princess Katherine's abode on the mountain above the ocean. She said she was no princess and that all of this was for my benefit.

"That's just what I got through telling Carl. What do you think of that?"

"Where's Jude?"

"I don't know. I miss him."

"I think he's gone," she said. "Come on, let me help you."

"Where're my boys?" I said, looking for the past in an uncertain future of her light blue eyes.

She led me in and told me that I was a warrior, and that I would have to stand down. There were others who would take care of things now. For now, I would rest.

Carl arrived at the prison psychiatric hospital complex located in between Mendocino and Fort Bragg, California, approximately two hours driving time from the city of San Francisco. He arrived at the proscribed time, namely 2:00 a.m., and the guard waved the bright yellow Porsche in. He then drove through the security gates and into the gated quadrangle of buildings, of which Vincent was in the east wing, lockdown for the most violent patients. As he made his way down the hall, he noticed indeed that things were different. The staff nurse was friendly, waving him in, as if she knew him—this would not hit him until later.

The lights in the corridor of Vincent's wing were dim, and where there used to be a series of patient's rooms, there was a new wall—a smooth wall with small windows nearly at ceiling level. Multicolored lights were strobing somewhat, with a constant florescent buzz, and inconsistently illuminated the dark hallway. He looked on with intrigue, and amazement—for it was not the same building that he had been in just a short while ago.

"Vincent, you must let me handle this. He is not stable. And you are weary."

Carl looked back at the nurses station puzzled to see that Hillary Pride was indeed there, reading patient's charts, not the least concerned.

For there was no way that major construction such as this could have been completed in a matter of hours. He turned the corner and approached Vincent's room; passing him were two fairly large nurse's aides, a large black man named Rob, and a short, squat but husky bulldog of a man named Fogier. Fogier looked him over and asked, "May I help you find something?"

Carl looked at him and indeed, his face looked familiar, but in the darkened hallway, it could have just been a passing memory. "I'm...yes, where's Vincent Del Monte's room, please. I'm the journalist—"

"We know who you are," Rob said, and took him by the arm. "This way..."

Carl removed his arm from Rob's grip and asked, "What the fuck is going on with the building—what are you using the rooms near the nurse's station for?" He stood back and watched Fogier look him in the eye with a long gaze.

Carl held his gaze, and this was joined by Rob's gaze, and Rob said: "Carl...don't you remember me?"

Carl snapped back. "What's wrong with you? I'm here to see Vincent Damien Del Monte—you might have heard of my work, *Time, Rolling Stone, Newsweek....*"

"Of course we have...and no, the building hasn't changed. It's what it was when you first came to us."

Carl moved around the hall and found the door to Vincent's room and opened it, only to find no one.

Nothing. He backed out and looked at Fogier, who stood at about shoulder height. "What's going on...maybe I'm dreaming, but...where's Vincent?"

"There is no one here by that name, Carl. Now...I want you to come with us, there is nothing to be afraid of, Fogier said.

Rob, the ex-49er's tackle, grabbed Carl and held him up against the wall, while Fogier stuck him in the wrist with a little Valium shot. "Just to make things a little easier."

They dragged him down the hall.

"I don't understand!" Carl was screaming.

"You don't? Surely, you'll understand this!"

As Carl looked at the nurse's station, Hillary, a middle-aged faux-blonde nurse, a bit menopausal, was standing, topless and nonchalant, going over the charts. "Oh," she said, looking at Carl, perhaps reading him: "The hot flashes make it impossible for me to remain fully dressed. It's policy."

"What's policy?" Carl asked, but got no response, as he was now walking between Fogier and Rob—knowing he could not run. But Carl recoiled when he saw that the strobe lights from the little ceiling-high windows was so intense they bathed the whole hall in an eerie yellow and blood-red haze that made Hillary's casual nudity seem even stranger.

It was coming back...there was a price, or something...he had, he was...there was an accident in the Porsche...or something.

When he turned the corner he was led into an observation booth where he was strapped to a chair. Two teenage girls entered the room and removed his shirt and pants, so that he was in his jockeys as the screen to the next room opened. An orgy, it appeared at first, until he noticed humanoid creatures, with erect genitalia double the size of a normal man's erection. In the room was his wife, Elaine, middle-aged and saggy and stressed, strapped to a table with her legs spread, and being raped by every conceivable being in the room. There were vats of blood in the corners where little children were playing, and soon Carl noticed that Rob, Fogier and Katherine were seated all around him. Katherine massaged his cock until he obtained the necessary erection. "You couldn't seem to remember anything...so we tried to make things look like they were back home, the way you used to be, Carl," Katherine said.

He shoved her hand from his crotch, and she smiled. "You can't be naïve forever, this is our world—you always wanted to know what you were involved in...here you are, Carl. Be happy," Katherine said. "I'm looking forward to your being humbled—we all are!"

From behind, Rob's hamhock hands began massaging his chest and Katherine stood up and watched while Fogier knelt down to give oral pleasure to Carl—who howled. Who howled in horror. Rob penetrated him from behind, since the chair had an open hole and Carl's underwear had no back.

Then he cried for mercy. "Please stop! Please! What did I do?!"

"What did *you* do?...YOU need to go back to sleep! *You*, Carl, need to be ordered, as from chaos," Katherine said. "I am *not* your mother. I AM YOUR MOMMY."

"Please tell them to stop."

"Who?" asked Katherine, and Carl looked around, though tied to a chair and a kind of armrest, he could see no one there. He looked down and indeed, he was in his underwear—no violation had taken place.

Then, when he looked up, Katherine was gone, but he could

see into the room that was recently constructed, and he could see himself, stripped to a black bikini thong, watching Elaine, his beloved wife, servicing this line-up of studly men. She was screaming and crying. The last one, instead of sodomizing her, cut her throat.

Carl, watching all this, a holographic image almost more real than reality itself, screamed and cried, and finally fainted.

I am your mommy.

Fogier woke him up with the smelling salts and then he saw something he could not fathom...Katherine standing over him on a table—he was surrounded by candlelight. "It's not real! It's not!" he rejoiced.

Then she smiled, "You didn't think you would go to Heaven, did you, Carl, after murdering your wife and implicating her in a sex crime? A sex-pot, you called her?"

"Am I dead?" he asked, coldly. "Am I...is this...you know...*that?*"

@   @   @

"He can't handle it!" said Kruzmar, in his 3K square foot office, standing in the forty-story penthouse tower build to house all the executives and bankers and child prostitutes hired by the studio for all its sundry and perpendicular affairs. "Whaddya mean you can't find him! Or Anastasia, or Vincent? Or anybody—well, go back to the CIA and I hope your number comes up zippo, you fucking turd!"

Slamming the phone, Kruzmar was literally standing in view of the soundstages where the global epic *Soul Survivor* was being filmed.

Lucy had returned triumphant after Stu's picture tripled the outlay of the hundred mil, and three other films had just broken even with no audience fall off. The music division's profits were up substantially after buying *all* the Christian Gospel recording studios and artists worldwide, to cash in on those who would soon be eradicated off the face of the earth forever. But they could change the message...slightly, and lead them to the true *God*...the reality of the earth, the power of *God* within all creatures...but this was long term. Suffice to say, all those losers buy a lot of religious music when the world crumbles, and the fear of *God* was rampant since the war in the Middle East had gone code red. It didn't help that there were threats daily on New York, Washington—and numerous right-wing extremist threats against the studio for taking the Lord's name in vain while making pictures, which were supposed to glorify, and not denigrate, in the constant supplication of 666 lucre—and sadly, all had a hand in it, the left, the right, and the *Family Fun Festival* (FFF, or 666), led by serial killers in Colorado Springs, home of the evil one parading around on TV in Jesus' clothing, whose job it is to launch protests against pictures with sex in it as a way to up ticket sales.

Already two months into production, *Soul Survivor* trailers were in the theaters and cut for excitement. After all, it was an action-adventure/thriller where a man is placed in the midst of humanity during the tribulation time foretold in the Bible, when taking the mark, or selling one's soul, was a matter of course. But this hero refuses to pay the price for fame, fortune, or even avoiding danger and pain, and glorifies in Jesus. The prophecy always foretold..."they would send a pureheart to lead them, Elijah the prophet, who will show the way for a frightened world, will show there is no such thing as selling one's soul in the first place. A world of pretend, a world of make-believe, irrevocable if you sell out, or was it?

All deception—all one needs to do is turn back to the living God. That the initiation was empty, and of no effect, that it was all an illusion—there is no magic mirror, never was. All just one big amusement park...but for what? What's the purpose?

And *they* could not kill this man, as God promised to deliver His own, even if it were only one—indeed, He would destroy the whole world to save one...or two, or three...

Just like Noah.

He would protect the one against the many. Therefore, there cannot be soul survivors on the planet earth, not if peace and tranquility, prosperity and sustainability were to continue, and thus the hero, Adam, played by the exalted two-time Queenie®

winner Russell Scott, and Queenie® nominee Diane Winston as his consort bride, Leona, seek to inform the world as to their state—the destruction occurs when people wake up to the idea that they are spirit, not flesh—saved by the messiah. Redeemed and unafraid, even of death. They find out that their souls were never "sold"—they were simply lost. Nothing could stop the power of the revolution, but the commander of the other side, a mercenary played by Tommy Taal, is able to cripple the opposition and bring down the assault.

And then, the exalted director, the lauded, three-time Queenie® winner, Rim Fish, because he was unhappy with the message, changes the story, where Tommy Taal, whose character name is Establio, the antichrist, becomes the true hero, and that Adam is nothing more than a Dudley Do-Right loser whose insensitivity to the needs and safety of others places the world in jeopardy. A dark turn, a kind of AC-DC current swap.

"Give the people guidance, not bondage—is it so wrong that women can feed their children? That men can go to work every day? Who is this fucking asshole who wants the whole world to plunge into darkness because he *thinks* they need freedom. They need freedom, alright—away from Adam Signal, and they need liberation by the beautiful messiah of *the-way-that-works,* which is the way of the lead character, Establio. This is replete of course with the dynamic and vital music of our evolving and exquisite culture heralding a new age of cooperation and peace," Fish told reporters in a press conference with reference to all the extremist threats against the studio and himself personally.

Add to that a statement by Kruzmar on CNN, "Who wouldn't want the beautifully talented Rim Fish to take them on a tour of our near future and the threats of extremism. That's why those wackos are mad at us—they would rather hate those who are different and who believe differently. Some of us simply don't need God in order to exist. Sorry, but I never gave it the slightest thought."

One reporter asked Kruzmar, who could not hide himself even with the red cardigan he so loved, the golf slacks and the tasseled shoes, "Mr. Kruzmar, is it safe to say that Lucy's job is still secure, now that she had her first hit?"

Kruzmar almost threw the microphone at her, but instead, with as feminine a demeanor he could muster, said: "You people all have a problem with a woman being in charge...well, let me tell you something—you'd better get used to it. This is a titan studio, the only one of its kind, the first to share film resources with the world. In a true spirit of equanimity and peace, we have sought to provide a place where filmmakers from the whole world over could come to share their visions with the most powerful distribution force on earth, so they can be seen. We in America are so sheltered, it is refreshing to hear and see other ways of life, other political systems at work, and if a few right-wing extremists think that being gay in Sweden is repulsive, then they don't have to see Sven Hilkek's movie about the Stockholm financial community. Perhaps they don't even want to know the way it really is on Wall Street..." Kruzmar instinctively awaits, and gets, titters and outright laughter from the press, who seem, at least in the absence of questions about Vincent, on his side.

Stu Wittie's hit, *Coup d'État*, about mind-controlling the population for the greatest good, along with the Christian rock and gospel sales, combined with the book sales, again in the Evangelical market, which *everybody* hated associated with Shangri-La were successful. But money was money, and now that the religious fanatics no longer had control of their products, it wouldn't take long to change the message of intolerance and paranoia into the correct "family of man" and "tolerance" formats so familiar to any high school student in today's world. "I believe that *Coup d'État* will strike a blow against the Empire of Intolerance, the scourge of right-wing politics and show how love involves putting people first, not some abstract God who hates pleasure. Right? I mean, what's wrong with love? Seems their God hates it. Look what a mess Vincent Del Monte turned out to be—"

He knew at that moment, in the shelter of Sound Stage One, out of the rain, toasted bagels and free coffee notwithstanding, that the press, all the press, every single member of the press would bubble over it all—the illustrious, bootstrapped faces and the forgotten over-the-rainbow losers had all seized on, like a bunch of blistering Piranhas, Leonard Cutlass Kruzmar's strange battle with the most heinous cold-blooded killer of all time, who had developed a fan base akin to rock stardom! And they attacked him for xenophobia, thinking that there is a right-wing extremist under every rock. They quoted Vincent right back to Kruzmar: "I wish him well, I'm not sure you can blame me for his mother. My message is this: 'Leonard Kruzmar, you should not have killed our mutual childhood friend just because he was different, just because it was an initiation into your big money world. All the money in the world isn't worth that boy's life— just because you had to find a way to show 'em that you mean business, that you are worthy of elevation to rarefied heights...still not worth a boy's life—the vengeance quotient is reap what you sow...and from the future I can already see that justice is done. You're a dead man, Leonard, a shadow of yourself. You died with that first murder."

It was a tale of vengeance, the little guy gains the establishment, and every time Kruzmar tried to stop it, they kept spinning the story with headlines like these:

KRUZMAR A MURDERER? MONEY MORE
IMPORTANT THAN PEOPLE?

KRUZMAR VS. VINCENT, SOCIETY'S ENEMY

KRUZMAR A BULLY THUG, ACCUSED OF
KILLING BEST FRIEND

KRUZMAR FROM WEALTHY FAMILY HAD
EASY TIME

KRUZMAR SPOILED RICH KID, NOW
RUNNING HOLLYWOOD

VINCENT DAMIEN DEL MONTE! HERO!
AVENGER! LOVER!

VINCENT DAMIEN DEL MONTE! TRUE
REVOLUTIONARY STRIKES AT THE HEART

OF CORRUPTION!

VINCENT—THE PEOPLES' REVOLUTIONARY!

WE LOVE YOU VINCENT, SCREAM WOMEN
OF ALL AGES

PROPOSALS OF MARRIAGE, DEVOTION
GIVEN TO VINCENT DAMIEN DEL MONTE

Kruzmar tried to stop the press conference to a flurry of: *"Is Ashley Blue an accomplice?"*.... *"Do you know more about Vincent's whereabouts then you're saying?"*.... *"Did you try to kill Vincent at Shelter High?"*.... *"Is Anastasia the next Patricia Hearst?"* *"Did you have sex with Anastasia, who is underage?"*.... *"Are you and your wife...on the rocks?"*.... *"Are you gay?"*

"No I'm not gay!" Leonard said. "That's just the extremist press—I love gay people, I work with gay people, does that make me gay? And what would be wrong if I were gay, or if Lucy were gay? I have a wonderful life, a lovely wife I cherish, great kids—I've been blessed because I can work with people based on their integrity, and not the color of their skin or the orientation of their God-given sex drives! Will you people grow up?! Why is the press so homophobic, so hateful anyway?"

KRUZMAR REBUKES 'HOMOPHOBE' PRESS

VINCENT A MAD KILLER, KRUZMAR STATES

LUCY AND LENNY—VERY MUCH IN LOVE,
STORYBOOK MARRIAGE, SHANGRI-LA
CHAIRMAN STATES

LUCY LOVES LENNY, ANY QUESTIONS?

VINCENT SECRET STAR OF *SOUL SURVIVOR*?

GOT VINCENT?

He could think only of controversy, so in a huff, in a flurry, in a frenzy, Leonard dashed off and disappeared into his work, into his empire, the one Lucy and Linda made *in vitro*, the one made for a song and a tongue, the one made like love, like wine, and like all good things made by the hand of man—beautiful, illusory, and strange. Surely the symmetry, the wondrous management of the new Shangri-La facility should not only earn respect, but be a light unto the world—indeed, Kruzmar's light OF the world. As Kruzmar fashioned himself the world, *du monde*, and needed nothing, not even the press to accomplish his wondrous vision as Caesar the Permanent.

NEETHGIE

Anastasia had enjoyed the Lake Arrowhead retreat, provided by Kruzmar and sustained by his security detail, mostly ex-police, FBI, and a few rogues. She would reel in Vincent once and for all. Anastasia's control of Blue made life much easier for both Lenny and Lucy, especially that one day when a certain reporter committed "suicide." It was Blue who broke into his suite at the Regent Beverly Wilshire, and it was Blue who facilitated securing a semi-automatic Smith and Wesson .40 cal from the street. His control, *Multiface*, a nickname for the White House mole during the *Experience*, as Kruzmar called it, fixed the serial number so it traced back to one Juan Delatosso, who had some extremist talk show. The show sought to expose Lenny and Lucy as corrupt and undeserving, tracing their monetary sources, attempting to expose the truth about someone more powerful than him. Delatosso, in the end, blew his brains out after swilling a bottle of bad rye. The police easily traced the gun back to Delatosso, and suddenly a Kruzmar critic was silenced, and then the rest of the press snapped into line, pretty as a rose stripped of thorns, with the symmetry of a line of pharmaceutical coke, with a countenance harmless as a dove, and no serpentine wisdom in view, not ever again.

Anastasia was guided into a series of training situations, where she was at once *Beth, Annie-Jean, Phyllis, Roxanne* and *Penelope*—prostitute, murderess, heiress, etc. Blue was hers, but Blue was retrained and taught that he was Vincent, for real. And that Anastasia was in love with him, and there was nothing he would not do for his queen.

Carl had found all this quite interesting, quite convincing—he even bought the stuff about the ex-government agents beholden to Kruzmar simply because of the vast wealth growing in their Cayman Islands accounts. Corruption, no. Freedom, yes.

And who wouldn't want freedom?

Who would not want autonomy? The mastermind was Bernstein, this, Carl could not understand. What was Vincent's shrink at Dozier Hospital For The Criminally Insane doing training Blue, Anastasia, and supposedly instrumental in fragmenting Vincent's personality into various parts, namely, Millicet, Jude, the Flagellator, and Silas? What the fuck was Bernstein doing treating Vincent anyway?

It was not a cabal, it was not a gestalt, it was not a panacea. There was no peace in the ranks. First of all, Blue wanted to serve Anastasia, and when he believed he was Vincent, he could do anything—with more support than a military operation! Blue did not want to serve something he felt queasy about, and at Lake Arrowhead all he did was sun himself, drink beer and massage Anastasia—that he liked.

When she was raped by several men and told to look at several multicolored lights, and they were trying for another personality who would poison some exec at a nightclub downtown, she *woke up. She really woke up.* "What the fuck are you doing to me!"

"Look at the blue light! Now!" the voice came from the paisley-papered room.

"Fuck you!" she screamed, kneed the man named Twist in the nuts, then tore from the room.

Truly, Blue was Anastasia's servant, tied to her mind, and so he took the MP-5 machine gun and killed all seven men, first the "friends," who claimed to know Blue from childhood, then the guards, and then the ones who called Blue "Vincent."

They tore from the room to the motor court of the mansion that seemed to have an endless array of rooms bent around the far end of the lake like a castle.

Blue took the Hummer, got it up on the road, then trotted back down to the motor court, dragged all the bodies into the living room, then set the house ablaze—and the 35,000 square foot mansion belonging to Shangri-La Studios went up—all of it igniting the night sky—in jagged flames and black smoke. Even the dock, even the boats. Even the money, even the guns, even the computers, even the books, all the knowledge—it was perhaps even perfect for Kruzmar. It played into his hand perfectly, he would come to embrace it, would come to declare victory.

"I'm sorry—I'm Blue..." he cried in Anastasia's sixteen-year-old arms. "I'm...I'm confused. I...hate Leonard Kruzmar!"

"Me too," she said.

"I'm yours, please *own* me," he begged, and cried.

She massaged his genitals, took his balls in her hands and said: "Whose are these?"

"Yours, my lady. Please take me back, I don't ever want to be Vincent."

"You're much better than Vincent. Now drive. I have a friend to visit, and I want you to take care of something for me."

"Okay...please don't reject me...please."

It didn't help that Kruzmar had planned it all. It didn't help that they were welcomed into the next hotel in Laguna Beach, where Blue was given tranquilizers and woke up in a hospital. Some of the nurses were laughing at him.

"We're preparing you for surgery," Molly, the head nurse said. "You understand what you are about to do?"

"Where is Anastasia?"

"In the waiting room, of course," the pretty nurse named Molly said. The curly mop-top with the fresh, twenty-five-year-old face said. "You should be able to work in a few days."

"What's going on?" he asked.

"You don't know?" Molly asked, as his pubic hair was shaved by an aide named Sybil, who was laughing a bit with her friend, Jane, but Blue only wanted Anastasia.

Soon, she was by his side. "This is what you wanted—I am

ZEPH E. DANIEL

so proud of you," she said. "You understand your place—most people don't. It will be painless. And I'll be there...in fact, I'm going to help...with the doctor's assistance. My friend is with me, you know, the one who gave us a place to stay."

"Are you sure this is right?" Blue asked.

The women all thought Blue was cute, and they envied Anastasia—they knew she was only sixteen years old and already owning a slave. It wasn't fair, as she understood what power was all about. She was in the clear, after all, since it was ascertained that Blue had copycat killed Peter Mallard, Anastasia's father. Anastasia had needed help and got it from relatives, and later from Kruzmar, out of his loyalty to the relationship he'd had with Peter Mallard over the past decade. Kruzmar knew little Anastasia, and even introduced Mallard to Sharon, who replaced Isabelle, Peter's first wife and mother to Anastasia. The press had given Vincent all the credit, and there was open debate about a copycat killer, and so far Vincent's kill ratio was far greater than any mass murderer in the world, many times over. Web sites had sprung up like weeds, all over the Internet, and kids proudly wore T-shirts of Vincent's timeless, if androgynous face.

Sociologically, Vincent had set off a wave of school shootings and knifings unlike any seen in the latter part of the 20th Century or even in the first few years of the new millennium. One thing was certain, children were getting the word, and the word was intimidation—the adults were not trusting children anymore. The fear of God had set in, the animals attacking their owners, and nothing could stop it now. It was Biblical, it was *judgment.*

Kruzmar likened it to the days of prohibition, and envisioned the much hoped for boost in his entertainment budget, in order to calm down the masses. Shangri-La was the answer. Shangri-La was the place to bring a whole world together.

Anastasia used the surgical shears, and the procedure only took a few minutes. In the recovery room she told Blue it was inevitable—she wanted him around for protection when she would date men, now that she was of age. "I want to fuck a lot of guys right now...and guess what—it won't be you!"

They laughed themselves silly as Anastasia held the plastic jar with Blue's testicles floating like rotten candy.

Blue could not talk—Blue could not feel. Blue understood what was happening on some level. He was being dumped; they played a sick joke on him—rejected, mocked, scourged, destroyed. He felt the baldness of his shaved head and stared straight ahead, not looking at her. Because if he looked at her with the long blonde curls and the teenybopper friend and the bouncy little cocaine attitude, he would leap from the fourth floor window.

"And the best thing is...it can't be reversed," she said, laughing with her friend, Cindy.

"Can I see it?" Cindy asked.

Anastasia ripped Blue's covers off to find the stitched scrotum, a flat sack.

"Like a little boy—will the hair grow back?" Cindy asked.

"Eventually. Blue, you weren't really good for much anyway—you have to accept it. Ask the nurse if you don't believe me."

"You castrated him, Anastasia."

"Because male testes have power—that I can use to get what I want. I am a witch...what did you think, Blue? We tricked you. With these on my altar, I can run the world!"

"This way we can get what we want—thanks Blue," Cindy said.

"Well, my gelding...I got what I wanted." She held the plastic jar containing the two clean testicles of one Ashley Blue. Waving them in his face. "Don't follow me, or you die," she said. "I don't need you anymore."

Then Cindy said: "Let's go to Steve's—he is so handsome, and you said his girlfriend moved out—"

"Okay," Anastasia said. "We can try these out, see if we can make him do what we want."

"He's got some really good stuff—that'll definitely help."

"I thought you needed my help," Blue said.

"Oh, Cindy, I forgot—one thing you can do with a neutered guy..." Anastasia was saying with an even colder, more cruel look on her face, "You can get totally like nude in front of him and he's a like a dog or a little boy."

Anastasia took her shirt off, rubbed her tits in Blue's face, while Cindy watched to see if he would pop a boner.

"Nothing!" she said, astonished. Then she took her shirt off and Anastasia looked at his useless member.

"Still nothing."

Blue started crying. "Awwww, is baby going to cry? You are nothing but a baby now, huh? I want you to kill a few people—and we can blame it on Vincent," Anastasia said, gleefully.

"You fucked my life up," Blue said.

Cindy pulled her ponytail around to look at the split ends, then looked him over and laughed. "You can still pee—go ahead, pee...go ahead, we'll watch," Cindy said, getting in on the fun.

The fifteen and sixteen-year-old girls left the room as former detective Ashley Blue sunk into a depression. It was an outpatient hospital, so he would need a ride. But he could not wait. It was a private room with a view of a park—men playing checkers, walking dogs, romantic couples taking strolls. It was a nice room with piped-in jazz and it was temporary...it was catering to transsexuals but he was neutered like a dog. It catered to sex reassignments, transforming men into women—those who could not see themselves as men, those who knew they were not men, and those who could not wield their manhood, those who hated their male organs, but not castration at the behest of a wrathful teenage girl! He had been had—his testicles were stolen, and he was abandoned by laughing teenagers. Payment was made through someone else Blue did not know, and indeed, they had no idea he was sought by police agencies on a secretive basis.

Vincent's fame simply overshadowed Blue's, and with the shaved head and contacts, no one would know—in fact, he had aged significantly since his time with Vincent. Oh, if he had only stayed with him! Oh, how foolish to follow Anastasia—was it jealousy? It must have been, and it led to failure.

The nurse entered and asked him if he had any pain. "None," he said, and she said, "You will—but only if you move around. May I ask, why did you do this? Sex reassignment? Monk?"

When he did not answer, the slim blonde named Tammy, who reminded him of Tanya in her better days, flipped on the television. And live, on the *Larry Cousins Show*, was Tanya! Openly showing her destroyed face, sitting with her doctor.

Openly pouring out the pain that Blue caused to tens of millions of people.

Showing the face that Blue destroyed by pistol at close range.
Openly *open* about *everything.*

Every little thing.

Blue reeled back...horror, shock, confusion, and a faint memory of truth. He started beating his head into the wall. "I...I will solve the case. Vincent, you asshole! I'm you....I'm....no more talking." And that was it—he did not utter a sound.

Cousins asked her, "Tanya, do you think you will be able to ever have relations with a man again after what happened?"

She spoke through a mechanical speaker lodged in her neck. To speak, she simply pushed a button at the top of her trachea, said: "*Nu-oh*, Larry.....I.....first I need a new jaw."

Her mother, Sandie, a lovely, tan mother who looked no older than her daughter, until one looked a bit closer at all the caked-on makeup, said: "First we want to find that sicko who did this—Ashley Blue, if you're out there...you're going down, you sicko!"

Blue froze, staring at the screen, no pain where his testicles had once been.

"Larry," Sandie went on, "we're trying to raise the half a million it's gonna take to do the surgery. Can I tell the people the phone number if they want—"

"Sure, sure—we have a card for it, and we'll show it during the break."

"Thank you, Larry..."

"Thaaank...you....*La-La-r-ry.*"

Sandie broke down and wailed, "She was so pretty! She was just like me."

The number appeared on the screen. Blue wrote it down with the pen from the satchel. "I love you, Tanya—I love you!" he said.

He got dressed, did not care about pain, not one bit. He knew where to go—Kruzmar, this was all his doing, and he'd be killing Blue next, he was sure. He marched across town. The fact that the FBI officially hunted Blue notwithstanding, he used his badge to confiscate several weapons from LAPD impound, one 30-06, and the other a .323 Remington deer hunting rifle. The first thing he did was to take the doll of Anastasia, which had been in his knapsack all along, and slice her head clean off, then he set fire to her and watched her burn while cars ran her over again and again. He hadn't believed Vincent when he said it was the world's most powerful voodoo doll.

Precisely at that time, during the cutting of the doll's head, Anastasia and Cindy crashed head-on into a Brink's armored truck on Sunset and were both killed instantly, rendered unrecognizable. Cindy's Camaro was laid flat, and like them, it was not recognizable as a vehicle.

Blue needn't look back, and he had no need of the news, and he would not need to know. "You will do as I say, Blue," came the voice of Vincent. Blue tried to shake it off, but found himself, with his knapsack full of blades and a golf bag full of guns, heading toward Shangri-La.

ə   ə   ə

Carl woke up and looked around the room at the Heritage House Hotel, overlooking the endless cobalt Pacific. The wind swept his hair, and it felt good to be sipping the room service coffee and crunching down on a toasted bagel. He had several faxes from his agent and also his assignment editor, Bailey Swank, at the Post—everybody wanted more Vincent. And they wanted more Kruzmar. They wanted to know about all the dead bodies surrounding *Soul Survivor*, about how it was filming for over a year with no end in sight—with numerous calamities, like Tommy Taal arrested for murdering the Christian woman. Indeed, all his scenes had to be re-shot.

But Carl had other concerns. When he shaved he addressed them thusly: "I am Carl Wendell Nunn; I am a man, Katherine is my girlfriend, and Vincent is housed twenty miles away in a prison for the criminally insane. He lives in a separate wing, and somehow he knows the mystery of the Shangri-La Studios, as well as the true story of Leonard Cutlass Kruzmar." He knows the true story—but the story is driving me to the very edge of utter madness, Carl told himself.

I'm not a shrink, I am afraid of him, I do feel pain; I think and ponder, and frankly, I'm tormented. As I write about Vincent, I fail. From the beginning, several years ago, even when he was "active," I tried to impress upon the public that this character is a sad chapter in our history, as he has spawned a generation of violent children who feel it is alright to kill their parents. Since my writing, matricide, patricide, and outright mass murder of seemingly innocent high school students and office co-workers has skyrocketed to the tune of 475% in just two years! Vincent, glorified apparently without intent, by me, has given rise, indeed has fomented a zeal for hatred and murder that has reached epidemic proportions. Or was it me? And who am I, Carl Wendell Nunn? An ace reporter? A novelist, playwright, amateur painter, sailor, tennis player? Jerk-off? Vincent has shattered my ability to dream my own dreams, as I believe I am somehow lost in Vincent's mind, along with him, and can no longer get out, as it were.

It was bad enough when the first series of stories in the *New Yorker* won literary awards, plenty bad enough that while lecturing at NYU I was asked about Vincent, nothing but Vincent—what he wears, who he likes, dislikes, what his mother was really like; and how much they hated Kruzmar's attempt to buy his way into Hollywood, and how he must have had it coming to him. It was terribly frightening, for example, that no one felt sorry for Kruzmar's mother. That no one felt sympathy for Leonard and his wife Lucy; no, all they wanted to do was tear them down and gossip about their impending affairs and pending divorce, the vitriol, the incendiary moment, the false and stolen power, the lie of Kruzmar—how could it come to that while writing about a serial killer? They wanted to gawk, they wanted to be voyeurs, they wanted to eat it daily, massage it into their feel-good memories, and Vincent was always saying the key was in remembrance. And they were all in my memory, before I could say, good morning, how ya doin'? What's shakin'? Howzithowzit? Before I could put down the morning wood, everything had happened, like initiation, like script, like fortune telling backwards...from the aspect of certainty. No, you should not ever listen to Vincent—and don't think I'm throwing in the towel, just because I lost my way. Just because I...I need to know so badly that my life depends on it, and yes, I now sit at the throne of Vincent Damien Del Monte and wash his feet...whenever he needs me to.

Whatever Vincent wants, in whatever way he wants it, I give it to him! Me! Motherfucker Me!

MacDonald, Joey, Stoddard, Monkey-breath, you boys know me...those wild days—and nights! Down at *The Breeze*, remember that? When Solty was our mentor and Diana with the big tits caused our compasses to collide! Oh, how I remember those times when...when it wasn't the End Times. I'm not a religious man, by no means. A fallen everything: lost Jew, stupid Buddhist—my buddy Gere couldn't convince me, I even tried to get into the idiot brigade of the born-agains, you know, Messianic Jews. Nothing. But now I seem to remember things I can't explain, nor can I ever justify. I remember being there now with Vincent when his nemesis Leonard Cutlass Kruzmar would lay in wait for nerdy innocent Vincent, who never did anything wrong, and didn't even understand there was nothing wrong with that. No, Kruzmar was going to make it a prerequisite for the peace of mind of Vincent, that all good boys would join the bad boys, but would forever be called the good boys and the bad boys would forever be the good boys. Oh, how Vincent held sway while others blew their brains out, crashed their cars into poles mysteriously...and got stabbed for no good reason. No justifiable reason. And I was one of those doing the stabbing—I'm sorry! God, am I sorry! I wanted to be accepted. I wanted to have a job! I wanted to make up for my insecurity, my lack of dashing male prowess, my...I wanted to get that pretty blonde bitch too—how could I compete unless I had friends, and how could I have friends unless I tried to humiliate and destroy Vincent everywhere I found him?

He was the wrong one to mess with, for he disappeared into a hard life and destiny brought him back and now what was sown is reaped.

That one day he told me...that one day he was under hypnosis, when we asked him what happened, and he said:

"They stole my clothes. The gym teacher told me to lie down for a massage after track practice and they locked the doors, and after he hurt me, they all called me a 'homo' and laughed about it. None of the girls would come near me...they said they didn't want me in their clique. They said I was the most likely to fail. My teachers told me to jerk off and I asked why? They said I was a girl, and my name ought to be Mary; and then they only referred to me as 'she'—like, 'we don't want her' around. Get rid of 'her.' Things like that." He sat silently in the chair waiting for the next question without any visible emotions.

"How did your high-school experience make you feel?" I asked.

He turned and said: "I'm a child of God."

@   @   @

Carl was full of himself, not knowing that everything was through remembrance. The walls had returned to normal; and he watched in wonder as I jogged around the track, followed by my contingent, and he knew that he, Carl, was not the patient, and he knew that he, Carl, was not the culprit, and he had no memory of my continued liaison with Princess Katherine, the beauty of the future. His face was full of remorse and so he had forgotten the truth of his incarceration and where he truly was. A second chance? Hardly.

He wanted to know about things no one knew, and he wanted to paint a picture of some sort of rivalry with one Leonard Cutlass Kruzmar, or one Lucy Gabrielle Kruzmar, and I forgot to tell him I wasn't done with Blue just yet.

First of all, Millicet, Jude, Silas, the Flagellator and I were back having lunch in a room full of ghosts on Hollywood Boulevard—the spoils of war were many. We had transportation, weapons, money, and we were having a brilliant fellowship, oh, my friends. The things of life I had never known to be so sweet. The ancient waiters were saying, "He looks just like him," but I was under no alarm.

For there was a convenient exit in the back, and another car, this time a new Mercedes 500 waiting for us. Millicet drove and the waitress was a nice gift for Jude, who told her he would not harm her. I began writing poetry to my Lord, who was in the future—or at least out of the country—where I could be but got lost in the heat of the moment as we cruised down Motor Avenue, where I found Blue just as I left him. Of course I knew about the doll and the fate of Anastasia. That was why I had the future Princess on my side, and (Carl would hate to know) this was Katherine. My consort in this life. Whom I had wondrous sex with by hijacking Carl's rather aged body.

But it was mind—sex. Sex *IS* mind. They communicated all through the hive with the use of the penis phone and the penis envy—the phone system, dialing for dollars and forging the straight path into the future. Oh, enemy. Mine.

Carl was *jackable*, and I was using him from the past when I called the press from the deceased woman who had owned the car we were traveling in, and I said, to a reporter at the *La Daily* (who was my friend, by the way), "Leonard had inherited millions, and all the contacts and the keys when he stabbed a boy named Whitley Marcus in the heart, but they made it look like suicide."

My word, there was a frenzy after that! Was there evidence that he had killed Marcus, my friend and fellow misfit, fellow birthright-blown victim? Fellow citizen. Fellow who is good. They grabbed a dog bone and ran with it all the way.

Leonard made an appearance with Lucy on the *Larry Cousins Show*, advocating human cloning and genetic manipulation, but Larry wouldn't let Kruzmar alone when he said: "So tell me about your relationship with the suicide victim, Whitley Marcus.

"Larry, I thought we were here to discuss the benefit of cloning and genetically ridding the human race of disease," Lucy said indignantly, and by now her hair was in dreadlocks and she still wore those tough leather jackets. Leonard was wearing a semi-see-through silk *blouse*, unbuttoned to show a little cleavage; his hair was weaved, streaked, permed, and his nails were perfect.

"Larry, that was twenty-five years ago," he said.

Cousins adjusted his glasses, looked out at the television audience. Took a few calls, and every single one, without exception, was pro me, Vincent Damien Del Monte, and against Lenny and Lucy—and against the movie *Soul Survivor*.

Several Christian extremist groups were up in arms about the message, i.e., not presenting the Gospel of Christ, and the Satanists (corporate welfare babies) were against it because it revealed a secret that made them feel unmasked. So Leonard could not please anyone.

"If there was nothing to it," Larry was saying, "then can't you tell us a few details of your relationship with Vincent and this other boy, Whitley Marcus?"

They went to a break and Leonard threw his microphone off and started screaming: "How dare you humiliate me and my wife on international television! You were told to help out. See if you ever work again."

"Heaven forbid I might be intimidated—you people are a dime a dozen—I'M STILL HERE!" Larry howled, unafraid.

Lucy and her makeup artist, a glitzy, petite woman named Belle Époque, dainty, feminine and in lust with Lucy, helped the wounded fake-biker who had gained a few pounds in the upper arms and legs. She was strong, but Belle was the one holding her up, all the way to the second limo, after Leonard's car arrived and he was gone.

The Board had their obligatory emergency meeting the next day, and no, they would not admit Lucy to the Board, as Leonard already had it stacked. But this was the first time they met *in absentia*, that is, without their chairman.

"Now this is what I want to hear about," Carl was telling me. "Please...Go on." He was confident that he actually had a clue how to break the cycle of fame and fortune that had come my way.

NEETENIN

"This is just incredible," Carl was telling Katherine while enjoying caviar, shrimp and champagne overlooking the San Francisco Bay at the Fremont Hotel. He had finally gotten the nerve to ask her a question.

Katherine was transformed in the Halston cocktail dress Carl bought her at one of the shops adjacent to the lobby. Katherine, changed into a cycle of design beauty from the facials and makeup artistry and the hairdressing, the gym workout and steam, a new person? Hardly. She was Katherine, beholden to Vincent, who was present behind Carl's eyes, but there could not be more reality foisted upon his fragile mind after this—how long did it take to explain the death of his wife Elaine?

"Tell me about Elaine," Katherine said as he nibbled on her neck, with the glistening city below.

"You look so beautiful—that's an ocean away, why bother with it now," he said, loosening the tie and hoping to put off speaking at the Pacific Journalists' Conference.

And the call came—Katherine answered, "Carl Nunn suite."

"Where is he? It's twenty minutes to his speech."

Carl took the phone and said, "Hello...Smitty, I told you I'd be there. Keep your pants on."

He pulled everything together and then opened his drawer and found the Holy Bible placed by the Gideons. "What kind of fucking idiots believe in this crap?"

Katherine remade her eyes, remade her lips, and remade her mind in that moment and said, "Vincent comes from God."

Carl nearly choked on his toothpaste.

When he arrived at the podium, to a reveling applause, he said: "I want to tell you, I was just consulting the Old Testament and came up with this line of scripture: 'All is vanity.' It is amazing when you think about it, what are our careers? Do they make up for what happened in the past? Do they open the way into the future—they make us feel good, is that it? The Pulitzer, the Hemingway, the New York Journalists' Association—what I can tell you is this: 'All is vanity,' as Solomon says in the Book of Ecclesiastes. I never gave the Bible much thought, and indeed, found the Gideons' Bible placed in my drawer by my bedside an insult. I'm a Jew. Another great friend, Dr. Marv Wali, is a Muslim, and some of you here worship Lucifer."

There was a pause for laughter and applause.

"I guess the Bible doesn't do us much good when we sell our souls for fame and fortune. But Solomon had it right—whatever we do is vanity, and someone will come along and take our place just as soon as we lose our step, and they'll do what we did, and that will be vanity too. In the end, friends, the fool and the wise man are equal, sad to say."

The applause was frenzied, as he plagiarized King Solomon for every bit of wisdom he did not contain himself. He ended with something like, "taking care of our fellow man...now *that* is not vanity—we should all be concerned for the welfare of others, and that is called love. And *love* is the only thing worth living for. That means, sometimes, giving back, and giving in...I don't mean integrity, but simply seeing it from the other person's point of view, whether it's religion, politics, homosexuality, women's rights and the right to choose—being more understanding, tolerant and loving. That is what we must strive for as journalists, so that the truth is represented and helpful to those making their way through this very rocky and dangerous place we call our world."

The applause never died down, and it was one more step into immortality for Mr. Nunn, replete with Saint Katherine *pretending* to be his biggest fan.

Carl and the crowd partied until all were tired of the exposure—and when he woke up Katherine was gone. There was a note that said: "Hello, Carl, this is your friend…Vincent. I have taken the Princess with me for the time being. I am still in the past, doing all manner of things that you won't remember. Interview me if you must, but my bride to be and I are taking a holiday."

Betrayed? Watched? Was *she* some kind of spy—an agent?

The drive back up the coast was difficult with all the distractions, particularly with some announcement that Larry Cousins was going to interview both Carl Nunn and Vincent. There was just no recollection of that, except for that time when Katherine put some sort of drug in my coffee, and I thought I had died and gone to Hell, Carl thought.

Arriving at Katherine's place was to no avail—as she was not home. Carefully, he pulled the screen door open. He looked around the bucolic paradise surrounding what was little more than a shack on a bluff overlooking the ocean down the meadow way. A green truck pulled up next to his bright yellow turbo Porsche. Two men in lab jackets got out as Carl was about to break the door open.

He watched them with incredulity. Dutiful. Coordinated. When he looked closer at their faces, he noticed something strange—they had no mouths…not that he could tell from a distance of perhaps thirty-five yards. They went around to the back of the truck and off-loaded some sort of portable generator with a cord attached. Before they came closer they zipped up their jackets, which hid half their seemingly *cloned* faces from view. Both men had standard-issue bodies and the identical semi-shaved hair cut. Each pulled a hood up over their heads so all that was showing was an eye-slit, and now Carl knew these weren't lab jackets.

He started away from the property, away from his car and especially them.

As soon as he was a hundred yards from his car and the truck, as far as the path through the tall grass would go, he noticed they had set up a large spotlight in front of his car and aimed it at him.

Suddenly, a thundering voice rattled his head and shocked his ears to ringing. *"Carl, look at the light,"* it said, in a computer generated sort of voice.

A sound like a train horn but close, as if coming up out of the ground, shocked his eardrums beyond the ringing sound—it was sheer pain. "Okay! Okay! Stop!" he yelped in pain and turned toward the light.

They shone it into his face—a blinding orange light that toppled him to the ground.

When he woke up he was on a gurney in a hospital. The two lab technicians rolled him lazily down the hall—and he recognized them from just a moment earlier.

When he looked up he saw his wife Elaine holding Katherine's hand for support. They all cried and he wondered just what he looked like, forgetting entirely in that moment that Elaine was dead. Forgetting in that moment entirely that he was altogether helpless.

He was wheeled into a room with a view of a setting sun and when the doctor came in he started smiling. He too had his nose, mouth and chin covered with his white coat.

Small children clamped Carl down to the bed—arms only. He felt a shooting pain in his legs, particularly his calves and feet. When the doctor unveiled himself, Carl nearly leapt out of his skin...

For what he saw was somehow buried in his subconscious, just waiting for a certain moment before arriving at the gate, and moving through the turnstile of destiny. And moving despite the death-grip of life.

For what he saw wasn't just the dense fact of flesh and form—a name and a face.

What he saw was not going to intimidate him.

Seeing that it was Vincent, and Vincent only, who was the doctor.

For how long? Was it a dream? Then he wanted to jump up out of that awful bed and strangle him once and for all—but he could not.

For when he looked down he saw that his calves and feet had been removed. What remained were simple, bloody stumps.

"Oh...oh, my...oh, shit, oh fuck! Vincent, you motherfucker, what did you do to me?!"

He had not the heart to tell him in that moment that Carl Nunn had taken out fifty pedestrians in the Bay area before intentionally crashing the Porsche into a trolley car, in a miscalculated suicide attempt. A miscalculated lie is what he had apparently been living since being in the coma.

Katherine came in, the *head nurse* of all things. And Elaine was only allowed to visit for a moment. Of course he was restrained—because he was under arrest, and he was on his way to the Dozier Hospital For The Criminally Insane...he would be there as a patient.

"Vincent...you...you're not really the doctor—this is some sort of dream," Carl muttered, incredulous and meek.

Elaine, crying, left the room as Katherine shot him full of Demerol.

"How long have I been...out?" Carl asked, in a moment of lucidity.

No, there was never a moment of lucidity.

It was not a dream. He had *been dreaming*, but this was no dream.

"A month—you lost the limbs the first day...lost a lot of blood. In the MRI you just woke up suddenly and we were all amazed. Do you know what happened?"

Suddenly, there was a memory—it was becoming more real. "I went into a rage and...oh, my God, what have I done?" Carl moaned, and wept. The emotional pain of that revelation tore though him and silenced him and he stared straight ahead and spoke no more.

Katherine said: "I'll call Dr. Bernstein."

Dr. Jonas Bernstein was one of the most prominent psychiatrists on the West Coast, and a specialist in criminal insanity. There were a dozen or so professionals in the room when Carl was recounting his testimony, including his lawyer, Frank R. Bunting, who had been involved in everything from the

Unabomber to Chuck Bailey, who killed nearly twenty-five people, men, women and children, before being caught outside a 7-11 in Atlanta.

Bernstein wore the tweed, had a mustache and smoked good cigars, perhaps inspired by pictures of his idol, Freud. He loved his profession and was the poster boy for sanity on every show from Oprah to Springer to Larry Cousins. He and Carl worked together on the Bailey case, and Bernstein, et al, agreed, the pressure just ate Carl up.

It made sense at this point that he would have seen his doctors, the nurse and others around him as culprits.

At least he had now accepted all of this.

Until Millicet and Jude entered the room, unrecognized by Nunn. Millicet looked down and said, "I'll bet you thought we were just machinations of a very active imagination, sir. My name is Millicet," the bearded bear of a man stated unequivocally.

Jude unmasked himself, out of surgical garb, and into an Arizona State sweatshirt, and said, "I'm Jude—please do not get the wrong impression...I am very loyal to Vincent."

"You...you're not real—I don't know where I am...but I demand my nurse! I want my nurse!"

"Shut your trap," Millicet said. "We're going to get you out of here."

"Oh? How?"

Jude and Millicet looked at each other and smiled. This was no ordinary smile, but one Carl recognized from his fraternity hazing days.

"Come on then—you get what you deserve!" Millicet shouted, as Jude had unshackled him.

"But I can't walk! Doctor! Help!" Carl yelped and stammered in vain but to no avail. Millicet was strong enough to hoist him out of that bed himself. Jude dashed to the window, eight floors above Madison Street, and as the last sliver of sun set over the calm bay with a billowy fog ready to return, Jude and Millicet let out a cheer: "The wicked witch is dead!"

With that they shoved one Carl Nunn out the window, and screaming, bloody stumps and all, to his concrete fate.

PULITZER WINNER CARL NUNN LEAPS TO
SUICIDE AFTER KILLING 51 AT FISHERMAN'S
WHARF

PSYCHO CARL LEAPS TO DEATH

THE END OF JOURNALISM AS WE KNOW IT?
CARL NUNN LEAPS TO DEATH IN
SAN FRANCISCO

INTERVIEW WITH SERIAL KILLER WENT TO
HIS HEAD

But he did not lose consciousness, no. He woke up on a cot in the hospital, slammed his eyes towards his feet, then went to the caged nurse's station to ask what had happened.

She, Nancy, told him that he needed sleep, so she gave him a room to sleep in. He had told her he was on a deadline for the new article that connects Kruzmar's cruelty directly with Vincent's demise—but he had to prove that Kruzmar then hired and trained him as a killer.

"Where's Vincent?" he asked.

"In the gym—with Larry Cousins. Isn't that exciting?"

Carl looked at his feet while talking. "I've just had the most awful nightmares. I'm not feeling so well lately, Nancy."

Nancy looked around, and offered him some Tylenol, but Carl refused and took a cup of coffee instead. He dialed up Katherine on the cell and got her machine: "Hello, this is Katherine...what a beautiful day! Praise the Lord. Leave me a message and I will return your call."

Nothing unusual, so Carl answered: "Hi, honey, it's me. You left me perplexed at the conference, and I...well I...I'm, I love you, I think...and that was no way to treat someone you love, unless of course, you don't." Carl was befuddled. How could he not be? Reality had slipped him a *Mickey*, and the truth serum was wearing off—but the lie was much more truthful than the truth at this point. Especially considering that Vincent was being interviewed by Larry Cousins and Katherine was waiting in the wings for him. She could barely hold back her gushes. When Carl caught up with her, to confront her, she shushed him. The stage manager pulled him back, and at the break, Larry said, "This is too fucking weird for me—but it's a twenty-three share!" They brought Katherine in to sit next to Vincent. Armed guards surrounded Vincent, whose hands and legs were chained. When he, Vincent, saw Carl he said, "Carl, how do you like being dead now?"

Carl reeled back, not knowing what to say or how to respond. All were looking at him and then Étienne, the makeup artist, said, "Mr. Nunn, we're ready for you in makeup."

"Why?"

"Because Mr. Cousins wants you on the show."

"Well, I can't do it."

"Okay..."

After she left the staging area of the gymnasium, two men in lab coats came over and revealed to Carl that they had no mouths—indeed, were the very ones from Katherine's place, from Katherine's nightmare place.

Then he heard: "Carl! My friend! Come on and tell people what you know—give me the questions, I won't hurt ya, I promise. For old times sake, man."

It was the voice of Larry Cousins, and it snapped Carl's eyes about, and when he snapped back the other way there were no lab coats about. No lab coats in the gym. Lots of technicians and monitors and lights and makeup booths and a few production guys playing hoops between commercials—

—and the thirty seconds became fifteen, and he stood up, right up into that Larry Cousins' post open heart bear hug. It hurt, and he looked at his feet again. "Ouch. Take it easy, Carl. By the way, you don't look too fuckin' well, man," said Larry.

Carl looked at Vincent, then back at Larry, while Larry fed the question—camera two was moving in awfully close. "The thing that makes me sick is that this guy is so damaged, and so in need of help, but the audience, the readers, indeed the world has made him into a sort of sicko-celebrity. And I want to apologize for that, if I had any part in it."

Larry smiled, and said: "Of course you didn't—to blame Vincent here for the escalation of school shootings and domestic violence would be quite a stretch, wouldn't you agree? Portland, hello."

The voice of a caller hit Vincent like a ton of bricks. "Hi, this is Anastasia—"

"What's going on?" Larry asked off camera to his screeners—"You're fucking fired!"

"Anastasia," Vincent was saying, "who was your father?"

"Peter Mallard, the screenwriter, who was under contract to Trundle Pictures and that Jerk-off Kruzmar! And he killed my dad!"

"Yeah! Yeah!" Vincent said. "You see that Larry, you see that? She's on my side. Anastasia," Vincent said looking into the camera, "you're like me—we're both in the future but they don't know it. They're already dead but they don't know it—but they're getting a glimpse."

"I miss my boy Blue," Anastasia said.

"Yeah, I miss all my boys, Blue included," Vincent said.

Larry looked at him, smiled and said: "Would that be Millicet, Jude, the Flagellator, or Silas?"

Bernstein, who had been silent, sitting next to Carl and sizing him up quite heavily, interrupted—"Larry, please don't mythologize his delusion."

"But everybody out there knows—"

"I can't take it!" Carl said, falling into himself.

Larry called for a hard break, but confusion reigned. Carl fell to the floor and started having a series of grand mal seizures; Radar and Pencil Neck got Vincent and took him from the stage in the gym and escorted him away from everyone else. The guards present drew their weapons and Bernstein was hanging over Carl under the glare of stage lights. *He's in my mind! He's in my mind! The world doesn't exist! The world doesn't exist!*

YTNEWT

Carl woke up in restraints, in a room, in a facility, in a situation not of his making. *Fifty-one pedestrians?* He noticed that he had no feet and no hands, just stumps. He smiled about the memories of depravity in New York, of how Elaine was used for sexual gratification and then how Elaine was murdered. He took relish in it. Katherine and Vincent dressed in lab coats fed Carl baby food while he watched yet again the orgy where Elaine had been enticed to a torturous death.

Or was that *fucked* to death?

Carl knew this was a dream, somehow, but the key was...a glimmer of that turbo Porsche off the cliff, with Katherine driving...*was that real too?*

It had all happened so fast, Elaine's death, followed by his slamming—was it a rental van? —into fifty pedestrians at Fisherman's Wharf. But *who* supplied the van, and the *idea?* It was Vincent—*because he beat me,* Carl was thinking.

"We're both dead, Carl—it's a time of reckoning. You can come into the future with me to serve, or you can stay here and things will get worse," Vincent had said.

As Carl tried in vain to remember what he had told him, he

caught the last act of Hollywood, the final death throes...without knowing the source of all his troubles was someone equally beyond this world. Below.

It was Blue, Ashley Vale Blue, Carl remembered now, who infiltrated the studio during the filming of *Soul Survivor*.

It was Steve Shredd, or S.S.—and Larry would never call him that—who said, "This is a story about doing what's right. This is the last story that will ever be told before they lock it down and Judgment Day comes. I am calling on everyone who can hear my voice...throw away all music and images of a sensual nature...it's for Peggy, Joe, Sue, Parsons, Figureheads, Butterworth, Anti-Mater, Dues Payer and *Aloe-Vera*—gotta watch that bitch!—but you just can't trust what the Dark Master can do with ejaculate—"

"—That's it, cut him off," the short, cigar-smoking director shouted in the production truck in the parking lot.

Shredd stands, looks over at Larry Cousins, who cowers behind his dynamo girls, Étienne and Michelangela (who was really a boy). "Fucking jerk-off! Didn't anybody ever tell you to grow up!"

"Where do you think we are, Larry? You like it, you dumb motherfucker? Don't you ever question reality, the honeycomb of it all?"

"Go back to your Bible-thumping white supremacy bullshit and don't you ever come back," Larry said indignantly while squeezing Étienne's ass with his pincer-like grip.

"Don't you want to know why the most expensive movie ever made is being sabotaged?"

Larry sat back, waved off his prized makeup and blow-job detail and said, "Well, yeah. I'd love to hear about that. Okay..." Larry looked in the camera and said, "Get Steve something to drink—we're going to finish this piece of shit."

Blue wasn't alone in climbing over the wall, was not alone in his infiltration—he had plenty of help from Vincent's men. Help that former detective Ashley Vale Blue did not want. He was quite tired of seeing Vincent's face plastered all over newspapers and dumb bitches holding up picket signs against the studio with Vincent's face on it, statements of devotion and self-sacrifice—of total commitment. He was tired of hearing about Steve Shredd calling Vincent a national hero, and indeed, he at times knew Shredd *was* Vincent, or had, perchance, projected Vincent, and he knew Vincent was like the doll, very powerful, but not necessarily real. Yet the entire world seemed caught up in the rivalry between Vincent, who should be stopped and killed, and Kruzmar, who was just another depraved earthbound fairy.

It was Vincent, and not Anastasia, who took Blue's most precious possession, and *somebody* would pay—the whole world would pay. If they kept on attributing Blue's kills to Vincent, which continued to fuel Vincent's fame, then he'd just have to figure out a way to do something...something that now seemed inevitable.

The thing about the new Shangri-La, at least from Blue's perspective, was that it was massive. They were even going to rename Culver City Shangri-La, as most of the housing in the area was leveled to accommodate what an LA reporter called, "The Whore of Babylon."

When they operate with impunity, what is that? When there is no law, what is that? When there is no God, what is that? When they are cut off and it's every man for himself, with consequences bendable by mind, what is that? When murder is lauded by society, *what is that?*

After all, they might have taken Blue's testicles, but not his mind. He could see Kruzmar and Vincent as two sides of a very ugly coin, the coin not of the realm he was born into. No way.

And a whore it was, Shangri-La—so many places to hang out. Blue felt right at home, as his face was not well known, especially with a wig and beard, as his wits were about him, even more now that he could not even think about sex. From the day of his castration, Blue had lived off Kruzmar, eating his food, sheltered near his productions on various soundstages—the perks were amazing, and he liked that idea. He knew who would get the blame for it, and he knew that he would disappear. It was abundantly clear that Kruzmar and Vincent had some kind of ego/alter ego kind of thing happening, and the whole world was in jeopardy because of it. They, not Vincent, not Leonard, but *they* probably put Anastasia up to the cruel joke of castrating him and then ditching him. When he saw her picture on the cover of the *LA Daily*, he realized the doll was real.

If the doll was truly real...then Vincent was unreal. If Vincent was unreal, then reality is what I think it is—exclusivity of purpose, singularity of mind, that is me, Blue told himself, perched on the scaffoldings high above the interior set depicting a secret government facility used for mind control in Shredd's book.

Blue would thank his backwoods roots now, for Achilles could not have yielded up so completely. Vincent, credit? Fine. As long as one of them goes down. As long as justice is served.

Yes, he had the high-powered WWII M1 30-06 Garand rifle thanks to a shadowy figure who must have popped up on the street when he looked at the yellow light. He remembered him as *Multiface*, named apparently for his face-changing capabilities. He did not remember garnering a beard and a wig, but he had them. He also had a cot and some foodstuffs in the corner of the vast scaffolding, a small city hoisted in the air. His "area" was behind a partition with a trick door, and it seemed completely prepared for him.

He felt rage, as he looked through the site. He felt nothing but incendiary passion, vengeance! All his life, all his dreams, all his hopes *gone*, cut off, stuck in some sewer, forgotten doll, no regrets, not anymore. No, he, Ashley Vale Blue would strike a blow against the empire. Oh, he was under no illusion here—he was dead meat.

Rim Fish swaggered around behind his bank of monitors while his director of photography set up the shot where Russell Scott, who plays Mumfield, discovers his friend and confidante, Gloyall, played by Diane Winston, incarcerated, as they are preparing to take her soul and replace it with one of Satanic origin. At this point, Establio, now played by the illustrious Thad Hackworth, attacks Mumfield, who is responsible for sheltering the soul survivor, the lone nut who single-handedly brings a killer nano-virus to earth called God's wrath, which takes all biological life and replaces it with machines who have God's favor.

In Rim Fish's eyes, this was the gravest travesty, and he of course harbored the total opposite point of view from the author, S.S.

"Boys and girls, it's just theocracy versus humanism. I'm human...so allegiance to some homophobic God who doesn't even jerk off is out of the question."

All laughed, and Hackworth said, "Concept's pretty fuckin' scary...what if something like this happened?"

"Why do you think we have monitors...to catch those who just don't get it, like you, Russ."

"Hey, I sold my soul a long time ago, when I blew you, re-member?"

"I know when it was, and it was not a pretty sight—but you're in denial, so it's okay!"

"Hey," Russell Scott, the handsome hero said, "I passed, right?"

"And then some—may I cop a feel?" Rim asked. "After all, we must live for today, because we're what? HUMAN!"

But Russell Scott, one of the highest paid actors on the planet, and certainly one of the most famous, said: "*You gotta pay now*, motherfucker."

Rim laughed, and said: "That's why you're playing the hero, motherfucker. You lost all sense of camaraderie."

Diane, the auburn-haired beauty standing by, restrained to her bed and waiting, said: "Can we just shoot the fucking thing, Rim?"

"Places everyone," the first assistant director said through a megaphone.

Before the first false blow to Russell's face from one Thad Hackworth, a smacking sound was heard. The camera operator, script supervisor and first assistant were all covered in blood, but they didn't know what it was at first, although the camera opera-tor got something in his mouth, which turned out to be brain matter.

Before the screaming could begin below, Blue had left the soundstage altogether.

Before the screaming could begin, Fish had a heart attack

right on the set and collapsed.

Before the screaming could begin, Diane Winston watched Thad Hackworth's entire head shatter, its contents evacuate—his brain blown to bits, leaving nothing but a cavity that did not even include eyes. A half-head reeling around and flailing about, as if still alive—a clumsy mannequin that stunned too many into leaving Diane Winston tied to her bed, while she screamed for all concerned.

Then falling, blood showering the floor.

The screams led the way to everything, from ambulances, Feds, police, and ubiquitous reporters, who launched into the main topic—*Vincent?* Could Vincent have done all this? Was Vincent somehow responsible?

They'd been shooting for two months...too far into it to replace talent. Insurance would have to pay, but the company decided that assassination was not covered. The studio was not able to afford a calamity that clearly was a result of Kruzmar's high school "problem," and that is exactly where the blame rested.

No amount of Larry Cousins or Sean Hutchings or Charlie Rowan could fix the damage. It was Lucy who had to get out amongst them. It was Lucy who had to convince the board of directors.

Stu Wittie and his lovely bride, Bandaloo, worked quickly. First, they began by partying steadily and with extremity. It was so nice having the Bel Air mansion—all that money poured into one huge project, even though undeserved. One by one, the international board of directors were wined, dined, fucked, sucked and plucked.

One by one, from the royal heir, Jimmy Milner, to Henry Wong, from Paola D'Agostino to Val Ormont, from Indonesia to Rome, from Buenos Aires to Toronto, from Australia to Russia...the globe: they all had the pleasure of Bandaloo, who was an instant hit anywhere she was wanted. And *so* classy, everyone still thought of her as warm, clean—the Wittie place was certainly better than the Century Park Hotel, certainly better than some leased condo in Brentwood, with all the girls and boys wandering around; it was Kruzmar all over again, only better.

Serena stirred the pot of the beef stew she'd made for Milaca and Asenath, the Ethiopian. The summit, held at the Sierra Towers above Sunset, was the perfect spot, especially on the Winter Solstice. Especially since they knew everything from the dick size of the King of Majorca to the strange calling of Vincent Damien Del Monte, and even Blue...

On the board, they had them labeled. There was Anastasia; there was Tommy Taal, "and here comes Bandaloo!" said Asenath, trotting her miniature doll across the board while taking a hit of hashish from the hookah.

Serena pushed her cornrows back and smiled. "So *Lucy* is the patsy."

Milaca adjusted her bra, stood tall in her mellifluous beauty, then looked at the two women and said, "Do you think any of them will wake up?"

"Vincent is awake!"

All laughed at this. They brought out a Ken doll and said, "Though we have no power over him, if I could, I'd kiss him, like this," and she kissed the doll, a lover's kiss, a romantic's kiss—the deep sex kiss.

Between them, a hologram appeared, at least on their internal mind-screens. "Our god is great, our god is wonderful," said Serena. "He is good, he is glorious, he is Satan."

"But they don't know they're dead," said Milaca.

Asenath added, while puffing on the hookah, "I want it all in my tummy."

"The whole world?" asked Serena.

"Just Leonard Cutlass Kruzmar...he is..."

"You'll stop *that* right now—he is tied to the top of the sun."

"*He is going to fall,*" Milaca said, singsong fashion, while billowing in the wind of the open sliders, drinking in the Los Angeles basin.

The doorbell rang, and soon there were guests, a few women, and a few men, of all different ethnic backgrounds. Three warlocks from Egypt—the Queen Isis crowd no doubt. Then there was a couple from Brazil—Santeria; and one lovely lady from China—Order of the Black Dragon....and on and on, the Who's Who, all tied to one thing: the son of the morning.

And why not? The tug-o-war between the enemy, Vincent, and the morning's choice, Kruzmar, had to stop.

"But Vincent...is he a human host?" Asenath asked.

"I thought we invented him to foil Kruzmar so we could shift the field of play."

"He fired me," said Serena. The other ladies agreed, "That bitch of a wife has killed him."

"Killed?" asked Asenath.

"Well, we're all dead, aren't we," Serena asked, as the guests were greeted. "The sun will make us live."

This was no ordinary party, no, this was no ordinary event—no, the paradigm had shifted since Vincent could not, would not be stopped, and indeed, there had to be some sort of concerted effort to stop him.

"After all," said Mixar, the warlock from Tangiers, "Our Lord is not compatible with his Lord, wouldn't you agree?"

At approximately 7:00 p.m., there would be a natural disaster in Chile, where it was anticipated that thousands would die in an 8.6 megaquake that would last for several minutes, with aftershocks for the next couple of weeks. This was not as it seemed, as it had been planned for months. A very propitious sacrifice to the sun indeed!" said Asenath, disrobing.

As the music swelled, the guards made no moves sporting their M-16's and sunglasses, no emotion as the orgy took place while watching the Chilean earthquake and the sat-cams beaming in all the death and destruction into the highest orders of the world. The city of Santiago was easily buried, as millions instantly became homeless. The quake had measured more than 10.5 on the Richter Scale, which was a conservative estimate, surpassing even the practitioner's spell casting for an 8.6.

"Now, together, look what we can do!" exclaimed Asenath, orgasmically pleased.

"To the queen!" said the Egyptian, while ejaculating onto the fire in front of the congregation.

At this point all were possessed with the true rulers of the world, the familiar spirits like *Ashteroth* and *Baal* and *Beelzebub*, and the like. Serena, Asenath and Milaca were no longer participants, they were using their dolls of Kruzmar and Lucy and Blue and Vincent, and even Carl and dipping them into slime of bodies and then into the cauldron, where they melted.

"We want a new world! Let us remake it!"

"It's Vincent," the man in the dark suit said.

All stopped and immediately fell to their faces in front of him, the suit, in worship. He then said: "Remember, they don't know they're dead—you do."

Soul Survivor had been shut down, the board had decided to replace Kruzmar with Stuart Wittie, but had not agreed on how they might do it. The smart money was on *Soul Survivor*—if they could somehow pull it off, even with the tragedy of losing two actors to tragedy, first Tommy Taal, and then Thad Hackford, both in the role of the avenger.

It did not help things at all that S.S. was on Larry Cousins that night spouting that Rim Fish had turned his story around and lost the meaning. And that is why the curse was on. "Vincent, if you're watching—thank you."

"Cut to break!" The director with the ulcer screamed.

Larry took a look a Shredd and just smiled. "Don't you ever stop? What's so wrong with this world? Why do you have to glorify Vincent? We're looking at an escalation of crime worldwide that rivals anything we have ever seen before—you're just a right wing patsy, a shit-for-brains loser."

"No, I'm with the Lord."

"Oh, no, not you *too*. Well, why don't you go out there and stop Vincent then—and tell him it's not godly to—"

"You're making it a theological issue, not me, Larry, *you know that*," Steve said. "Are you betraying your oath? These people don't know they're dead."

That was when Larry woke up, got frightened, and said: "I'm sorry—don't say anything, please. You're right—they don't know how the world really is, and I don't want you to tell them."

"If they can't figure it out in the book, fuck 'em," Steve said.

Larry fumbled around and went back on the air with S.S.

"Now for your calls—Bridgeport, Connecticut, hello."

As Larry looked at Shredd, and Shredd looked at Larry, the eeriest call began, and began in a way that was unseemly. "First of all..." It was the voice of an elderly, perhaps erudite gentleman. "...You caused a paradox problem, and both of you know that I played each of you..."

Steve chimed in, "And who the *bleep* are you, *the Devil*?"

Let me replay it for you," he said dryly, and at that moment the monitors went blank.

It unfolded quickly now, Shredd driving in his Lexus convertible along I-70 near Vail, Colorado. He had his Rossignols tied on a rack and the silver bullet glided up the mountain. His girlfriend, Axena, was tall, dark, and perfect. She was the epitome of beauty and looks, stunning in her gold and pearls. "Baby, turn the music up," she said, and Steve let her know what he was thinking.

"Axena, I...I can't turn the music up right now because I want to ask you to marry me."

She melted just as the flash of light hits and the firestorm envelopes all the trees, an avalanche of fire roaring down the hill and vaporizing them, and everyone else, instantly.

Shredd reels back, as does Larry Cousins. "What's going on?"

"You idiot—*Vincent caused the war*," the caller said bluntly. He cleared his throat, and guzzled something, as they could hear.

"What the fuck is going on?" Larry asked. "Cut him off."

"You can't have Vincent on the planet because that will trigger my opponent's wrath," said the voice, and then he hung up.

The lights were suddenly off—and no technicians, just Cousins and Shredd, were left on the stage.

"Larry," Steve said, "it's time we took our masks off—I'm a double agent."

"I've got a double mind," Larry said. "And I'm sick and tired of it. Is there a way out?"

"I miss Axena—she was the—"

"She's a knockout, no question."

Before they could further contemplate the elasticity of what they thought was the collective unconscious (a silly concept designed to confuse the masses) they were brought collectively close by a mystery caller who brought true reality right down to the tarmac, painfully close, and now a single spotlight shone just off camera 1. There, bathed in light, wearing a formal sequined dress with an open back, was the lovely Axena. A gift? A demon? A punishment?

"My love!" Steve said, and went to her and sank to his knees..."Oh, how I've missed you, but I—"

"You have another chance. Vincent has to go."

"But Vincent isn't my—"

"You have another chance, but Vincent has to go," Axena, the tall dark beauty, said.

The lights suddenly struck brilliant, and the sun shone through as it set through the makeshift cardboard curtains, and Larry said, "I...time out—call it quits, that's it, kaput, goodbye, fuck you all, I don't care, I'm outta here, baby!" With that Larry deserted his set with fifteen minutes left in the program.

"I'll do it, I'll do anything for you," Steve said.

Axena rubbed his head and said, "It's time to stop the charade—it backfired."

"Yes, Axena, I love you—I love you so much."

ᘔ   ᘔ   ᘔ

They led me in, this time in chains, which was strange, as it had been a week that I had been in seclusion for attempting to lure the makeup girl with a simple nod.

"You exposed yourself to the nurse," Steinman said.

"You want to rehabilitate me, Steinman?"

At that point, Millicet and Jude entered the room and when I spoke to them, they asked about the chains. Steinman pretended they were not in the room and made notes. We got between his ears real good and started to chant, "Carl's a psycho, Carl Nunn is a rapist, Carl Nunn is sick, Carl Nunn needs *your* help, badly."

"Vincent, the chains won't budge."

"Jude, did you have to kill the doctor—I needed him for

Carl—you fool!"

Soon, Radar had let me loose and we proceeded to Princess Katherine's abode above the sea, and I found her remarkable, and she believed I was not responsible for what happened to the studio.

Carl and I arranged to meet secretly, because he had to know what happened in the past. He said he thought there was a plot to kill me in the prison...and that Steve Shredd called him and reminded him that I was the most influential man in the world, and the cause of all the strife. That I was a blight *on the mind* of the world. He also said that Steinman had had a heart attack after my interview and escape, and that the world once again applauded me, Vincent, and hated the police, Kruzmar, and others. And would of course hate Steve Shredd if I ever *outed* him as a hypocrite.

It was another time, and I was onto bigger and better things. The world, as I knew it, was gone. It was time to recount it for those who had an ear, that they might be delivered out and into the future with us.

I needed forgiveness, and I needed to forgive myself, but that was the one person I could not forgive.

ENO-YTNEWT

T hings had settled down at Shangri-La, at least for the moment. Globally, there was a peace treaty in place between the world and Israel, whom the world hates because of the true God dwelling there. One born from my experience as a non-human entity spanning the Spirit—knowing who *Jehovah-Jireh*, the *El Shaddai*, the *I AM* truly is. Here is a clue for you, stiff-neck: *Soul Survivor* is a metaphor for Israel. Rim Fish is anti-Semitic, not a Jew as he passed himself off to be, not a Jesus freak—an *agnostic*, which means, in ancient Greek: *Ignorant*. So when Rim Fish announces to the world he's agnostic, you can laugh, because it means intellectually lazy or compromised, one who has never questioned his own existence or ever searched for the truth—even one too stupid to know better, stupidity personified, stupidity enthroned, glorified, a testimony for the just cause of murder—that detestable blight. Pruning. How do people like Fish walk around dead to all things above and below?—no good for either side, indeed knowing nothing of *sides*, of *war*, of *heaven* or *hell*, a gross piece of dead meat on the mall of dried-up potential. Well, let me spoon-feed it to you, Mr. Fish: *Israel IS the soul survivor*. The *soulless*—that's you, genius—serve the Mistaken.

Yes, Rim, Mistake is your savior, and when I kill you, you'll go off to serve Mistake forever and ever. Oh, don't run from me now! Listen, anything connected with the true God of Israel, by way of *messiah*, is hated by the world—even by Hollywood, who replaced Elohim with *Personalism*, Gloryism, Infatuationism, a'groanin' and a'moanin,' a'covetous and screamin'.

You can't turn back—*El Shaddai* kills all who are not His. I say: Worship the Creator. You say, Worship the creature. I say, Fear God. You say: Worship the member, let woman divide the root. You say it in layers, you say it without speaking, you say it wise in your own eyes. You say "yes," I say "good bye."

You say, Why?

Him, not you.

You say, Why?

And I say, "You're so right! You have a right. Right you are."

So right.

Right and strong.

Only someone in the future can tell you, don't you know that by now?

In my confusion, I had a change of heart. They had me looking at blue lights, orange lights, and purple lights of all things. Captivity held me captive, once again. I was living in downtown Los Angeles. They had stuck me back into the midst of the problem, had understood my need for forgiveness, had understood that I led my men astray, that I had led a depraved life, that I was no national hero, and the fact that I took on that mantle, conducted interviews, was photographed like a movie star, had inspired children to turn against their parents, had encouraged those in bondage to throw them off, was more than a puzzlement to me in retrospect. When, on Bill Jenkins' show on the Monsoon Channel, I stood up and told all of corporate America to quit their moral prostitution, when I myself was guilty of moral vagrancy. Forgive me. But I was trying to alert them that the corporation was nothing more than a giant mausoleum.

I told them to burn their churches, torch their synagogues—and they did.

And they blamed everything on God. On Skinheads, on extremists, on Satanists!

They are Satan, beloved!

My screams went unheard, because I was shown how I failed, how I was a hypocrite, how I used a personal vendetta to foist us all into captivity. How I let Jude become a man of the world, how I led Millicet to a bullet at the hand of Blue, another creation of mine.

Well, the question, then, is how to undo all the damage I had caused? I was truly sorry. I had never had the gift of self-consciousness before. I had misunderstood the world, that it really was a pretty wonderful place. I had misunderstood. It could be one's oyster, if one played their cards right, if one stood in the light of the sun with appreciation.

The sun of the dawn was what we all had to face, at one time or another. And did I face it? No, it wasn't necessary. So how could I possibly tell anyone else to turn away from the brilliance of warm sunlight? And more light?

And more light.

Even more light.

I was self-illuminated; I never turned away!

But as I said, a change of heart was in the offing, if only for a short while. All I had to do was be kind, warm and supportive to all those wonderful people out there whose hearts were made pure by their acceptance of the way things were, the way they could be in perpetuity. World peace, sustainability, harmony, with no religion, a brotherhood of man! *"You may say I'm a dreamer, but I'm not the only one. I hope one day you'll join us, and the world will be as one."* Oh, prophetic, my brothers!

That we could have one big circle of inclusion, that all our brothers and sisters were just waiting to come out and play...if we would only be kinder. If we would only pull together as a team.

What were the kids so upset about anyway? Why did they steal weapons and shoot their classmates and their teachers and parents? Why were they so much against the establishment? Why indeed were there so many haters in the world? But instead of labeling me a hater, who killed his own mother in the name of something invisible, higher and clearly of superior purpose, they deemed me a saint, as evidenced by the fact that I was loose, and was front page news on a daily basis. My poster was up on Sunset Boulevard by the new movie, *Vincent*, starring Tommy Taal (they'll let him do a movie on a day pass from prison if he donates the money to the victim of his crime). When I wanted something, I simply appeared at the cash register and it was given to me.

I came here from the future, I had said. And there were definite slips in the fabric of space and time, caused by me, of course...the ripple effect. There were those who were visible for a moment, like Jude and Millicet, like parts of Blue's personality, like Anastasia...and then they were gone. Mysteriously. Clandestinely.

Remember, dear reader, the past is not certain. You always have to worry about people like us being dropped in to stir things up and produce a certain outcome. The god of this world doesn't like me. Not like he likes you...if you cooperate with him.

Conformity.

Duality.

Flesh-covered—no worries.

But he hates me.

I am the cause of his pain. I am the foil of his plans. I am the blight on his crop of souls. My soul is made of something inhuman...I have handlers who for a season will employ me to take out targets they deem worthy, but they failed to realize they are not themselves, that is, they do not own themselves and have not free will when they are in my presence.

I don't know why this is the case. I know I serve my Lord, and do what he tells me, as the orders come in through my men, through the television, through little slips in space, through all the anti-people, those who worship the earth and die in the process.

To those who worship mankind and die in the process, I salute you! For you wasted your lives, and you saved me a lot of trouble.

I have been given temporary authority over death. Not your god.

I am a destroyer. I cause the end of things. My presence brings down nations. I cannot even be in the world. I am a poison, acid in the fishbowl.

I, the angel of death, am here to defend the meek, the lost, the soul survivors wherever they may be! It would always come to this. After all, there is no point for the bully thugs to be on earth if not for the existence of God's own, that is, those who still have souls. When their numbers decrease, mass death and destruction comes to those who prey on the beloved ones.

What gives your life so much importance, that I should not upset you, or kill you? Why should you live even one more day? What difference would it make? She was not my mother, Margot, the queen of the past, who used the candles and the phalluses, but to no avail...what was the point of her life? To move a few objects around for her comfort and benefit and then croak either by the tip of her son's sword or the Reaper himself...who the fuck cares? She was detritus, took bread from the poor, candy from babies' mouths, sure, a defiler of innocence, absolutely, the destroyer of self-esteem, a mean, mean witch who piled her money to the moon. Her death was ordained and I carried it out happily. I honor her by causing her to sin no more.

I honor my father and mother when I pull the trigger, the kids now say. You can't follow that commandment without causing death, as my Lord commands!

I love my brother as myself when I pull the trigger, the kids now say.

I make the office party a special event when I use the machine gun and go for the pregnant women first. I am showing mercy, for their lives would be wasted if they continued to strive with the god of the world, with the human filth of their wombs, growing up to be like them, a blight on Creation itself! I saved the world from that kind of sludge, after all.

I told you, I made mistakes, and this wave of killing is exactly what the enemy wants. I played into his hands, and I apologize. Yes, now you understand—mass death suits the god of this world just fine.

I killed a lot of people who were in my way, and couldn't manage to have sex with a woman without killing her. Let's be honest. I am no better than your master...your pied piper. You who sold your souls, you know. You know, rich man; you know, hate monger, you know, institutional death, big or small. You know, guys chasing the skirts right up the queen bee's leg, you know, liars, muzzled; you know, self-abusers, upwardly mobile in chains—you weren't free at all until you used violence, am I right? Not only that, you were muzzled, perverted, desperate, lost. Leaking all manner of eternity—now you are a countdown. You were told to keep your head down and hate them who did not agree, and I told you to push them over the edge! Oh, vanity! You were told you were on the winning team and that all the others were losers. You were told it was an exclusive club that guaranteed success, food and medicine for your children, life insurance, retirement benefits, endless winning lotto numbers, pretty panties anywhere, anytime. More pussy than you could imagine. You used to tell the wife, fuck off, now because of me you put a bullet in her head. Look how I aided and abetted mine enemy! Before me you were taught how to run the table, I showed you how to *be* the table. To own the table, to burn the table. To create the table again and again. To eat the table, to fuck the table, to shackle it and abuse it—to glorify it and worship it. Oh, my, it was glorious, *your future.*

Remember?

I'm talking to you out there—never mind my particular training in carnal warfare, never mind all those hypocrites in the churches, synagogues and mosques, never mind the wide-world system that insures your freedom from here to shattered dreams. From innocence lost to power boy, a three-hundred yard shot, a real comer, oh, my lad! Watch him...then leave him when he fails to dazzle. Let him keep his head down. Then forget him.

ā ā ā

Do not listen to Vincent anymore. I am the one you have been listening to, and indeed, the only one you should ever listen to. I have many names, but only one purpose...your happiness. Haven't I provided? Haven't I made a world where the best can be best, the worst can be worst, where you know something—

you have knowledge? Didn't I cause you to measure yourselves and the universe—wasn't my mystery so much greater, random chance...swayed by the luck I would provide. Do you know to whom you are speaking?

Do you know who you are—as gods? Don't believe Vincent for a second!

You are God. Gaze into your mirror and seek the light—you! Glorious you! All this bile spewing out of those misfits' mouths...shun them forever!

Because I can make your dreams come true, or I can bring the very forces of creation itself to move you where I wish, and like that loser Vincent, I can move you around the board for my purposes. Which Vincent is...oh, he'd like to think of himself as a rebel, as a liberator...but he has nothing. All the killing—misfits! Yes, I am your Master. This world is for peace, prosperity, to find yourself, indeed, exalt yourself today and realize your dreams today—don't wait, precious one. Don't put off your dreams...tomorrow may never come!

Didn't every single person have a chance? Don't blame me for those who didn't make a better go of it. And you who worshiped the sun and saw its splendor, bless you. Love and light, I always say. Beauty and sustenance. Fecundity and purpose, puerile and focused, Mother Earth forward, God is Woman. You make luck with a snap and a twitch, a look and a nod. With a howl and a gasp.

With a sledgehammer if you want.

Aren't you all living longer, isn't the world becoming a place of tolerance, isn't sex out of the closet, isn't it more of a brotherhood without the dumb notion of some angry father who wants to shackle us all and then judge us after we die? You are beholden to no one, men and women. Notice how I always include women. I include everyone. You might not have a chance, but if you play by the rules, I'll make your odds. You play by my rules, I'll increase your luck. Look at how women are exalted in my world, but not in Vincent's! Look how all religions, except one, are not only tolerated, but *encouraged*—we love all people, and all traditions.

Except one. That's a very high percentage. Please do not be

distracted by the word *one*.

Vincent would have you believe there is only one path to truth. My friends, all your ways are true, that is the mystery I illuminate before you now.

Who could lift up a bunch of poor boys to the highest status since Jesus Christ? Me.

Who is the all-time winner on this earth? Me.

What are you who follow me? *Winners all!* Yes, your dreams become reality; wealth and fame straighten your path before you. Exalted as gods you are, with spiritual knowledge beyond anything you could learn in that monotheism of a small region of the world that became the way of losers and charlatans.

Now it's time to call in that favor I told you about through that sound you heard. Oh, please do not be alarmed. *That sound* wasn't just something to scare you into total compliance. Or to prove my reality, validity and purpose. *That sound* you heard had a twofold purpose: One, to let me, the angel of light, enter you. I can be an angel, or...I can be your lover, the most sensual and beautiful girl...

...And two: to lead you to total empowerment, self-love— women, *that sound* meant power. Secret power. Sisterhood. Children advancing to great heights, as doctors, lawyers and politicians: society's best and brightest. Of course *that sound* wasn't for free. You wouldn't want it for free either, but the price is relatively small. When you crossed over—Rubicon, Styx, Bridge of Sighs, The Road, Into the Glass, Darkly—you became a joint-heir with me of all in my earthly Kingdom and my paradisiacal world of the future, the meta-system. Did I stop you from going to your churches and worshiping the all-time loser? No.

Some of you got deluded into thinking that the note would not come due, that if you worshiped this Jehovah character through Jesus or mumbled a few words of confession or repentance that you would somehow escape what you did back...don't you remember?

Back when you were a child...

When there was a way home...

Did I stop you from acting pious while you gave your wealth to charity...of course not, especially all those sexual charities, the casualties caused by the ones who sent Vincent.

You also knew that one day you would owe me a favor...from many of you I asked nothing. From some of you I asked you to do what one might call a deed, which of course would be kept confidential (I am not without dignity and fairness), just to insure your loyalty. That of killing Vincent, for example. I offered great reward...just like others who had come before.

But you failed. You rebelled. You thought, for some silly reason, that you were enslaved and that you needed to be liberated. Ha! Don't you know that *I* liberated you? What would it be like not having sexual magic—I'll bet none of you would go to Vegas if you didn't have my little secret in your pocket.

It wasn't free, children. And you're not supposed to be so virulently ungrateful. Look where you are now! Up in the hills, a mantel full of awards of appreciation. Job well done. Civic leaders, mayors, senators, presidents, kings, monarchs...look at you all. You have all, *all without exception*, paid my price. None of you has complained...until now. Now you doubt me? Don't you know I'll always take care of you and make you safe in your beds? Don't you know why we have never had a nuclear war on this planet? Because of me, and because of my keeping those fools who don't have a clue down, way down, that terminal cloud over their heads—as it should be, as it is and forever will be. And weren't you assured I was the only way to fame, fortune, to the realization of all your dreams?

Look how charitable and helpful I am to all people. Look at all the foundations and charitable organizations and fraternities that tirelessly work to make it a better world, all the while increasing their social status. When you gave money to my charities I gave you a plaque on the wall. Vincent would have you do it in secret, like the One he follows.

We keep them down, the homeless, the poor laborers, those who never get a promotion, the hypocritical religious people like Christians—oh, you laugh at them, at least those who take it seriously enough to follow those intolerant rules!

Of course they need to be poor. Imagine...no gratification? No friends in high places, only their own sorry huddles. Would you like to be scoffed at, mocked and made the scapegoat? Abused, lied to, ganged up on, cheated? IRS audits, police harassment (and well-deserved, yes, my loved ones?), occasional rape (mainly of men who are idiots). Is it any wonder why *you* are the winners and *they* are the losers?—might it have something to do with using the *mind* I gave you?

You are to be saluted, for you have used your brains, your minds, minds that control the world…the remote control for every conceivable channel—your wish was always my command…well, perhaps not *completely*—but I gave you power.

And yes, perhaps it is a sad truth, but the mind, the Mind, is mine. My will and your will must conform—but with enough distraction, you'll still believe you're the captain of your own ship…and isn't that the important thing?—to get what you want?—to want what you get?

Who does the abusing, the raping, the pillaging, the plundering, the mocking, the scapegoating, the lying, cheating and stealing?

YOU DO! AND YOU GET AWAY WITH IT EVERY TIME!

And you love to do it—you never had to leave the fun of the playground. You got even with all those bullies of old…look at them now—your footstools!

It's a perfect system. And you love it.

Why in the world would you ever want to listen to someone who is against everything we have built—a true hater of all that is just, moral, true and righteous? Why would you follow *him*? How can you not inform your children of my reality so they can prosper and grow? Why have you turned away from the truth now?

It's your fault that this world is coming loose at the seams (and it is because of Vincent and other misfits), but don't you dare look for a savior to help you now!

Don't you dare!

Do not look toward *that* direction.

You want to be religious, fine, you can have any number of other options. Besides, as for salvation…you don't deserve it anyway, not after what you've done. How could you think otherwise? Just serve me and you'll do fine. You know you're part and parcel with what I do in secret chambers, higher up...you have an inclination of what it takes to be at the very top, don't you? Oh, you must have a feeling that there is a very *terrible* secret...that there is a very big shoe that could drop on all of us, yes?

Well, let me tell you this, you ungrateful peons, you are guilty of the same crimes as the worst of them, all partaking in the magical covering of the shining...for you do shine, do you not? You look new every single day—as if you have never done anything wrong...isn't that nice for you all?

And if you want out, know that the dark and terrible secret, the truth is that you are guilty for all the evil in the world—but since no one brings it up, why worry about it?

I will tell you what you all have done, through proxy, the terrible truth: you are guilty of pedophilia, pornography, mass murder in every single war, the Holocaust, genocide around the world, drug running, gun running and slave running, child sacrifice, institutional rape, assassination and torture all as worship to me. You worship me through your greed and lust and power-mongering...and you did what those above you and below you did. And that one called The Creator will judge each of you, despite your charity work, as guilty of all the cumulative sin of all the world since man emerged. That is the deep dark and terrible secret. I don't care if you have given your life to feeding the poor, you are painted guilty by an insensitive God who is no respecter of persons.

Whereas, I respect you. I love you.

And as for Vincent Damien Del Monte...well, *he hates your guts!*

And even more, in my temples you built the eye of the pyramid, you built the Temple of Isis, you built my monuments to my big dick and worshiped it everywhere in exchange for your mystery girl, your secret girl who wants your life mucho, *mucho*!

You put my stamp on your dollar bills. And you act like a virgin on her first spring? You want to demure now and cry out, help me! How dare you! How dare you insult me or our covenant together! How dare you be so stupid as to even look for a way out!

I'll kill you if you even deign to say something evil against my kingdom. You go back into your hole or wherever you crawled out of, and let me worry about the soul survivors.

Put it this way, don't be surprised if I ask you to kill them all soon. That may be the only way to avert a disaster you have caused by being too soft. Namely, thermonuclear war on a global scale, followed by famine, earthquakes, drought, and the mass killing of 4.5 billion people—that is what that jerkoff called God would do to you, and all his so-called children of light.

Whereas I protect you. I am the only light you will ever need.

And Vincent laughs about it, says death is gain.

Think about it—what side is your bread buttered on?

Don't you be so foolish. You continue to be fearful, as that keeps you reasonable. Continue to listen to your women, let them dominate you, as I have designed. It doesn't have to be overt. Let your children become sexual, as I have ordained. It's not skin off your nose is it? I want souls, I want supplication—or I'll kill you where you stand.

Continue to corrupt yourselves for the greater good when called upon.

Follow all my commandments or risk exclusion, hatred, and death.

Any questions?

Do I have to show you the iron fist? Why can't you just live in the peace I have provided? Go find your answers in the New Age bookstores, in the churches, the mosques, the temples, the ashrams—especially the ashrams! You know what spirituality is: we're all one. One for all and all for one. When you hear this doctrine, you know it's Me calling.

We're all one spirit—except for those lousy misfits.

Worship Gaia, dance around the Maypole, do your rock and roll, it's all Me, all Me all the time!

It's all One. Remember? All is God. You are God. This is eternity. There is no death and nothing to worry about. Go back to your world and enjoy. Please.

You saw that new day dawn. You heard my shrieking sound. You propelled yourselves up the ladder. But you say I made it too easy, now everybody's in on it? How dare you talk to me like that! It just means that you can go a lot higher. So get busy, future kings and queens! *Enjoy*, that is an order!

You ask me about death and Hell.

You and I are going to be together forever and there is no way out. There you have it—the truth I tried to hide from you so you could have a nice life, but look what you made me do! Because of your insolence and disrespect you made me stick that sad awful truth in your craw, and I did.

To repeat, for those of you who somehow missed the gist of my tome: *There is no way out.*

You knew that. And yet you still think you can somehow be good and escape the penalty?

I don't think so.

So be happy with your lot in life, go fuck a nubile nymphet or jerk off to the *Sound of Music*, I don't care. Taste the fruit I gave you to eat. Taste the liberation of desires beyond your wildest dreams. Sex, permanent vacations, your best friend's wife, anywhere, anytime...a 1996 Cab, a DB-7, fondling a teenage pecker in Morocco, buying pearls in Mauritania, using slaves for your safari—all the fun, all the time...*and do not complain now!*

Or *ever* again.

You take what I gave you and go on with your life till the end—and no more questions. Lest you have a run of bad luck yourself.

Here is my warning. Anybody caught following, glorifying, exalting, cherishing or imitating Vincent will be framed, thrown in prison and executed, worldwide.

You leaders, this comes from the top down.

Any of you tell them about me, I will personally kill you on the spot.

Get rid of Vincent.

Kill him, and his spirit.

Kill Vincent completely, that is all you have to do.

ə   ə   ə

Don't you hate it when you know all about what's going to

happen but you can't tell anybody? In my case, my Lord commands it. Meanwhile, Blue has just picked off Diane Winston, and Steve Shredd's nightmare tale about a man who refuses to sell his soul to the devil has come to a dead halt.

Kruzmar had hired me, and someone else had hired Kruzmar, and there is a mystery to this. As I wait in my room at the Peninsula Hotel—again, top suite, goons everywhere, high-powered rifle and my trusty friends. I am aware of the fact that the world has been upended, and there is a greater destiny, but to put it all on me, to make me the centerpiece, the centerfold, the poster boy, the finger-wagger, the inspiration to young idealists worldwide, is just plain shameful journalism. You all know who you are.

It's true; I never really escaped Kruzmar's grip. In fact, I have a confession to make. I have been in the unfortunate fold of Kruzmar the entire time. Though he sold out long ago, he was the perfect vessel to use as a battering ram on the world's mirror, or power, or illusion mistaken for reality.

Serena, Milaca and Asenath had done their temple worship and awakened the wrath of their lord and master, the great Dark One, who now appeared in my room, a shining prince—a beautiful woman, or a man, it was hard to tell which. Perhaps this was because of my own abuse or transgender issues. Kruzmar was his boy, and his boy was bloodied beyond recognition. No, he did not like that one bit.

He, the Ruler of Darkness, welcomed me to the balcony and made the concrete appear like a swimming pool. She wore a beautiful thong bikini, or I should say, *she* was beautiful...and then she was Jude. Now, I know what you might think—perish the thought. Jude is strictly off limits, and *sex* for that matter is off limits. I was attracted to his beauty or age because I lost that, oh, my friends who are in this world but not of it. I am informed that there is nothing but concrete below, and the shining sensual beauty of the angel of light suddenly becomes a winged reptile, a dragon who hisses and sprays electrical current from his mouth and anus—I fall back onto the balcony and then I am whisked away by limo to some trendy fish taco place on Melrose for a banquet room emergency meeting.

Leonard kisses me on the cheek, which means he will kill me after this is done, or at least try again, as he did when I split the studio chief's head open in Beverly Hills.

"Vincent, you have to get me out of this. Have you heard?" he asked, pacing. This time there was no lisp. His voice was high, he had little mounds for breasts (these I hadn't seen before), effeminate, sure, but not flaming. Just very, very nervous. "Even though I raised all the money, I'm being dumped."

"I thought you were dumped before."

"Threatened, plotted against, ordered to cease and desist under the threat of murder."

I walked around and several photographers took pictures of me. "Lenny, why all the coverage?" I asked.

"You kidding? I can sell your photos for millions."

I wanted to kill him, but I was outnumbered. The Flagellator had stolen another car, and had Millicet, who apparently was not dead, in tow, along with Silas the *punk*, as I now called him, and beloved Jude. Believe me, I'm turning myself and Jude away from the idea of becoming like Kruzmar. Enough said.

"There is *no* Millicet—you're a stark-raving lunatic, thanks to all that time in the loony bin! I resurrected you! ME! I made your delusions pay off. You're sick. That's why you never made anything of yourself. Because you're sick. Your existence is annihilation of all that is decent."

So much for blind cows.

He laughed and so did all the black suits who held me at bay with half a dozen M-16s.

"Why all the security if I'm so easy?" I asked, thinking about Princess Katherine in the future.

"You killed your own mother. You escaped my best men...I think you qualify as a threat," Kruzmar said, pacing around in black silk trousers and a semi-see-through blouse.

"That's good, because I'm taking over your mind," I said. "And when I'm you, I'm going to commit suicide."

I was whisked, *whisked* back to the guarded hotel room, handed a set of ninja clothes, my trusty plastic rifle with the stupid sniper on it and taken to the evacuated studio lot, where there were contingents of FBI military and Special Forces personnel—all without the advantage of true sight.

One amusing detail I must tell you about. The number of picketers against Kruzmar and holding posters of my face had now grown into the thousands—and the police had to use tear gas and rubber bullets. They were my people; they were good people, and their roar was growing louder—could this be the voice of my Lord?

OWT-YTNEWT

While Leonard was being exposed, Vincent was being mythologized. While Lucy was doing damage-control P.R., Vincent was sipping Montrachet in posh spots and jubilant getaways. Those were all rumors—little did I, Carl Wendell Nunn, know, it was more about a global coup, and that is why they fucked with my head. I told you before to never listen to Vincent, *whatever* he is. While I'm interviewing him in this prison for the criminally insane, he's out killing women and children. He's eating 'em and laughing as he tosses the bones off the balcony! He's a loser, but for some reason he's paraded in front of the world as a winner. All I wanted to do was find out what the fuck happened to Shangri-La, the largest movie studio in the world, the biggest business coup the world had ever seen. I wanted—and you check me on this—to find out what happened to *Soul Survivor,* you know, the movie that could not, would not, and probably will not *ever* be made. The movie that destroyed Hollywood forever.

And look where my investigation got me? No one believes that he, Vincent, took my mind. I was co-opted, absconded with, taken, and the heinous things I did were after I met Vincent are truly unbearable! How do you explain that one? That's evidence, *more* than evidence—it's collusion, it's intersection. Look, how can you explain the amputation of my feet and hands so that I have to dictate all this into a friggin' tape recorder?

He's shedding his skin, he's free for Pete's sake, and I'm in here! I was the one hired to interview him and yet I got—or my mind got—messed with. *I'm* the one who didn't know, who didn't go, who didn't see, who didn't get, who didn't fly away—how fast it all went! I came here; I fell in love with Princess Katherine— no! Her name is Katherine, just plain Katherine, but now he's got *me* saying *princess*...it was Vincent's idea that she is a princess. You see the effect he's had? My idea was that *she*, regular Katherine, was my girlfriend after the divorce from my wife...or at least after we were separated. Elaine and I were best friends, that was the problem. Well, that was *always* the problem. That was always the situation—and that of course precipitated the womanizing, let's be honest. I hate to call it that. Let's just say, a little dating. That's all—just a little relief...is that so wrong?

About the orgy, she set that one up. Of course I knew what was going on. The open relationship. And she used it as a chance to get even—one big moment in front of me, and I was...I didn't know what to do, I didn't know what to say—I couldn't stop it. All those men—did *she* hire 'em? She OD'd, man, she OD'd. It was heroin; it was something more serious, more provocative at the center of it. It was something severe. It was something difficult to understand.

I stated it—I understood it for what it was. Don't let anybody tell you it's not a cause and effect situation, grounded in time—all that bunk about the future...that's how he got me! Don't let him do the same thing to you.

Don't let him think he's winning.

@ @ @

And then he shot Jay Rawlson, the mogul agent who signed Harry Batzer and others, while he was walking back to his

Mercedes...and he shot Rim Fish right through the heart—and when he shot Rim Fish right through the heart, they shut down the studio.

That was when it all ended.

All production halted. All pictures, all television, all transportation, all traffic in and out of the studio. It seemed like the whole world stopped. It seemed like the whole city ceased its heart beat, for the time—it seemed that even God Himself halted the rain, the fog, the sunrises and the sunsets...and it was the way of the future. It would be portentous. But it wasn't the future. It was now. It was spinning forth, the colors of the rainbow—reality...and Vincent was riding it.

The FBI told him what to expect. The Special Forces team leader, MacBeth, told him how to react. Hostage Rescue Team sniper, Rudy McCauley, filled him in on how to take the shot.

Vincent laughed at all of them as Leonard sponsored a party for the board members and their families in Kapalua, Maui. Diversion, perhaps—Leonard becoming a college Joe all over again? Impossible. Lucy, meanwhile, already had the votes to enter the board of directors; she had taken a penthouse suite in the Heritage high-rise on Wilshire. It was speculated that the shutdown of the most expensive movie ever made, the one upon which the hopes and dreams of the entire world hung in the balance, was done in secret.

But Lucy was nobody's fool. There had to be some plan of revival, or their ship would certainly sink. And it was *their ship*, after all.

Vincent was too cool for all this. He was the undisputed king, the champ, the brave one. The noble, the honest, the revolutionary, the messiah.

Celebrity shootouts?

Fuck the rich! Fuck those elite SOB's, Vincent did. Stuck it right up their hypocritical noses. All about equanimity and tolerance—how about homelessness, how about ugliness, how about ordinariness? How about the fact that if you were famous, now you got shot? How about the fact that the public turned on all celebrities en masse, in honor of Vincent? Irony?

Divinity.

In the fifteen hundred-acre facility, Vincent was supposed to find Blue and kill him—simple as that. But Vincent only *allowed* Kruzmar this idea that he was in charge.

It was a duty—it was his mission. This was the fulcrum, the axis, the *imago-mundi*, Shangri-La was. All eyes on the dying whore. And all eyes disappointed.

Vincent said goodbye to Millicet, Silas, the Flagellator and even Blue. Oh, he found Blue, high up on a scaffolding, waiting for him. Blue was beauty personified. He was fit, honed, aware, living on air—needing nothing but his own breath to spin existence around any way he chose. He had finally found peace, miles above the fallen mortal state. High above romance, and clouds, and brides and children, far beyond the rage of stupidity, and Vincent could see it in his eyes and he kissed him on both cheeks. "I've sent my men to see you through, Ashley," Vincent said.

"I was jealous of you, Vincent. Please forgive me."

"I love you, Blue. My Lord wanted these good men to see you through, understand—all the way to the End."

"The End will come?"

Vincent, with knee-high boots and a black oil raincoat, three knives, two pistols, his sniper rifle, was every bit the image of Guevara, or Mohammed, or Lawrence of Arabia, but *not* Jesus. Because, as Vincent would say, "Who, pray tell, do you know my Lord to be?"

So when a security guard asked, "Christ, what the fuck are you doing here?"

Vincent shot him in the head and said, "No one takes the Lord's name in vain."

Of course it helped Blue, in the beginning. "Why don't I get any press? They know about me."

"They're suppressing you instead of me. But they're supposed to stop me—to villainize, to scrutinize, to block, to kill me in some way."

"Blue, I am sorry—my Lord is changing me. I have to lead them...despite my violent past as a mercenary from Bel Air. You know my men, Blue?"

Blue got his chips and dip going, along with a few Diet Cokes and offered them to Vincent's men. They were glad he finally received them; they truly were, beings of substance. Beings of light. Beings of perpetuity, fully visible, if you had an eye to see.

"You got the credit, Vincent, but I shut down the world."

"Blue," Vincent said, watching one lone FBI agent strolling under the scaffolding, "let me."

Blue watched Vincent take aim, saw his regal form, his eye through the scope—every bit the professional. Every bit the best sniper the world has ever known. "This one's through the heart of the world—then I begin my ministry," Vincent said, enigmatically.

It was a perfect hit—right through the heart, and he fell almost in slow motion, painlessly, with no effort, lying on a bed of feathers, the Special Agent was, and then he was not.

"They're not what they appear. They work for the other side. They don't know about the future," Vincent told Blue, who was living from scaffolding to scaffolding several stories above the concrete floor. Soundstages had to have tremendous height, and these were higher, wider, with more juice, with sitting areas on top, which were really exquisitely-built walkways, stairways, small offices, storage tool rooms—all existing up on walkways hugging the ceiling of the soundstage, with every light, every flag, every rigging apparatus at some forlorn grip's disposal. Blue was no grip; and he never killed one either. He could only look at handsome, charismatic Vincent, and he saw the glowing white beauty of Princess Katherine, standing in the air a hundred feet above the concrete floor. And he wept. "It's all true...it's all true."

"Of course it's true. You can't touch her, Blue. You can't touch her. She's not the doll we shot up with power, remember that?"

"That was a voodoo doll."

"No, it was a God's doll—and what happened to Anastasia was God's will, as you had no idea of the potentiality of such a doll, a Barbie doll named Anastasia."

"Fuck...fuck, it's like being run around the fuckin' board, but by who...you, Vincent?"

Vincent could hear the walkie-talkie of the Special Agent blaring, and saying they were going to send in some backup...

"Well, kid," Vincent was telling Blue, "you're a good and loyal subject, and I will return to take you home."

"This voice in me—"

"God," said Vincent with a warm smile.

"He told me to kill anyone who tries to come back to work."

"They won't even go to their offices since you took that executive—excellent shot by the way," Vincent said. "But look, the people understand...it's not all in vain. They're following—multitudes, all over the world. Don't worry, dear friend," Vincent said.

Blue was grateful for everything Vincent had done for him.

Vincent had disappeared among the crowd, as they could not follow where Katherine of the future took him. Into the midst of their picketing, where he told them: "You shall spare no one—you shall never be in bondage again!"

A member from the crowd saw a limousine, and screamed: "Look, there goes one of 'em now!"

The crowd rushed the stretch-Caddy stopped at Motor and Washington. The police showered the now rioting crowd with rubber bullets and tear gas, but would not venture in on foot, as the crowd had grown to a multitude. It was none other than Leticia Wiles, blonde goddess, who had been called to replace Diane Winston, and the irony was that they were going to finish the shoot in Mexico City, but Leticia just had to have a taco at her favorite stand to celebrate Winston's death...a private pleasure.

They pulled her out of the mistaken limo, cut her clothes off and taunted her as she ran around in circles, all while the press videotaped without the slightest thought of intervention, shooting print film, digital film, slides. Close-ups, legs, arms, throat slit SLO-MO, as she reeled, screaming for help, trying to keep the blood from spurting out of her neck—and they just let her spin in circles of her own waste, naked, alone—and even her driver was spared but forced to watch the celebrity taken down.

Vincent stood on top of the car and the crowd cheered wildly. "My Lord greets you, my people!" he said. They were crying in their fervor, they were crying in their rise to front page, big screen, premier venue. "You all stopped this abomination—now you can think for yourselves! They are the enemy—*not* you, my beloved! All of you...I want you to seek forgiveness...to seek not the lusts of your own heart, but in the life hereafter!"

The chants were overwhelming, even with a megaphone:

VINCENT, VINCENT, VINCENT, VINCENT!

And headlines to match:

SHANGRI-LA SHUT DOWN

SOUL SURVIVOR BRINGS DOWN
THE STUDIO

KRUZMAR IN SECLUSION, NOTHING TO SAY

LENNY AND LUCY—FALLEN FROM GRACE,
DIVORCE IMMINENT

Vincent slipped away before the tanks and helicopters arrived and killed 20,000 people and said there were no injuries.

"It had to be put down in the strictest possible terms," said the President of the United States.

"There was no other choice," said the Mayor after speaking with Kruzmar.

Lucy and Lenny were unseated, and the board of directors filed for bankruptcy.

And the proceeds would be sold to a cartel in Toronto, Canada, home of the New Hollywood after the slaughter to come.

Carl paced around and was sick of all the photographers, makeup artists, personal trainers—sick that the entire hospital for the criminally insane was turned into a private mansion for the benefit of Vincent Damien Del Monte.

"Carl, I can help you," Vincent said.

"Look, you little fucker—"

"Stop torturing yourself, Carl. Doesn't your god tell you to take the money and run?"

"My god?"

"Satan."

"Fuck...fuck!" Carl shoved Vincent, straight-jacketed, over onto his back and kicked him in the head until Radar and Pencil Neck, now both dressed in Oakland Raiders togs and with tattoos of Vincent's face on their upper arms with this caption: *The future through remembrance.*

They grabbed Carl, and Vincent ordered them to leave the room, that he would finish the interview with Carl, that Carl would find out what he wanted to find out, once and for all. "Listen, sorry," Carl said.

"You have a violent streak...you're an angry man. Elaine's in danger, Carl."

"So it was Blue...who..."

"Yes," Vincent said, smiling.

"But you're the hero? Look, I'm losing it, Vincent. I'm...my sanity has definitely slipped."

"Then let me help you—join us, before it's too late. Don't you know my Lord will send a sword, me, and say 'No Mercy' and that means no mercy? It's because he made all this. But you want your own understanding...and your own leader...and he's fooled you, the son of the dawn, and all the gods of the earth and air. And in the sea, the reptiles breed like rabbits and they hate you, they hate every fiber of your being, dumb schmuck."

"I have no leader, except myself," Carl said, a last ditch effort at saving his fracturing personality.

"Exactly."

Carl responded: "So Kruzmar hightailed it to Mexico and tried to finish the movie...after you escaped. And you're saying it was Kruzmar who trained you to assassinate his opposition, and you turned the tables on him, would that be safe to say?"

"Carl..." he said. He leaned back, comfortable in the straight jacket that would soon be Carl's, he knew. "Join us."

"Shut up a minute! So tell me, they never found Blue...did he really exist? I mean, I know he existed, but some thought he'd committed suicide...after the castration." Carl sat back on that—

how could he print it? Castration. What the whole story hinged on. Castration of males at the advent of a perverse god and a matriarchal matrix over a false social order loosely based on the patriarchy of the Bible. Yet, Vincent represents that patriarchy.

Carl wrote it like this:

> Vincent's theology is what drives him. He serves an ubiquitous and yet invisible Lord, and claims that Satan, in the form of an angel of light, or a lovely woman, as a feminine system, runs the world, indeed, has run it from time immemorial. He claims to be here at his Lord's bequest...as a sword of judgment. To kill everything he is ordered to kill. Unwittingly, he became a global hero, mythologized in magazines, comic books and new movies, now produced in foreign countries, since Hollywood has effectively been shut down.
>
> It may be that Vincent, *a sword*, as he calls himself, has felled the big whore called Mystery Babylon: Hollywood, den of iniquity. Home of broken hearts and shattered dreams. Kingdom of perversion, queen of eternal damnation.
>
> God knows this reporter is damned for now and ever more. Ladies and gentlemen, please forgive me for what I have done regarding Vincent. This is the last piece I will file. I withdraw in shame, as I have no one to blame for the wave of worldwide violence except myself. I created Vincent, and if I live another day, which I hope I do not, I will pray for God to torture me, as I well deserve.
>
> Turn to God and ask his forgiveness. That is my last word, fellow citizens of the earth. I am not a god, I am not God; I never will be, no matter how many people I hurt.
>
> Carl Wendell Nunn

He filed the last story but was thinking about Elaine, how he needed to be rid of her. There were voices in his head, voices that began when he would black out during conjugal activities with Katherine, whom he eventually called *Princess*, in his memory.

EERHT-YTNEWT

Serena had prophesied: "He who came to kill cannot be killed. He whom the lion would devour, devoured the lion; a hateful woman is now hated, a king would be a prostitute. Our Lord shall not be mocked, he shall regain control...and we will help him."

Asenath took the dagger and thrust it downwards, and the flames of the fire at the Los Angeles Coliseum were leaping lizards, branches of brilliance, torrents the color of light—rainbows and pantomime shadows. All surrounded under the stars by armed guard, the old guard—the true guard. The august guard. For there was order to sustain, and the flames of sacrifice would peradventure be quenched this night!

And they would see him, once and for all the shining prince would appear, the Lord of the Air, the true ruler of the world, the bestower of power, the son of the dawn, the light of the morning—one who makes all who follow stars in their own right to shine on forever and ever—hallelujah!

The multitudes came from the far reaches of the globe; these participants were nothing short of royalty, in deed, in manner, in appointment. For miles around the streets were lopped off, as the

City of Angels would remember its dawn, in *California*—which is to say, *Kali-Fornica* = Fornication to the goddess Kali...the Divine mother who slays the men of the field as a means to bring about a new cycle.

How could they not understand the truth of the world? Kali-Fornica. The angels of destiny. The angel of light—the Shining Sun.

It had to be done, as the world had started to become chaotic, or at least the programming of the world had started to slip. Those who knew were not supposed to tell, and those who told were not supposed to know. But as it happened, those who knew were telling those that told, and before long, those who knew and those who told were one and the same. Vincent, sent by the God of Hell, Asenath would say, disrupted the entire beauty and symmetry of the world—he actually bloodied Lucifer's nose, the swine!

Indeed, it was matriarchy that made Africa the world's killing fields, and yes, death was important—no, these African ladies of the world did not want them to *live* in Africa, to Live Africa. To Life, in Africa. To Be In Africa.

The death was necessary, and the Africans were fueling it—destined to be the greatest holocaust the world had ever known, not due to Vincent, but the population control junkies, the Civilized World, *Imago Mundi*, just as the wars of the white people were fueling it in Europe. Millions upon millions dying in battle for the sake of their Lord and Savior, the Dawn! The Light of the Dawn. The New Day of the Dawn! The one who is cool. The one who brings...legendary success.

The one who opens the doors to Asenath, in Rome, in Tangiers, in Tokyo and Beijing, the One who is without parallel, who is beauty personified and spiritualized. The one who fooled Freud and Darwin and Plato and Nietzsche, and Hemmingway and Joe DiMaggio, and John Lennon and Larry Cousins, and Princess Di and Lady Chatterley.

And Leonard Kruzmar, who was seated on the stage with his wife Lucy—at the top of the ladder, though it was Asenath who held the dagger of paean majesty, the dagger of palpable immortality.

Though this was ceremonial.

First, all the boys of the new millennium ejaculated to the cheers of a hundred thousand worshippers.

And then the orgy of valor, a dance with sexual dominance over virgin anuses.

Followed by the wedding of virgin girls and beasts of the field, big horses too.

Followed by the blood sacrifices of sheep and goats and monkeys.

And finally a man...

His name was Carl Wendell Nunn...

The cause was the effect, as the oracles of eternity thus would state.

A wish was granted, and he would return to where he belonged, forever.

ə   ə   ə

They had to burn them, one by one. How else could they lure them back? I told Carl. I was no longer to be trusted, as you can well imagine. Blue was a soldier after my own heart, a believer, no less. Blue became the boogie man and they knew it was not me; it was something to behold.

"Tell me why they trusted you to go in and eliminate Blue?"

"You wouldn't understand. Carl, there is no reason for me to be in a straightjacket—as I do not require one at any other time, except in this room." I gazed on what would become Carl's playroom in the near future, as I had already glimpsed him from the multiple future. As I understood that the executioner was always an ubiquitous man no one knew, who was truly a monster, whose name, you may recall, was Multiface.

He was the one I would have to watch out for, he was the one who could do more harm. But he never knew the truth—to die is gain!

"You wouldn't understand," I told Carl. "But one day this will all be yours."

"It's a black hole—where the studio, indeed, Hollywood had been—it's a friggin' black hole!"

"Scorched Earth" came out and won Carl another prize, as his personality changed more rapidly, as he was moving toward the multiple future that I had in store for him. "But they cheer you, Vincent. And now..."

Carl began to cry, holding his head in his hands.

"My life's messed up," he went on, "My life's a joke. The world is different—not sure I want to be in this world anymore."

"Carl," I said, "this world is the one you made, spinning reality out of your typewriter—a valid form no doubt. You, who turned from the Creator to the creature, you were going to do it your way. Whereas I, and those like me, do not live for ourselves.

"You can't call yourself a good person! You're a mass murderer! You have no remorse for all those you harmed."

"I beg to differ," I said in the small quarter that would soon be used by Bernstein to interview Carl. "I like the yellow walls in here. And I like the lights—they think I respond, but you'll respond. Don't worry—they'll do it to you too. They do it to everybody."

"More double talk."

"Multiple talk, Carl," I said with a smile on my face. "You thought it was double talk because you have a double mind. But those of us who took the real brunt for you have a multiple mind—and that got me into the future right quick. Look, reality is pliable, formable. You are a co-creator as long as you submit to the Creator."

"There is no creator...you mean God? There is no God," he said, sitting back in his chair confidently. Looking at the two-way mirror where he had his usual gallery of society's dutiful: a secretary, an assistant, a photographer, Dr. Steinman (who had been of late studying Carl!), and of course my two lovely handlers, Radar and Pencil Neck. "Now you're the messiah—and no matter how long they keep you locked up, your mystique grows. On the Internet, there are thousands of sites dedicated to you. They want your words, Vincent. But I won't give it to them. I will make you sound stupid—I will make you sound feeble, wanton, selfish, prideful—and that would be truth, because you are a narcissist, and that is what happened when you committed matricide, and I'm sure if your father were alive, you would have committed patricide. Am I right?"

"You speak of yourself, Carl. You need help."

"So tell me how it got burned—did *you* do it?"

Vincent sat back and began to tell Carl about the first soundstage, burned by none other than Kruzmar himself; Multiface was involved, Blue and Vincent knew. Blue could see everything from his vantage point. The man who did it definitely had blond hair one day, and a long nose, then for the second soundstage he had dark hair and a pug nose. This went on, and then the FBI and their friends joined in, burning everything in sight, under Kruzmar's watchful eye.

From Kruzmar's office he watched it burn—and he was alone. A city of fifteen hundred acres, burning before him—ending. He had hired Multiface to kill the new Bank of England man, Jenkins, a devout man who could not and would not corrupt himself, or let others corrupt him. After the stabbing, the rest of the Board was supposed to vote to rebuild and install Kruzmar again as chairman.

When Bandaloo and Stu were installed as temporary co-chairs, it was simply too little too late. But this, and this only—jealousy, avarice, greed, but mainly avarice—got Kruzmar to begin the scorched earth policy. All the equipment, and every facility, from scoring stages, to recording studios, to producers' offices with all their belongings burned, and it was easy because the studio was empty. Because no one would walk on the grounds all as a result of this boogie-man...whom they knew was not Vincent, as Vincent had escaped and submerged into the will of the people, their messiah, who sojourned to a mountain to ask for forgiveness.

Lucy had filed for divorce, and the press was merciless in exposing Kruzmar's bullying past. It seemed that all his boy-toys came forward and spoke of the perversion...of how they were only twelve and were made to do things so their parents could work at his studio, or on a particular movie; actors whose careers would be forever soiled if the truth came out, came out and told all. To Larry Cousins, to everyone.

Kruzmar's career was ruined. There was no loyalty in the

brotherhood who could burn living children at the Coliseum, no loyalty if you sucked his dick on Monday and stabbed him in the keester on Tuesday with any media outlet available. It was a feeding frenzy. Even Lucy came forward to tell of Kruzmar's *hermaphroditism* and that sent it over...that sent the first can of gasoline in, and that sent them all in.

He watched it burn and waited as there was a warrant for his arrest, for arson, for the murder of the Bank of Britain's Linda Periwinkle. Lucy had garnered her forces, had holed up in the Holmby Hills estate, had hired a security detail every bit as connected as Kruzmar's, and indeed, Kruzmar's chiefs had abandoned ship.

But when Lucy sat there, straight-faced and intimated that Kruzmar *had* somehow, or *was* somehow manipulating Vincent, and could have manipulated him into killing Abacazzia for money...that sent shockwaves around the globe. Carl was the lead, and he was able to publish more quickly because he had Lucy exclusively, before Vincent's arrest and incarceration.

As it burned, Vincent appeared in the office behind Kruzmar, the orange glow leaping across Leonard's face, as he massaged his "genital package" in glee while watching it burn.

"I hate to interrupt your pleasure, Leonard, but you're not the one burning it..."

Kruzmar would not turn around. "You're happy, they love you—what the fuck do you have to worry about? I'm making history. This is the end of Hollywood—they want to run me out, no problem."

"I'm from the future," said Vincent.

Now Kruzmar turned around and was joyous. He pulled his pants up, zipped up and poured himself a glass of wine. "You're just a crazy homeless bum who pissed on Goering, and the rest is history.

"Behold, it's not too late for you to join me, Leonard."

"You! You?! Stupid Vincent? Homeless crazy Vincent!"

"*Crazy?*"

"I cured you—I made you what you are today, and this is the appreciation you show? Coming in here and acting like some sort of know-it-all?"

"You know why I came, dear boy. Troubled child. Remember when we were in high school, and you were the class president..."

They took the journey, happily. Kruzmar dating Larissa Moore, whom everybody wanted, but she could see that boy Kruzmar was going places. Always commissioning the dance, the next event, the world. Always in charge. Vincent showed him a holographic movie of how he, and others would laugh at Vincent in the hall, and how they would scapegoat him and a few others. And he watched Vincent cry quietly at home.

"Personally, I would have gotten a machine gun and blown all of us away. "I'm sorry I did that to you, Vincent, but you were a moron—you wrote fucking poetry for shit's sake. You were an idiot."

"Was I?"

Vincent approached Kruzmar, who stood his ground, and Vincent hugged Kruzmar, kissed him on the lips... "This is for Whitley, motherfucker," he said, then hurled his serrated blade straight into Kruzmar's heart. Yes, the studio burned below, as Kruzmar's life ran out of him...

He smiled at Vincent, for a moment, a brief moment— "You're still a faggot loser—I'll always be the winner," he said and reeled around his desk and smacked himself against the floor to ceiling window, the blood washing down as the orange flames of two dozen mega-stages burned, stabbing tongues of flames now reaching the office building. "I killed that fucker, Whitley, because he was weak!"

Leonard pulled the knife out and turned, a goner, to face Vincent, but Vincent was not there...and he quickly thrust the knife back into his heart where it stayed as he died.

The press was in a flurry.

KRUZMAR COMMITS HARI-KARI

LUCY KRUZMAR FINISHED IN HOLLYWOOD
IN WAKE OF HUSBAND'S BIZARRE
SELF-MUTILATION

KRUZMAR FOUND TO BE PART WOMAN

KRUZMAR A HERMAPHRODITE,
CORONER REPORTS

LUCY K. CAUGHT IN BED WITH LESBIAN
TRYST AND DRUGS AFTER

HOLLYWOOD BURNS TO GROUND,
BOARD VOTES TO DISBAND STUDIO

So Carl wrote it from Lucy's perspective. Stu and Bandaloo presided, all right. Over nothing. Lucy became delusional and was admitted to the Transmore Clinic in Palm Springs...as her insurance dictated. Carl met with her there and offered to pay enough for the interviews and to pay for her medical. She would bounce around and say, "My mother works at the Deli."

And Carl would ask a question about Linda Periwinkle... "Did Leonard actually..."

And she would say... "Daddy was a nice man, and he taught me this: that you have to figure out the way the world works, and then get along with it."

She became violent one day, bashing her head against the wall, and had to be transferred to a long-term facility in Topeka, Kansas, where her new book deal with Carl Nunn would pay the bills—some $3,000 per day.

It didn't matter where she wound up...because she could go where she wanted to go. And indeed, she loved Vincent. "I want to marry him," she told Carl, who became disgusted as early as that.

"Vincent visits me in my room and has sex with me...you see? I always needed a real man to satisfy me. The men today are sluts, prostitutes, they're *women*...how can I be satisfied with a man who wants me to fuck him in the ass?"

Carl wrote article after article of Lucy's fall from grace. But it was more than that. It was a window into the messiah of the hour...Vincent. The rise of school shootings, the rise of celebrity homicide was staggering. *If you see one, kill one* became the motto of the day.

ə   ə   ə

And yes, they fled. All of Hollywood fled. Even Stu and Bandaloo knew the end was nigh, and they packed up for Mexico City where they presided over the Antony Figueras movie, dubbed into English with Spanish as its original language.

Other countries adopted the Italian style of having everybody speak in his or her own language, then dub for whatever country the film would play in.

The board members had simply launched a coup d'état.

Didn't they, Carl Nunn would ponder? After all, they were all from foreign countries.

And in the meeting the man from Sweden said, "I vote to disband the studio, sell any salvageable assets to us—including libraries, equipment and especially qualified personnel. I could certainly use some of it in my country."

Which opened the door to Japan and Australia, who agreed with Sweden.

But this was all formality. In the clubs and dark holes of Los Angeles, it was known, it was well known, that Europe and Asia had installed the Kruzmars because they were weak.

They had overseen this Vincent phenomenon and fueled it.

And eventually used it to get rid of Kruzmar, the evidence, all of it.

"It has always been our plan, Inayana, the industrialist from Japan said. "Why should we take a second seat to the United States when we produce much better movies and television? You had it coming, you were weak and we simply destroyed you for the greater good. All of us feel this way."

No, you did not listen. You thought Hollywood was immune, unsinkable, permanent—but you did not heed my call when I told you to shut this *Vincent thing* down," said the man with the goatee, sitting next to Multiface, whose face was tan, whose nose was peeling, whose hair was streaked, who looked like he had never done anything wrong his whole life.

"Back to one," the director said. "Let's get a close-up."

The handsome man turned to the camera, with a smile that reeked of eternal power. He was timeless, impeccably dressed, the ruler of the world, as he was known, delivering a stern warning through satellite television to his honchos worldwide:

"Now let this be a warning to you. I told you there was no way out...and now you've destroyed the greatest industry the world has ever known. Well...not destroyed it, but put it in the hands of those better than you. I told you I would restore order. Yes, and look back on it now—all the killing and burning, and indeed, even your beautiful worship at the altar of love in the stadiums across the continents could not stop me from forcing the peace. As a result of your disobedience, I have decided to end the economic prosperity of the United States, unless you round up all dissidents, and especially those, like Steve Shredd, who glorified the enemy, and those like Vincent, whom you seem incapable of stopping, and this is your punishment. Los Angeles doesn't mean shit to me. It's now Beirut with nothing to quell the riots, twenty-five percent unemployment, and a permanent National Guard curfew...welcome to my wrath! Your only escape is to serve foreign rulers, foreign bosses...you are finished. Serve me, or I will kill you all. You are only here to...."

And suddenly, the airwaves were interrupted.

The shining, beautiful face of Vincent broke through, overriding the bully tactics of one who shall remain nameless. Vincent was clothed in white robes, and as he looked at the world, and the world looked at him, said: "Beloved, love each other as you love yourselves, for that is what my Lord teaches. I ask for your forgiveness, I ask for your mercy, I ask you to turn from the one who hates, and to my Lord and Master, who is love. What does it matter if you gain the whole world but lose your own soul? You only have a few years left anyway—if you die in his snare you will go to where he is and serve him for all eternity. Come with me, into *eternity now*—don't believe the evil one's lies...he can neither create, nor destroy. Everything that happens on this planet is for my Lord's pleasure. But he is no respecter of persons. I love you...put down your guns, as I have, stop killing those who have more than you. Stop hating. As you forgive me, please forgive each other, love each other. Help each other. Your enemy is without, not within."

This was followed by scenes of Vincent kissing little children and walking along the Colorado River with his apostles.

The whole world was in love with Vincent.

The forces of darkness, indeed, those behind the mirror of deceit, were gathering about him, the second greatest revolutionary of all time, who single-handedly put an end to the greatest spinner of lies, Hollywood.

Do not listen to all that propaganda about Vincent, or even the rumors about the devil or Satan or Lucifer showing up on private televisions to issue warnings to his flock. Look, I have my own problems, of an escalating nature, but I can tell you that Vincent is only a man. Did the Board collude to destroy Hollywood? Yes, but it will never be proven. Did the talent disperse in what I am now calling Diaspora II to the far reaches of the globe? To Spain and Mexico and Japan and Italy? You bet they did! Sure, after the top actors were gunned down like cardboard cutouts in a cheap gangster movie, they all fled, and who couldn't or wouldn't? You cannot prove a conspiracy just because the Board decided to sell the only studio in the world to the highest bidder. Kruzmar burned it to the ground and committed suicide. Any questions?

There was more to gain for the foreigners by being on the board at Shangri-La than to disband it. I believe one day it will be back. With all the history of Hollywood, how can it not come back? Already we see signs of its return...but without the talent, perhaps it's a mere pipe dream.

Did Vincent bring her down? Absolutely not! These forces were economic forces and very hard to pin down. I don't see why all this fuss about Vincent. I have told you who he is—a psycho-murderer, that's who! He is where he belongs, in a prison for the criminally insane, where he will reside for the rest of his life.

All those images of Vincent dressed in robes as the messiah are false—he's in the hospital for the criminally insane and that's where he's been much of the time. His arrest and conviction were well documented.

That day when Hollywood burned, he was found not preaching to his disciples, of which there are none, but having a hamburger at Tommy's and looting like everybody else. He was nothing more than a two-bit rioter vying to loot a TV set or something. Before he came to Los Angeles, where he killed his mother in cold blood, and his high school rival's mother, I might add, and hundreds of others in a random fashion, he was on the streets of Phoenix begging for dimes at the local Greyhound. Get real! Quit making this story more than it is. Quit buying the books, the magazines, the newspapers, even quit buying my articles if it'll make it easier for you. Just stop. Do you want every city in America to be controlled by the National Guard because the kids try to imitate their leader and kill all those in authority? Do you? Turn away from the media, turn away from violence, keep your kids in at night. Do the right thing, Civilization, before you all go the way of Hollywood.

RUOF-YTNEWT

My name is Vincent Damien Del Monte. I am from the future, which to me is the past. I am with you until the end of the age, and I am not with you at all, but here, with my trusty men, Millicet, Jude, the Flagellator and Silas, I AM HERE FOR-EVER.

The facility that houses Carl is a state psychiatric institution for the criminally insane in which he believed he was interviewing me, and that I was the source of all his troubles.

The Princess and I were trying to help him that day, but he rented a Ryder van and killed fifty-one people on Fisherman's Wharf. He confessed to murdering his wife at a party where he had forced her to participate in an orgy. All these things occurred while I was here, as commanded, pretending to be the patient who killed over a thousand men, women and children—all innocent—beginning with matricide, beginning with my own mother, Margot.

Carl believed that I—and by extension, *he*—had single-handedly destroyed Hollywood. He created a phenomenon through trying to discredit me...and yes, it's true, that *was me*, all right. A version of me. I was sent, and everything that happened was to lay the path straight for the return of my Lord to this planet, or so I believed—now I know I was also deluded, that is, lied to. I believed I was human; for a season, I was convinced I was human, after all. I felt like a man, like a brave warrior man sent to liberate the whole wide world. But no, that was a lie. I am not violent by nature, but as a spirit, I am a destroyer angel. I take no personal pride in killing, nor am I afraid of it—the closest I came to human emotion, indeed, was when I was killing, though it was a duty, an assignment. For I am the angel who burned Sodom to the ground. I am the angel who told Dr. Oppenheimer and company about the atom. I am the angel who sank the Titanic. I am the angel, a servant to my Lord, and ultimately a servant to the human race itself, who has bestowed God's judgments on the wicked, which today is most of the planet, as most of the humans on this planet have turned away from God and are thus fair game. It's true, many turned to Lucifer, to Satan, to the sun god, if you will, the Eye of Horus, for their protection from my Master, but to no avail. It is true, not one sparrow falls from the sky without God's prior approval.

So, I am hardly all those things Carl says.

I destroy, and if you see me, then you had better run. No walls can contain me. Satan has no dominion over me.

I am here to tell you that Steve Shredd was arrested today, for no good reason, and that he was perhaps the only *defender* in all of publishing. Though he turned when they threw more money at him, and claimed he was a double agent. This was a lie, meant to save his life.

Perhaps his life is not worth saving after all.

But my Lord wants him alive. So let this be a warning. If one hair is touched on his head, the same thing will happen to the publishing industry as happened to Hollywood. I will burn it to the ground. Manhattan, for that matter, will cease to exist as you know it. You are warned.

Anyone touching or in any way attempting to destroy the *survivors*, i.e. the innocent ones who belong to my Lord, will be killed on the spot. By me, by my men, or by any number of means—by what you call bad luck, we call divine intervention. Watch when you take that plane, or that limo...or cross the street—nowhere are you safe. Whether you ever learn the truth about this world or not, look into the eyes of innocence and there you shall see Truth. His name is God.

Any of you who think you own your bodies, go visit a grave-yard, for that is who owns your body. Anyone who thinks he can have peace of mind on this planet and in the dark one's system, go pick up a newspaper. For you are a fallen, evil race. Wrathful children, if given the world, I would kill you all, even you children, and the sucklings, quick and painless for the innocent, as a method of escape from you, prideful defilers. If that is the only way goodness and mercy can be preserved, if that is the only way to save these children from your dreadful clutches, then it seems perfectly reasonable that my Lord would act, though I do not know his ways. I worship Him alone.

For He alone is worthy. And your friend, Satan, is not.

For now, I am Vincent Damien Del Monte, and I was with Carl the night that the Princess, my consort, invited me through him into union. Because this is forbidden of Carl, as she is one of us, and not human at all, his mind was attacked, and he was given over to his depravity.

As I walk down the hall, in this ridiculous straightjacket, he waits for me in the little room a few yards from the nurse's station, which is behind a partition and not a room at all, but some sort of stage, where satellite feed is beamed around the world so they can study Carl Wendell Nunn.

When I enter he looks at me, while sitting in his wheelchair, and smiles. He starts dictation into his tape recorder. "This is Carl Nunn. Interview with Vincent Damien Del Monte, August 28, at 10:00 a.m. Hello, Vincent," he says.

"Hello."

"Sleep well?"

"I did. And you?"

"Oh, you know, the pain of recovery."

Then I put it to him, while looking at Radar and Pencil Neck, "Please remove the straightjacket."

They accommodate me most swiftly.

"And place it on Carl."

"Hey...what are you doing! Hey! Don't you know who I am?"

"Yes, Mr. Nunn, we know exactly who you are."

They fasten him into it and seat him back in his wheelchair.

"So what's real? Did I...I knew I shouldn't have come back."

"All those things happened, just as you wrote. You're a famous man," I said. "It's just that things have changed. The story is over."

"It's..." He choked a bit. Then he looked at me and said: "You made me do all those bad things...you got in my head, and now I'm in your place."

"Do you ever wonder how I was able to be here and then gone, and then here again?"

I told him how I turned myself *into him* on national television, on the *Larry Cousins Show*. He was a hero, with arms and legs intact.

We talk awhile longer and then other men enter the room and tie him to the chair and wheel in a blue light and an orange light. "Carl, you look at the orange light."

"Vincent, you look at the blue light."

These were the faceless ones, the cloned doctors who spoke directly into our minds. Carl looked at me and I looked at Carl, both of us liars, both of us cheaters, both of us carnal.

Both of us trapped in something we might never understand.

ABOUT THE AUTHOR

Zeph E. Daniel is a novelist, speaker and activist currently roaming the U.S. His first novel, LAMB, has drawn acclaim around the world.

He hosts the controversial website and ministry, The Zeph Report (www.zephreport.com), which, in his own words, is dedicated to feeding the lambs and freeing the slaves.

CPSIA information can be obtained
at www.ICGtesting.com
Printed in the USA
LVHW030811240419
615365LV00001B/100